The Songbirds *of* Colliers Row

Jennifer Hart lives in London. When she's not writing, Jennifer loves to dance, and is often found tripping the light fantastic at her local Lindy hop class.

Jennifer Hart

The Songbirds *of* Colliers Row

First published in Great Britain in 2018
by HEADLINE REVIEW
An imprint of HEADLINE PUBLISHING GROUP

1

Cataloguing in Publication Data is available from the British Library

ISBN 978 1 4722 5039 1

Typeset in Janson by Avon DataSet Ltd, Bidford-on-Avon, Warwickshire

Printed and bound by CPI Group (UK) Ltd, Croydon, CR0 4YY

Headline's policy is to use papers that are natural, renewable and recyclable products and made from wood grown in well-managed forests and other controlled sources. The logging and manufacturing processes are expected to conform to the environmental regulations of the country of origin.

HEADLINE PUBLISHING GROUP
An Hachette UK Company
Carmelite House
50 Victoria Embankment
London EC4Y 0DZ

www.headline.co.uk
www.hachette.co.uk

The Songbirds *of* Colliers Row

Prologue

As Josie looked at the headstones she noticed that they were all laid much closer together than the others in the graveyard. Their noticeably different formation intrigued Josie. She scanned the dates of death and saw that they were within the brackets of the six-year nightmare that had changed the world they lived in for ever. And just as her mind was ticking over a low and husky voice behind her made her near jump out of her skin.

'Those are our boys lost in the war, poor sods. They never made it home, not even the skins they were born in. Sorry love, didn't mean to startle you there.'

Josie turned to face a scruffy-looking man in overalls with a shovel in his hand. The sight of which should have been menacing but his soft and twinkly eyes combined with his gentle smile immediately put Josie at ease.

'Do you work here?'

'I do. Everyone deserves a nice place to rest. I like to keep things nice for them.'

'You do a lovely job of it, I can tell.' Josie looked around the graveyard, as she complimented him on his work. Her gaze returned to the stones she'd been studying before she realised she had company. 'What did you mean by their skins not making it home?'

'Their bodies, love. Either too blown to pieces on the battlefields or lost for all eternity. Nothing there to send home, not that they would anyway. Wasn't the done thing. The stones just mark their lives so that the families here have somewhere to come to remember them. There's no one buried beneath those headstones.'

That's why they were laid so close together. A reason so sad Josie had to stop her mind thinking about where these men might be, alone on the battlefields somewhere, dust among the dirt now. It just occurred to her that Matthew might have a stone here. She had never had a body to mourn or place to go to remember him by. She hoped there was one for him here.

'Is there a stone for Matthew Williams here?'

He nodded and led Josie away from Dylan's headstone and towards one a couple of yards away. Josie knelt to the side and ran her hand softly along the top of the stone and across every crevice of the carving.

She looked around at the other headstones close to Matthew's. The village was aching with loss. If reforming the choir would make even the tiniest difference, if it would soothe for even a moment a little of everyone's pain, didn't she owe it to Glenys, to Peggy, to herself to do it?

She held on to Matthew's headstone, hoping to feel something from her husband that would guide her. 'What should I do, Matthew?'

There was no magical answer from the afterlife for Josie. But she didn't need one. Her heart, steered by the souls resting in this pretty graveyard, had told her everything she needed to know . . .

Chapter One

Josie opened the heavy carriage door and stepped down on to the platform. She immediately felt the sharp bite of the cold Welsh air as she left the warmth of the carriage behind her. According to the rota of the seasons, spring was about to clock in for its shift after the darkness and icy frost of winter, but there was still a sharp chill in its breath as the light wind whipped around her. Shuddering, she turned to her six-year-old son Sam and clutched his hand to help him disembark the train, only picking up their two small trunks containing all of their worldly possessions once he was safely on the platform. It wasn't until the train had departed that Josie looked around her and took in what was to become their new home. Well, their home for now, at least. Nothing was certain and Josie no longer had any idea what the future might bring. If the last six years had taught her anything it was that Fate wasn't concerned with fairness when dealing out its blows; it didn't care how many one person got over another. And Josie had had plenty. The most recent one being the reason she was now shivering on a platform in Wales, miles from the city that had always been her home.

She quickly realised they were the only people there on the platform. The station was empty and the silence of the surrounding countryside felt so strange after the constant hustle and bustle of the streets of London where she had spent her whole life. The quiet was another thing she'd have to get used to, she thought as she took in the rolling hills and endless stretches of green that framed the tiny platform at Llandegwen station. She'd hoped she'd feel more relieved to have escaped the mess she'd somehow made for herself in London. The thought of what might have become of her if she hadn't got Glenys's letter, enclosed in which was a lifeline in the form of the train fare to Wales, made her feel sick. And she was relieved, but it didn't mean she wouldn't miss her home. London might have been cruel to her these past months, or even years, but it had been the backdrop to some of the happiest days of her life too.

But those days were over; that chapter was finished. Wales, specifically the village of Llandegwen, was her only option and her only hope now. She would have to make it work, for both her sake and Sam's. No more mistakes, there was no turning back. She'd been gifted a little bit of luck and, given how thin on the ground luck had been in her life recently, she was going to grab it with both hands.

'Isn't it pretty, Sam? And just breathe in that lovely clean air!' Josie declared, trying to inspire something resembling positivity in her son who had dragged his feet all the way to Paddington station in London and sat staring sullenly out of the window of the train for the entire journey to Wales. The frown hadn't budged from his face for a moment, even when they had had to change trains at Cardiff to catch the smaller, and less comfortable, train to Llandegwen.

'It smells funny,' Sam said, scrunching up his nose. 'Where are all the buildings?'

'Well, I think it's lovely. And there will be houses in the village. Just think of all the room you'll have to run around and play. You wouldn't get that back in London, would you? You can kick your football as hard as you like here and you won't have Mrs Groves coming out and shouting at you for scuffing her door using it as goalpost!' Josie said, nudging him conspiratorially in the hopes that her powers of persuasion and the mention of the comically and eternally miserable Mrs Groves, their old neighbour, would convince him that this big move to Wales was a good thing. But Sam only shrugged at this, his frown unmoved. She needed him on board. She had to believe this was going to work out for both of them.

The war had made things hard for everyone – a hardship no one had known before and a hardship that lingered years after it had all ended, like ripples of water forming ever bigger circles on the surface of a lake long after the stone that broke its stillness has fallen to the bed below. Josie had been fortunate to have been relatively unscathed by the devastating consequences of the war for most of the years that it dominated the world stage they all trod on, and if she'd known that Fate had been racking up the blows for its final act and the years following, she might have savoured those times more. The first blow came when she lost her beloved husband Matthew six years ago. She missed him terribly. She could still remember every detail of the night she first met him. How she didn't notice this tall, self-assured man when he first entered her ma and pa's pub in the East End of London, she'll never know. She had been busy helping out by collecting glasses and washing up out the back, while the regulars and a few new faces she didn't pay much attention to gathered around the rickety old piano her father insisted on keeping in the corner of the pub. Music was her father's greatest passion and that piano was his prize possession. They didn't have much, but that piano was everything to him. He taught Josie to read music and play his favourite songs on those ivory keys, and even though the paint was peeling from the wood and the stand that held the music was wonky and half falling off, the sound was still magical when he sat down to play. That night, the night Matthew lit up her world, her dad was in particularly high spirits. He'd probably had a decent win at one of his regular card games, being partial to a flutter as he was, Josie remembered with a smile. He'd sat down at the piano while his wife held the fort at the bar, and began taking requests for a sing-song. Soon the pub was filled with the sound of song and laughter, the sound of Josie's happiest childhood memories. There was nothing like music to soothe and lift the soul, she had always thought.

While she carried a tray of freshly washed glasses out of their kitchen towards the bar, the notes to a tune Josie wasn't familiar with floated to her ears, soon accompanied by a beautiful, deep and melodious voice singing with such longing and sadness that she instantly stopped in her tracks. *Who was this?* she wondered. It wasn't one of the regulars, she knew their voices as well as she knew her own. And whoever it was was singing in a language she didn't recognise. But even though the words were foreign to her she understood that they spoke of love and loss, just from the way their singer delivered them to his audience.

Curious to get a glimpse of the man who could sing with such heart that he had moved everyone in the pub to tears, Josie walked slowly to the bar where she could join the crowd already mesmerised by this singer. Next to her father, who was perched on his stool and utterly lost in his playing, stood a man with hair as dark as soot, leaning his solid-looking frame against the piano. He was handsome, yes, but what Josie noticed first was his presence – he exuded strength in a way that made her feel immediately safe. And his pale blue eyes were full of kindness. Their gazes locked as he seemed to sing for only her, and in that moment Josie knew she was done for. He had her heart there and then.

When they first met, he had been in London recovering from a broken leg and wrist that had put him out of action temporarily, and it was just as he was getting back on his feet, literally, that he had walked, or hobbled Josie later learnt, into her ma and pa's pub that night. She wouldn't swap those glorious weeks they had together, spending every moment with one another, each hungry to learn everything they possibly could about the other, their love deepening by the second, for an easier life now. They were married just weeks later. With the war raging on, lives being lost were a constant reminder that every moment was precious and it was foolish to hesitate or waste time. Josie and Matthew had to grab every second they had together, and they did. And thank God they did, as it wasn't long before he was snatched cruelly away from her. She'd loved him with every piece of her heart and with every bone in her body. She still did, even though he'd been gone for six years now. It broke her heart that Matthew never got to meet the beautiful boy they had created together. She realised she was pregnant a month before Matthew was killed in action. He'd had to return to his regiment two weeks after their wedding. And so he'd never met their boy who was the image of his father in every way, from his dark hair to his icy blue eyes. He even had Matthew's swaggering confidence and cheeky smile, which at the age of six were so funny to witness in Sam. Sam was like a little old man sometimes, and this never failed to make Josie smile.

It was her little boy who had kept Josie going. And Matthew lived on in a sense in their beautiful Sammy, whose existence she would always be eternally grateful for.

But losing Matthew was only the beginning of Josie's woes. There would be more heartache to come and it would land her in a dark and sinister place. A place she had escaped from by the skin of her teeth, and had paid the price of uprooting herself from the only city she had ever known, and Sam from his home and his friends, to bring them all the way to Llandegwen.

Standing on that chilly platform in the middle of the Welsh countryside, Josie began to recite the mantra *Everything is going to be all right now*, which she'd been repeating all the way to Wales to convince herself that it would be.

She heard a tentative 'Josie . . . ?' from behind her. Turning, she was met with a tiny woman, her hair tinted with streaks of silver, looking at her with instantly familiar pale kind eyes – the same eyes she saw when she looked at her son and she would picture when remembering her husband.

'Yes! Glenys?' Josie asked, relieved and nervous at the same time. She had never met Matthew's mother before but she felt straight away that this woman, who seemed immediately as warm in the flesh as she had in her letters, was going to be their saviour.

'Have you been waiting long? Oh dear, I'm so sorry, love, I had so wanted to be here to greet you. You must think me a terrible woman to leave you waiting, but I bumped into a friend of mine from the village who just doesn't stop talking once she gets started and, anyway, I'm one to talk! Listen to me rambling.' Glenys laughed at herself and in doing so put Josie completely at ease. 'It's just so wonderful to meet you finally. You're exactly how our Matthew described you. And this must be Sam? Hello, young man, I'm your grandma and I'm just so happy to finally get the chance to spoil you!' Sam, who had uncharacteristically shrunk behind Josie at the arrival of this cheerful, tiny woman, peeped up at Glenys with just the hint of a smile.

'We've not been waiting long at all, Glenys, please don't worry. Sam and I are just so grateful to you for taking us in, aren't we, Sam?' Josie looked down at her son, who to her surprise was nodding slightly, but nodding all the same, having not taken his eyes off his grandmother since she addressed him.

'There's nothing to be grateful for, pet, I can't tell you how happy me and Harry are to have you here. Now, let's not stand here in the cold. I've a lovely fire lit at home and a pie in the oven. Follow me. Let me show you your new home.'

And in that moment Josie felt the first flicker of hope that things were going to get better.

Chapter Two

Dusk was starting to dim the light in the sky as Josie and Sam followed Glenys through the rickety gate that led up to the small cottage they were to call home for the foreseeable future. Two houses up a neighbour called out 'good evening' to Glenys as he fixed his front gate in the fading light. His miner's hat sat on the wall as he worked and his face was dusted with soot. Josie figured he'd been sent out to mend the gate before he'd had a chance to clean up after his day at the pit. She knew this was a mining village but even still the startling contrast of the whites of his eyes against his soot-covered face took Josie by surprise.

They had taken a shortcut around the village to avoid dragging their luggage too far, but Glenys had promised to give them a proper tour of Llandegwen the following day. After a long day travelling with a sulky Sam, Josie was relieved to skip the village – she was longing to sit down and to get some warmth into her bones.

As they stepped through the front door they found

themselves immediately standing in a cosy living room aglow with a hearty fire and cluttered with threadbare but inviting furniture. Books and photographs lined the shelves either side of the hearth. The top of a grey-haired head was just visible from behind the large armchair closest to the fire.

'Harry! Drag yourself away from whatever you're doing and show some manners. Josie and Sam are here at last,' Glenys declared to the back of her husband's head.

As Harry rose slowly to his feet Glenys muttered to her, 'He always has his head buried in a book. I could throw a party in here and he wouldn't even notice, he'd be so engrossed.' At which Josie smiled, but her instincts were telling her that it was more than the book Harry was reading that made him so slow to greet her now. He looked quite shocked to see a six-year-old boy standing in his living room; at least that's what Josie took from the expression that suddenly appeared on his face when he clocked Sam. And when Harry could barely look her in the eye as he said a gruff hello, the flicker of hope that she'd put so much weight on only minutes before trembled within her heart, at risk of being extinguished.

Glenys, seemingly oblivious to any tension, bustled around them all and got Harry to take the trunks up to the bedrooms while she laid the table for tea. But Harry had put Josie on edge, and no amount of cheeriness from Glenys could disguise his cold welcome.

'That pie was delicious, Glenys. I'll have to pick up some tips from you while I'm here if I am to cook you a meal to match that,' said Josie after she and Sam had practically licked their plates clean. They were understandably starving after their travels. Glenys had chatted easily throughout dinner, asking them about their journey and what they saw along the way. She seemed so excited to have them there, Josie almost didn't notice the opposite feeling Harry was exuding. He hadn't said a word other than those Glenys had prised out of him with her forceful prompts. Watching them that night, they were like chalk and cheese. Josie had had an idea in her mind of what they'd be like based on the stories Matthew had told her about them. His mother was just as he had said, warm, bubbly and could talk for Wales, but his father wasn't the open and easy-going man he'd described. She had tried to see even a glimmer of her husband in the man sitting in front of her, but though Harry bore a strong physical resemblance to Matthew, his stern silence was nothing like the confident warmth of his son. Matthew must have got that from Glenys, Josie reckoned.

'I'm sure you're a great cook yourself, Josie. It's so nice to cook for a full house. It's been a while since I've been able to do that. The house has been so quiet since our Matthew left.' Glenys paused for a fraction to swallow the sadness that had laced the words she'd just uttered, before she composed her face and beamed again. She leant across the table and took a hand each of Sam and Josie and said, 'I can't tell you how thrilled I am to have you both here. It means so much. And Harry is sick of my food at this point, aren't you, Harry?'

'Hmm? No, no. I'm happy enough.'

Josie glanced over at Harry shifting uncomfortably in his chair. Was he shy maybe? Perhaps he wasn't good with new people. She would work on softening him.

'Harry, I'm definitely not as good a cook as Glenys, but

maybe I could cook you one of my mum's recipes one night, as a thank you for having us.' Josie smiled at him but only got a nod and a barely audible 'thank you' in return.

'You must be exhausted after your long journey. Why don't you both head upstairs and get an early night? I've made up your beds. And Sam, would you like a cup of cocoa before you nod off?' Sam's eyes lit up at Glenys's offer.

'Yes, please, Grandma!'

'Such a polite boy.' Glenys got up and hugged her grandson before picking up their empty plates and taking them over to the sink.

'That sounds wonderful, Glenys, but first Sam and I will help you clear up, won't we, Sam?' Josie watched with amusement as her son began quickly collecting dishes from the table, knowing it was the idea of getting a cup of cocoa that had made him so suddenly keen to help. He usually ignored her requests. Perhaps Glenys would be a good influence on him, she thought as she piled up the empty glasses that had been left on the kitchen table.

'Mummy? Is Glenys my grandma?' Sam asked from beneath the covers of the bed Josie had tucked him up in moments before. She was standing in front of the tiny mirror above the washbasin in the room she was sharing with her son, pinning her honey-blond hair into curls for the following day. The novelty of suddenly acquiring new family members for the first time in his life was clearly occupying Sam's mind.

'Yes, that's right. She's your dad's mother. Remember how I told you that this is where he was from? This used to be his house and this was his bedroom.'

Sam was silent for a moment while he considered this, despite having been told this information several times. The meaning of these facts suddenly had more importance for him now that he was here.

'I like that she's my grandma. She has twinkly eyes. Do you think she likes me?' He was so earnest that Josie's heart melted a little.

'I think she likes you very much, sweetheart.' Unable to resist the urge to hold her little boy close to her, Josie moved away from the mirror and snuggled up to him on his bed. 'And how could she not? You are the most precious boy in the world. You know that, don't you?'

Sam rolled his eyes, but his smile gave away his delight.

'You *always* say that, Mum.'

'That's because it's true.' Josie smoothed his dark hair from his brow as he looked up at her.

'Grandpa Harry isn't as nice as Grandma.'

'Well, we don't know him very well, do we? He might be shy or maybe he needs to get used to us being here. Some people just take a bit of time to get to know them.'

Sam looked unsure. 'I still like Grandma best.'

'OK, well let's be nice to Grandpa Harry and I'm sure we'll all be great friends in no time.' Josie kissed his forehead. 'Now, lights out and sleep tight.'

'A song first, Mummy! *Please!*'

'OK, but then sleep, promise?'

Sam nodded his head and snuggled under his blankets in anticipation of the lullaby Josie would sing him, the same lullaby her own father had sung to her when she was a child.

* * *

In the darkness, as Josie climbed into the warm and comfy bed that Glenys had made up for her, she thought about the quiet Harry who had shuffled off back to his armchair in silence as the rest of them moved around the kitchen clearing up after dinner. She didn't feel that she'd got any sense of the man who was allowing them to stay in his home and she worried that maybe they weren't as welcome in his eyes as they were in Glenys's. As she lay there in bed in the room at the back of the house, she smiled to herself, wondering what Matthew would have thought of her being here now with their son Sam sleeping soundly in the bed next to her. Josie tried to imagine Matthew sleeping where she was lying, wondering what he used to dream about and think about as he stared up at the same ceiling she was looking at now. It was an odd sensation but a comforting one.

Being in a proper home with Matthew's parents, especially the wonderful and warm Glenys, had reminded her what it was like to have family around her. She missed her parents every day. They had been her rocks after she lost Matthew and after Sam was born. Josie had remained in the East End pub she'd grown up in after Matthew went back to join his regiment in France, the idea being that when the war was over they'd make a home of their own. They hadn't decided between London and Wales at that point, Josie had been so stubborn about wanting to stay close to her family and her roots. It's funny how things turn out. Matthew would have been delighted to know he'd won this battle in the end, just not about the hardship Josie had had to endure to get to this point. God, she was glad he wasn't alive to learn of the mess she'd got herself into, the mess that had led her to flee London.

Her cheeks burned with shame at the thought of anyone finding out how stupid she'd been and what she'd almost been forced to become.

Maybe it was being in a strange and unfamiliar place, or maybe it was the fact that being around Matthew's parents had made her think more deeply about her own, but in order to block out the thoughts of what might have been if she'd not left London, she found her mind wandering into the other dark corners it usually avoided. For a long time Josie hadn't thought about the day that the war had snatched away another piece of her heart. For her own sanity she had to put it away in a box in the far corner of her mind. But now, lying in bed, she found her mind taking her back to that day, the images of it forming a moving picture in her mind. Complacency can be a cruel punisher. It had been so long since the night skies had rained bombs on London that they'd all believed the German air raids to be over. They should have known not to take anything in that war for granted, for of course they had been wrong. And on the day that complacency sought its retribution, Josie had taken Sam with her to visit her best friend Rose in west London. She hadn't seen Rose for ages and she was excited to hear all about her new life out west with her new husband. They'd had such a lovely day, Josie didn't feel the time go by and darkness had begun to fall as she made her way back east. In the weeks that followed Josie wondered if she'd ever feel lightness or joy again as she had laughing with her friend earlier that day. Before she'd even turned the corner on to her road she knew that something wasn't right. The air was too still, too dense. And then she saw the rubble, the dust, the devastation. Huge portions of the street had been obliterated, houses reduced to their mere bones. Josie's eyes scanned their way to the corner at the end of the street where her home should be, not wanting to look but needing to at the same time. The Crown pub was nothing more than fractured bricks heaped in a pile. At first she couldn't quite put together what had happened. She just stood there, frozen, staring at the mound of stone that used to be her home. And when her mum's best friend Dot put her hand on her shoulder, she didn't need to say the words for Josie to know, just by looking in this woman's eyes, and by the sickening pull in her own stomach, that her parents were under that mound. In the blink of an eye her home and her parents were gone.

When she thought back now to the weeks that followed, Josie had no idea how she got through it. She had one brother, Billy, but he had taken the boat to America in search of a better life just before the war had begun. He couldn't have come home even if she'd asked him to, or even if he'd wanted to. He'd been drafted by the US army and was deployed with his regiment at the time the bombs dropped from the skies above London killing his ma and pa. She'd felt so alone and so hopeless. If it hadn't been for the kindness of Dot, Josie shuddered even now to think what would've happened to her and Sam. And now Glenys had extended the hand of kindness to her in her latest hour of need. Her ma and pa would be as grateful for this kind, tiny woman as she was, she thought now, smiling to herself, wiping away the tears that she hadn't even realised she'd shed.

'And so here I am, Matthew,' Josie whispered, as she stared at the ceiling of his old bedroom. 'I finally came to your beloved Wales and I hope we'll be happy here.' Glenys had already made her feel so at home. And it was nice to be living in a proper house again, rather than a damp and depressing room. Harry was another story though. If only she could work out how to crack that sullen exterior. *One thing at a time*, she thought as she closed her eyes and let the exhaustion of travel and emotion finally lull her into sleep.

Chapter Three

Their first days in Llandegwen were challenging, to say the least. Glenys had shown Josie around the village as promised. The heart of Llandegwen was Colliers Row, the main road that ran right through the middle of the village and out into the surrounding hills one and a half miles to the coal mine where so many of the village's men worked. As they reached the road and before they headed into the centre where Colliers Row was lined either side by the bakery, the village shop, the post office and the village hall, Glenys pointed in the direction of the mine, too far away to see in the distance from where they stood.

'The men head off up that way every morning to the colliery. If you're here at the right time you'll see them marching up there like a little army, hats and all. Though there're less of them now with the mine struggling these days. And after we lost so many in the war.'

Josie had nodded but she hadn't really been able to imagine what it might look like now, let alone before the war, to see most of the village's men all heading off to work in the same direction. In London there were so many different ways to earn a crust – both above and below board – the idea of all the men on her street doing the same job was a strange one.

As they'd continued their tour of Llandegwen Josie had met some of the villagers as they'd passed them by. Though most were friendly and welcoming, not everyone seemed delighted to have them there. Harry had continued to avoid any interaction with his houseguests and would make himself scarce at every opportunity. If it hadn't been for Glenys's constant chatter, the atmosphere in the cottage would have been close to unbearable. And though Josie hoped Sam would make new friends at school, if she'd had any notions of making some pals of her own they were soon dispelled at the school gates on day one.

Sam had started at the local school on their very first Monday in the village. Josie had thought that if he had a routine as soon as possible, and if he could make friends with the other children from the village, he'd settle in much more easily. The guilt she felt over dragging him all the way to Wales because of the mess she had made of things in London gnawed at her constantly and consequently she was desperate for everything to be OK. None of this was his fault and she didn't want him to have to pay the price for her mistakes.

'Are you excited to start your new school, Sammy?' Josie had asked in an attempt to put a positive spin on a morning that had them both a bundle of nerves. Sam had been quiet all morning, a clear sign that he was anxious, and the nerves knotted tighter within Josie as a consequence.

Sam's only response to his mother was a shrug and Josie's heart sank.

'Think of all of the new friends you'll make! Then you won't have to be bored with me and your grandma all the time.'

'What if they don't like me?' He lifted his gaze from his dragging feet to meet Josie's. He looked so worried Josie almost couldn't bear it.

'How could they not like you? You are such a special boy, you never need to worry about that.'

'But what will I say to them when I get there?'

'Well, you could tell them about London. I bet most of the children here haven't ever been to London before so you can tell them what it's like.'

Sam nodded but his gaze had dropped to his feet again, his steps getting heavier and slower the closer they got to the school.

'Just be yourself, Sammy, and you'll be just fine, I promise.'

If only it had been that simple. Josie had believed her own words when she'd spoken them to Sam, but when she'd attempted to make friends with some of the other mum's at the school, she'd realised that being yourself could count against you with some people.

She'd initially been relieved to see a group of women her own age when she had dropped Sam off at school. Growing up in a pub had gifted Josie with an easy manner with new people. She made friends easily, so it was without any trepidation that she had approached them at the school gates on that first Monday morning. It was only when she'd got closer to their huddle that she saw they were gathered around one of the mothers in particular who was seemingly holding court, and that they were all listening intently to whatever this woman was saying.

Whoever she was, she was dressed in a lovely green wool coat with matching hat, her hair immaculately styled into smooth brown curls that sat perfectly beneath it, and she didn't seem to be pausing for breath. Josie had started to feel a little silly standing on the outskirts of their circle. She didn't want to appear to be earwigging either, if any of them happened to notice her lingering there, and so she had decided to announce herself to the group.

'Hi there! I'm Josie, Sam's mum. We've just moved here so I thought I'd come and say hello, given we'll probably be seeing a lot of each other.' The natural smile Josie had given them all now froze on her face as the perfectly put-together woman at the centre of the group just stared at her, the other women either looking at the ground or expectantly at their queen bee. 'Er, I'm Glenys Williams's daughter-in-law . . . ?'

Another beat of silence followed before the queen bee suddenly produced a smile that didn't quite meet her eyes and said, 'Of course you are, how nice to finally meet you.' Something in her tone meant that Josie wasn't quite sure she believed her. 'I'm Anwen Lewis. And how are you settling in? Girls,' before letting Josie answer Anwen directed her next comments to the women around her, 'this is who I was just telling you about. The one with the son who kicked his football up against Mrs Duffy's freshly painted gate on Sunday. He is quite the bundle of energy your Sam, is that what you said his name was?'

Josie cringed internally at the memory of Sam's mucky football. Despite the trouble it had caused with Mrs Groves in London, he'd insisted on bringing it with him, slamming it into this woman's gate just as she opened her front door to leave the house the previous day. Her husband had painted it that morning and the wet red paint was now smeared with dried caked mud. She'd apologised profusely and had made Sam say sorry also. She'd taken his football from him as a punishment. Though Mrs Duffy obviously wasn't thrilled at the state of her red gate, she had accepted their apology gracefully, Josie had thought. But clearly the impression Sam had made had got back to the mothers of the village somehow.

'Yes, he's Sam. And I felt so awful about that. Boys have more energy than they know what to do with sometimes!'

'Well, I hope he won't be teaching our children any of his bad manners.'

'He's actually a really good boy—'

'Hmmm, well, let's hope so.' And with that Anwen turned her back on her. The other women, who hadn't uttered a word, quickly followed suit. Josie stood there like a lemon, staring in shock at the backs of these women and once again on the fringe of their circle. She'd been snubbed and she was stunned by such a cold reception. But the tough East Ender within her quickly reminded her of her pride so she turned and walked away with her head high in an attempt to show that their snub hadn't damaged her.

In the days that followed Josie had tried approaching one or two of the other mothers in the hope that she might find an ally, but one look from Anwen and they quickly shut down any conversation Josie had managed to draw from them, anxiously excusing themselves. Yesterday, she had heard Anwen commenting loudly enough to ensure that Josie could hear her perfectly, on the state of Sam's shoes: 'Have you ever seen such scruffy shoes on a St Luke's pupil before? I'd be mortified to let my girls out with shoes in that state.' Josie had pretended she hadn't heard her but this woman's strange and instant dislike for her was starting to wear thin.

Now, as she approached the village she wondered, not for the first time, what Anwen's problem was. From what she could see the woman had the perfect life. She was very pretty and always immaculately turned out. Not a chestnut hair out of place from her perfectly sculpted curls. Josie found this especially annoying, as her own thick blond hair was a daily battle for her to tame. Despite their sour mother, her two children seemed like such darlings and Josie knew she'd been lucky enough to have her husband return from the war unscathed. So it wasn't as though Josie had something she could want. What could she have possibly done to make this woman dislike her so much? Josie sighed. She had been naive to think that slotting into village life would be easy. She'd seen Glenys's invite to Llandegwen, complete with the train fare, as fate, a sign from the universe that this was what she needed to do to escape the nightmare she had found herself in in London and to give her and Sam a better life. But Sam was miserable – he'd begun refusing to get out of bed in the mornings and mysteriously, or rather, conveniently, losing his shoes – and she had made enemies before she'd barely opened her mouth. Maybe coming here had been a mistake. But then it wasn't as if they could return to London. Yes, she had friends there, friends she missed dearly and couldn't even write to because she couldn't risk anyone knowing where she was. And that was the worst of it. She was in Llandegwen out of desperation, not choice. Glenys had taken them in out of kindness and a pure wish to know her family better, but Josie was sure that if her mother-in-law knew the real reason Josie had bought those train tickets at the very moment that she had, if she knew the shameful truth of what Josie had left behind her in London, that she wouldn't want her in her home. And Josie wouldn't blame her, but for Sam's sake she had to keep that secret to herself. When she thought of the horrible damp room she and Sam had been forced to live in for so long, unable to afford anything better on the pittance she earned playing and teaching piano, her heart sank further. Llandegwen really was her only option. If this didn't work, well, she couldn't even bear to think of what would become of them both. It had to work. And if she could escape the shady East End figure who was holding her life in his hands, she could handle the cold shoulders of the villagers of Llandegwen. But as she turned on to the street to return to the little cottage to help Glenys with her morning tasks, she didn't feel at all as tough as she was telling herself to be.

That afternoon, as Josie proved to be more of a hindrance than a help to Glenys in her task of baking several sweet pies and buns for the local bakery, Glenys took Josie into the village to pick up some extra flour and eggs from the local shop, thinking the walk might do her some good. Mr Driscoll, who owned the bakery in Llandegwen, worked alone and was grateful to have Glenys as an extra pair of hands preparing her delicious cakes at home for him to sell along with his own baked goods. And for Glenys, this task kept her busy and put some money in her pocket too. With Harry unable to work properly in the mines, these days it had fallen to Glenys to earn some of their keep. She didn't earn much baking for Mr Driscoll but it was enough to put food on the table and coal in the fire. They'd been surviving on rations for so long now that frugal living barely felt like a sacrifice any more.

As they strolled through the village Glenys, who seemed scarily able to read Josie's moods, probed her to find out what had her in such low spirits. Josie, unable to tell Glenys the truth, that her heart was in knots over the events that had led her to Wales, instead stuck to a more superficial truth.

'It's silly really. It's just one of the mums. Well, all of the mums actually, but mostly one. Anwen Lewis? She seems intent on giving me the cold shoulder and forbidding any of the other mums to talk to me. They all seem petrified of her. She was so nasty about Sam's shoes the other day. I know they are a bit rough around the edges now but he's growing so fast, I can't get him new ones till he really needs them. She just made me feel a bit useless.'

'Oh, don't mind her, love. She's just a bit of a madam, as I'm sure you've noticed!'

'Normally I'd be more than able for someone like her, but this not being my home and . . . oh, I don't know. I miss my friends too, I suppose.'

Glenys looked up at Josie with a pained expression that made her feel almost guilty for saying anything about how hard she was finding it settling in. It was obvious to her that Glenys wanted Josie and Sam to be happy in Wales. She had been doing everything possible to make them feel at home in their first few days there.

'It's natural to feel a bit homesick. But please don't let someone like Anwen upset you or make you feel unwelcome. You and Sam are family and so you're welcome here for as long as you want to be here,' Glenys said as they walked into the village shop.

Josie smiled at her. 'Thank you. That means a lot.'

'What's Lady Lewis been up to now then?' a voice called out from behind the counter.

'Hello, Peggy, how are you, love?'

'I'm all right, thanks, Glenys. So what's this about Anwen then?'

'Oh, she's been giving Josie here a hard time.'

Josie had met Peggy briefly earlier that week when Glenys gave her a tour of the village. The shop had been busy that day and she'd not really had a chance to speak to this bright, curly-haired young woman, but she'd liked her instantly. She was friendly and full of chat and now Peggy seemed to be suggesting they might be on the same wavelength when it came to Anwen.

'I'm not surprised she's been giving you a hard time. You are quite the thorn in her side.' Josie must have looked a little horrified at this as Peggy laughed warmly and said, 'Oh, don't look so worried, it's not a bad thing. In fact, it's a great thing. Not a lot ruffles her feathers so I'd take it as a compliment.'

'What do you mean? How could I have possibly ruffled her feathers when she won't even talk to me?'

Peggy looked between Josie and Glenys, her brow furrowed in confusion.

'Well, because she thought she was going to marry your

Matthew, of course. She practically had the wedding all planned when he wrote to her to say he'd fallen in love with a girl from London and broke it off with her. Didn't you tell her, Glenys?'

Josie's head whipped around to face the older woman. 'What? Matthew never told me he was engaged before we met!' Her head was spinning.

'No, no, he wasn't engaged to her,' Glenys corrected, giving Peggy a look of impatience, annoyed at her for making the matter worse.

'Sorry, Josie, no, they weren't actually engaged. But in Anwen's head they practically were. She'd set her sights on Matthew when they were at school together, everyone knew that. She wanted them to be the golden couple of the village. Anwen has always cared more about her image and being perfect than she ever has about anything else. Believe me, I've known her all my life. Anyway, what Anwen wants Anwen usually gets, only this time she didn't and I don't think she's ever got over it.'

'Thank goodness my Matthew came to his senses and fell for a lovely girl like you,' Glenys said, soothingly. She seemed very uncomfortable with where the conversation had gone, probably because her son was coming out of it looking like a bit of a heartbreaker.

'I feel a bit bad for her now. Having your heart broken is awful and if Matthew had chosen someone else over me, I'd have been devastated.' Anwen's behaviour made a lot more sense to Josie now.

'Don't feel sorry for her. I'm not sure she's capable of heartbreak. She managed to brush her rejection under the carpet for years and look down on everyone else from her ivory tower, but now you're here in the flesh you are a walking reminder to her that she didn't get what she wanted, and to the village that she's not as perfect as she seems,' Peggy explained. 'She's a silly cow. Glenys is right, just ignore her.'

But Josie did feel sorry for Anwen. She knew Matthew was too good a man to hurt anyone deliberately, but perhaps he hadn't handled things in the right way. They'd fallen for one another so fast and so hard, maybe he hadn't been able to explain this to Anwen. Either way, Josie had sympathy for her. Perhaps she could try to show her that she wasn't the kind of person who stole other women's men. Maybe there was a way to get Anwen on side.

'Now I know what her problem is with me, that makes things easier. Thanks for explaining it all, Peggy.' She sighed and rolled her eyes. 'Bloody Matthew, only he would have women falling out over him when he's not even around to see it.' It was a risky joke to make with the man in question's mother in the room. There was a fraction of a second of silence before Glenys started to cackle. Her laughter was infectious and it went some way towards making Josie feel much better about the whole situation.

'Stick with me. Any enemy of Anwen's is a friend of mine.' And at Peggy's words Josie felt lighter for the first time in days. She might have finally found an ally in Llandegwen.

Chapter Four

Talking to Peggy that afternoon had been both enlightening and a bit of a boon to Josie. Nevertheless, her previous downbeat mood hadn't entirely lifted and nor had that fact escaped Glenys's notice. When they'd returned to the cottage the older woman strategically brewed some tea and set up a quiet moment for them to chat before baking resumed. All of their talk of Anwen and Josie's feelings of homesickness had clearly sparked some concern in Glenys. And Josie hadn't even told her the full story – and she knew she never could, not if she wanted any chance at happiness for herself and Sam. She'd tried to show Glenys that her mood had improved, but the older woman's ability to see beneath the surface was both disconcerting and strangely comforting at the same time. The fact remained that she and Sam were struggling to settle into village life. Josie was sure Glenys had picked up on this and that she wasn't going to be content until she was sure that Josie wasn't about to jump on the next train back to London.

'Now, love, I know you've had a tough few days settling in but I hope what Peggy said has eased your mind a little.'

'It has helped, in that I now understand what's going on. But it's still hard knowing there are some people who don't want me around. And it's hard being somewhere so different from what I'm used to. And it's not just Anwen and her gang, Sam hates school – he's not making any friends as far as I can tell. Like mother like son, I suppose! I just didn't expect it to be so hard to fit in.' Josie instantly regretted being so open with Glenys as the older woman's face fell at her words. Josie rushed to reassure her. 'I mean, you have made us feel so welcome, Glenys. I am so unbelievably grateful to you, please don't think I'm not. It's just, it's harder than I thought it would be.'

Glenys was quiet for a moment, considering her words carefully. 'It must be very strange for you, love. London and Llandegwen couldn't be more different, I expect. And I know you've gone through so much hardship since marrying my son. I could tell in your letters that life wasn't all roses, even though you put such a positive spin on everything.' She smiled as she patted Josie's hand from across the kitchen table. 'I was so pleased when you answered my letters after we lost Matthew. He'd told me all about you, of course, and about how he couldn't wait to bring you home to meet us if only the war would end soon. I just had to write to you to know the woman who had made him so happy in those last months of his life. And then when you told me I was to be a grandmother, well,' Glenys threw her hands up in the air in delight at the memory, 'I was thrilled. I just always wished I could help you, especially after you lost your own mam and dad, you poor love. You need family around you when you have a little one and you're on your own. I know Matthew would've wanted me to look after you and Sam, and that's what I've always wanted to do.'

'I know, Glenys, and I'm so grateful—'

'But will you give me a bit more time to look after you, love? Give Llandegwen a bit more time? Reading between the lines, I don't think life was giving you much of a helping hand in London.'

Glenys didn't know the half of it but even so, Josie couldn't help but smile at how much this wise little woman had gathered from her letters. Josie hadn't told her the room she was renting in London for her and Sam was riddled with damp and was so small it felt like living in a cell. She'd said instead something about it being a little in need of cheering up and being snug, if she remembered rightly. She hadn't told her how she'd been scraping a living together from playing the piano at weddings and in pubs while a neighbour looked after Sam for her, her war widow's pension not enough on its own to put that dank roof over their heads and bread on the table. She hadn't told her how she'd not been able to get much work in recent months and was facing eviction as a consequence. The shame she'd felt at not being able to find even the small pittance required to call that hovel their home was only topped by the shame she felt about the way she'd finally found that money. She was paying the price for that shame now, though, and it was a lower penalty than the one she'd managed to escape by leaving London. Clearly Glenys had seen much more beyond the words Josie had written on each page. *Hence the train fare in the last letter*, Josie thought wryly.

'Oh, Glenys, you're a tough woman to disagree with! I suppose I haven't given things enough of a chance and for Sam's sake, and yours, actually, given your generosity, I promise I will.' Josie said this as much for her own benefit as for Glenys's.

Glenys beamed at her. 'That's made me very happy to hear! And listen,' she dropped her gaze to the table, 'I know Harry might seem a bit quiet to you, but don't take it to heart. He's got his own battles to contend with.' And with that she patted Josie on the arm and rose to clear the table, marking the end to any line of questioning Josie might have wanted to pursue on this matter.

After her chat with Glenys, Josie decided she wasn't going to be beaten by playground bullies. It was ridiculous to her that at her age she was even referring to Anwen as such, but that's what she was, a bully. She wouldn't be driven out of the village and on to the streets just because some woman was holding a grudge against her for something Josie hadn't even been aware of. And Harry might not want her and Sam there, but Glenys really did and that would have to be enough for now. She hadn't given up hope of winning Harry over, she just hadn't yet worked out what was going on inside that stern, serious and silent head of his. Fighting battles of his own, Glenys had said, which made her see Harry as an even more complicated puzzle to be worked out.

She looked out of the kitchen window to see the man in question working away in the small square of yard that allowed them to grow some herbs and vegetables. He had been tending to the plants for some time now, seemingly lost in the task.

Completely unaware that he was being observed, Harry paused in his work for a moment to look over the fence and into the distance where green fields seemed to roll on endlessly towards the horizon. From the safety of the kitchen Josie was able to study his face freely without fear of being seen. She was taken aback by the raw pain she saw etched in the older man's brow and which haunted his eyes. Josie couldn't be sure from her position behind the kitchen sink, she was just that bit too far away and the glass of the window was in need of a clean, but Harry appeared to roughly wipe away a rogue tear before it had a chance to fully escape his lashes. He then sniffed sharply and went back to caring for his plants. This man was in pain, Josie realised. She had no idea what thought had brought a tear to his eye, but she had seen a different, softer side to him in that moment. Maybe there was some way to connect with him. It was hard for her to watch him suffering, even in that brief moment. But he thought he'd been alone and Josie instinctively knew she'd be the last person he'd want to comfort him. He obviously wanted to carry whatever cross he was bearing alone. But now that she knew that he had this sensitive side she had more hope that she might be able to open him up to her and Sam being around. Sighing, she moved away from the window so as not to be seen when he eventually came back into the house. Clearly she wasn't the only one who had her struggles.

Now that Josie had resolved not to let Anwen or her difficulties with Harry stop her from making the best of her new life in Llandegwen, the next thing she had to do was to make herself useful. She needed a purpose. She was always in better spirits when she had something to focus on. And she also wanted to earn her keep. She knew she wouldn't be able to teach or play piano as she had in London – work was scarce in Llandegwen and everyone seemed to survive on very little, so no one would have the money for lessons – but she could help Glenys with her bakery orders, perhaps, and she could do more around the house. She said as much to Glenys that afternoon. As it turned out, Josie wasn't the greatest baker. After Glenys prevented her from over-beating the batter by the skin of her teeth, she put Josie in charge of the less risky task of checking supplies so that Glenys could make sure she had enough of everything for the orders she'd committed to.

'Was your mam not a baker, love?' Glenys asked as they worked.

'Not really. She helped my pa out behind the bar so much she didn't really have time for things like that. She did make a lovely apple pie though.' Josie smiled, thinking about her mother.

'Working in a pub must have been an interesting life. I bet you meet all sorts of characters doing that in London. What was she like, your mam?'

Josie looked wistful as her mind filled with images of the woman who had been a rock for her until the day she died. 'She was the most charming person I've known. She could even charm the most notorious East End gangster into behaving himself in our pub. They'd do whatever she'd ask of them. I used to watch her as a girl, trying to learn how she did it. I think she was just born with it. I never cracked her secret. But she was made of steel too. She was tough, a survivor, you know?'

Glenys nodded. 'That must be where you get it from.'

Josie smiled. 'She was so glamorous too. I never saw her without her lippy on or her hair perfectly set. I used to think she just woke up that way! My pa adored her, he called her his princess. Pa was the sweet one. He was a bit of a dreamer. I think if his life had been different he'd have been a musician, but he seemed happy enough to play the piano in the pub and sing with the locals, as long as he had Ma with him. It was Pa who taught me to play the piano and sing. He was an amazing teacher and he could play anything. I learnt to play classical pieces as well as show tunes. I don't think I could've had better training even if I'd been allowed anywhere near somewhere like the Royal Academy of Music.'

'They sound like wonderful people. And I knew they must've been, to have raised such a lovely girl like yourself.'

Josie felt the familiar waves of loss crash into heart. Even after all these years they still knocked her sideways with their force. She'd needed her parents more than ever recently, and she'd felt so alone without them. And though Josie knew that she was incredibly lucky to have someone like Glenys, she missed her old life with them in London and she missed the buzz of the locals chatting and laughing in the Crown. The sounds of the pub would always float up to her room in the flat above and the noise was always a comfort rather than a disturbance. It was the familiar sound of home. Llandegwen was so quiet. Josie had never known such quiet. Everything here felt quite alien to her. But there was no point in lamenting leaving London. Her parents were gone and all that was left there for her was someone who wanted to harm her, not save her.

A cold and sickening shiver ran up Josie's spine as the thought of her mistake following her up here to Wales crossed her mind. But no, she told herself, she'd been so careful. Only Rose knew she was here, and Rose lived on the other side of London now. Her friend didn't even know the real reason why Josie had left London, she'd been too ashamed to tell her. Instead she'd said she wanted Sam to get to know his grandparents, which wasn't entirely a lie. Josie was safe and if she stood any chance at happiness she had to leave her past behind her.

Glenys, thinking her sharp shudder and sudden quietness had been brought on by all the talk of her parents, gave Josie a sympathetic squeeze.

'Oh, you poor love. You've known so much loss. Life isn't fair, is it?'

Josie was only able to shake her head, she didn't trust herself to speak. There were too many words that could never be spoken.

It wasn't until the following day that inspiration struck Glenys and a plan to give Josie something to focus on and to help her feel more involved in Llandegwen life formed in her head. She and Glenys had taken Sam to the shop to buy him a treat to celebrate their first week in the village. Sam had continued to be difficult about all things Llandegwen and though he had worn her patience thin each morning, Josie's own struggles to settle in meant she felt she should go easy on him and give him some of the encouragement that she had got from Glenys. She knew it was all very hard for him.

Peggy, as usual, was behind the counter and when the

purpose of their visit was revealed to her she made it known to a delighted Sam that she had kept a few pear drops back especially for him. Of course Sam was thrilled and Josie was relieved that his spirits had been lifted so dramatically by Peggy's kindness.

'Have you heard, Glenys, that old Mr Rhys has taken a turn for the worse? He's in hospital, and I think the feeling is that he won't be coming home,' Peggy said, as she removed the lid from the large jar of pear drops.

'Oh that's such sad news. Poor Mr Rhys.' Glenys put her hand to her heart.

'It is sad. Especially given all he's done for the village, what with running the choir for all those years before the war. I remember we used to get so excited when they'd perform concerts for us in the village hall. And they'd go off to all these exciting competitions. Do you remember? I always wanted to join them so I could travel, but I was too young then. It sounded like such a thrill.'

'That all seems like so long ago now.'

'What happened to the choir?' Josie asked, her interest piqued by this detail about the village's past.

'Well, the war happened really. A lot of the singers went off to fight, and lots never came back. I think our hearts were too broken to think about getting a choir together again. It's such a shame though, I do so miss the music they used to bring to the village,' said Glenys.

'Me too. It's funny, I saw a flyer for a choir competition in the Valleys the other day, actually. It was stuck to one of the boxes we got in our delivery this week – it must've blown in to the van from one of the other villages they deliver to. Anyway, it reminded me of the glory days of the Llandegwen choir and I felt a little bit nostalgic. And then with the news about poor Mr Rhys. I suppose those days are over now.' Peggy sighed.

'Oh, but that's such a shame! To have stopped singing even after the war was over . . . it's times like these we need music the most,' Josie said, genuinely saddened by the idea of music being lost to a community.

And while Glenys and Peggy were lost in a bittersweet memory of the days of the old choir, Glenys appeared to have some kind of epiphany.

'The choir! Of course, it's so perfect! Peggy, you're a marvel.'

Peggy looked too confused to fully take this praise onboard. Josie was equally unsure of what Glenys was getting so excited about but she was keen to hear about it nonetheless.

'Don't we have a classically trained pianist and songstress living among us in this very village right now?' Glenys had an almost wild look in her eyes as they danced from Peggy to Josie. The two younger women were still waiting for Glenys to let them in on what on earth she was talking about. 'Oh, for goodness' sake! Josie, you'd be perfect for the job. Weren't you only telling me yesterday that you've played the piano since you were a child? That your dad taught you classical pieces and how to sing? You could reform the choir, get the village singing again.'

Josie was so taken aback she didn't know what to say at first. She'd never run a choir, she'd never even sung in a choir. Sure, she'd sung with her pa and some of the more musically inclined locals in the pub. They'd even put on a few performances in the past. But running a choir was another thing altogether.

And a Welsh choir at that. She only knew one Welsh song. The idea was ridiculous.

'I had no idea we had such a musical talent living among us!' Peggy clapped in delight.

'No, I mean, that's very kind of you to say, Glenys. But I'm not qualified to form a choir.' Josie shook her head to make her point, she hoped, even firmer.

'But why not? You have a lovely voice. I've heard you singing Sam off to sleep at night, so I know you do. And weren't you taught by an excellent teacher, your dad? You'd know how to pass the knowledge down, I know you would. Plus there's no one else better qualified here to do it.'

'Oh, please say you'll do it, Josie? The village needs something like this. God, *I* need something like this. It might be my chance to finally get out of Llandegwen and have some fun. We could enter competitions, travel the country, be the pride and joy of the place!'

'Imagine if we won competitions again! Josie, you'd be our saviour.' Glenys looked at her pleadingly.

'But aren't there rules and traditions? I wouldn't know about any of that. And wouldn't the village be a bit funny about a girl from the East End swanning in and trying to take over?' Josie was desperately scrabbling for solid reasons for why she absolutely couldn't do this. It was too much pressure. She had too much to lose. The village hadn't entirely welcomed her and Sam with open arms, and they were hardly likely to if she made a mess of their choir and humiliated the village all across Wales. And that was if she even managed to get anyone to join. No, this was not the way for her to carve her space in Llandegwen.

'Having a choir, even with a slightly less traditional choirmaster, would be better than no choir at all. And we could teach you the rules. Lord knows we've all had some dark times since the war, and didn't you say yourself that music always eased those times?'

'Maybe we should let Josie think about it, eh, Glenys?' Peggy had clearly seen the look of desperation on Josie's face and had correctly determined that they were more likely to twist her arm if they let her be for the moment.

Glenys reluctantly agreed and Josie felt relief to be off the hook for now.

'My mummy has a very nice voice,' Sam piped up from where he'd been examining the other jars of sweets. All three women looked at him in surprise. They'd forgotten he was there in all of the talk about the choir.

Josie kissed the top of her boy's head and said, 'Thank you, Sammy.' Glenys and Peggy wouldn't push her any further on the matter for now, but even though Josie felt convinced that her reforming the choir was a terrible idea, she also felt guilty about disappointing them. They'd both been so excited and Josie knew the joy that singing could and would bring back to their lives. But they didn't know what they were asking of her, she just couldn't take the risk. If she failed in her attempt she might have to leave the village, and she couldn't let that happen. She wouldn't.

Chapter Five

Josie took a deep breath. She felt a strange relief to be outside the tiny cottage and leaving the scene within it behind her. Glenys had been reading Sam a story in the front room and Sam had been in raptures listening to his grandma's lilting voice as she told him the tale. Harry had been pottering in the yard again. But Josie had found it hard to sit still or to settle into any task. The talk of the choir had unsettled her more than she'd realised. Or more specifically the sense that she'd let Glenys down in saying no to an idea that she was so excited about had unsettled her. Glenys had done so much for her, more than she even knew, and Josie couldn't do this one thing for her. She was finding it hard to justify her position in her heart, even though her head was perfectly clear on the matter.

She had needed to get out of the house and to clear her head. She had no idea where she wanted to go, but found her feet taking her towards the village and then following the pull of the pretty path that led around the side of the church which she hadn't yet entered. Churches had always been strange and foreign places to her, and she felt like a bit of an intruder entering one. Josie was much more interested in the uneven but well-trodden dirt path that was full of brambles and the buds of wild flowers on the verge of blooming, and where it might lead. When it opened up to a neat graveyard she laughed inwardly at her own silliness. Where else was a path along the side of a church going to lead to? A secret garden?

Graveyards were usually creepy places as far as Josie was concerned, but this one had a prettiness about it that diffused any unsettlement. She wandered between the headstones, scanning the names and dates and ages of the souls that lay beneath the ground, their lives marked by such basic details, yet those details conjuring up stories of who or what they might have been.

She paused at one headstone, the age of the soul it marked catching her eye. He was just nineteen. Dylan Rhys, died in 1943. He was so young, barely a man. Josie ran her hand across his name, wondering if he might be a relation of the old choir master Glenys and Peggy had spoken of and feeling a strange connection to this lad she had never known and would never know. She thought of his mother and wondered if her heart had ever recovered from his loss. Maybe he had a sweetheart. Had she ever found love again? This matter was the most curious for Josie; she didn't know how she felt about finding love again after losing her sweetheart. Part of her hoped, if Dylan had had a girl waiting for him at home, that her heart had found happiness again. The idea gave her hope, if nothing else.

As she looked at the headstones positioned around Dylan's she noticed that they were all laid much closer together than the others in the graveyard. Their noticeably different formation intrigued her. She scanned the dates of death and saw that they were within the brackets of the six-year nightmare that had changed the world they lived in for ever. And just as her mind was ticking over who might lie beneath these stones and why they were laid differently to the others, a low and husky voice behind her made her near jump out of her skin.

'Those are our boys lost in the war, poor sods. They never made it home, not even the skins they were born in. Sorry, love, didn't mean to startle you there.'

Josie turned to face a scruffy-looking man in overalls with a shovel in his hand. The sight should have been menacing but his soft and twinkly eyes combined with his gentle smile immediately put Josie at ease.

She composed herself so as not to make him uncomfortable thinking he'd scared her. 'Do you work here?'

'I do. Everyone deserves a nice place to rest. I like to keep things nice for them.' He puffed his chest out a little as he said this and Josie smiled at the pride he clearly took in what many would consider a bleak job, wandering amongst the dead all day.

'You do a lovely job of it, I can tell.' Josie looked around the graveyard, as she complimented him on his work. Her gaze returned to the stones she'd been studying. 'What did you mean by their skins not making it home?'

'Their bodies, love. Either too blown to pieces on the battlefields or lost for all eternity. Nothing there to send home, not that they would anyway. Wasn't the done thing. The stones just mark their lives so that the families here have somewhere to come to remember them. There's no one buried beneath those headstones.'

That's why they were laid so close together. A reason so sad Josie had to stop her mind thinking about where these men might be, alone on the battlefields somewhere, dust among the dirt now. It just occurred to her that Matthew might have a stone here. She had never had a body to mourn or a place to go to remember him by. She hoped there was one for him here.

'Is there a stone for Matthew Williams here?'

He nodded and led Josie away from Dylan's headstone and towards one a couple of yards away. Josie knelt to the side and ran her hand softly along the top of the stone and across every crevice of the carving.

'You must be the girl he married in London. I heard you'd come to stay with the Williamses.'

Josie nodded but didn't take her eyes from the headstone.

'He was a good lad, Matthew. I knew him from when he was a boy. You must miss him, love. Terrible business that war. His memory will be well looked after here, don't you worry about that. It's not much comfort, but hopefully it's some.'

Josie turned to face him, her smile sad but full of gratitude. 'It is, and thank you. You are a very kind man. I don't even know your name?'

He blushed a little at her compliment. 'Jerry. Jerry Collins.'

'Thank you for what you do here, Jerry. I'm Josie.'

'I'm glad to meet you, Josie. I'll give you some time with him.' Jerry nodded his goodbye, the look in his eyes so earnest, Josie felt a little humbled by him. He spoke of the dead as though they were still present and in need of care. He was a simple caretaker, but he clearly felt responsible for those resting in peace here and took pride in helping those who had experienced loss. Josie knew what it was like to have experienced loss but yet she was too scared of her own uncertain place in the village to do her bit to help.

She looked around at the other headstones close to Matthew's. The village was aching with loss. If reforming the choir would make even the tiniest difference, if it would soothe for even a moment a little of everyone's pain, didn't she owe it to Glenys, to Peggy, to herself to do it?

She held on to Matthew's headstone, hoping to feel something from her husband that would guide her. 'What should I do, Matthew?'

There was no magical answer from the afterlife for Josie. But she didn't need one. Her heart, steered by Jerry and the souls resting in this pretty graveyard, had told her everything she needed to know.

Josie walked with more purpose back through the village this time. She was a little jittery with thoughts of the risk she would be taking in reforming the choir and she knew that once she'd agreed there would be no turning back. But it was the right thing to do and she knew she'd only feel guilty if she didn't do it. Music was her gift, one her pa had given her. If she was being asked to pass on this gift to help lift the spirits of the place she was trying to make her home, then she couldn't say no. Her fingers crossed instinctively behind her back as she hoped with all her might that she didn't mess it all up.

She was walking so determinedly that she almost steamed

right past Peggy, wiping some smudges from the shop door as she prepared to lock up for the day.

'What's got you in such a rush then?'

'Peggy! I didn't even see you there.'

'Clearly.' Peggy gave her a wry smile. 'Anyway, I'm glad to catch you. I just wanted to say I'm sorry if me and Glenys went on a bit earlier. We got a bit carried away with the idea. I would just so desperately love to have the choir up and running again, and the chance to sing in it. I always saw it as my chance to escape, to travel in the way I dreamed I would but never did. That's why I was a bit pushy, but it's not your burden to carry, so just ignore us.'

Josie looked at her new friend. She was genuine in her words but Josie could see the disappointment behind her gutsy exterior.

'How come you need the choir to travel? Can you not do it anyway?'

Peggy dropped her gaze, hesitating a beat too long to suggest she was comfortable with where the conversation had gone and Josie felt immediately guilty for prying. 'That was really nosy of me, I'm sorry. You don't have to answer that if you don't want to.'

'No, it's OK. I don't mind telling you. I just don't want you to feel sorry for me, all right?'

Josie nodded. 'All right.'

'I can't leave my mother. She's not very well, in her mind as well as her body. She hasn't been since my dad passed. He died suddenly – heart attack, just before the war – and it broke her heart. She will only let me, Glenys and a handful of others see her, and she would panic if I left her for too long. So I can never leave Llandegwen, not while she's like this. But if I was in the choir, she'd love that. And I'd only be away for a little bit at a time. I know my older sister, Carol, would look after Mam for a short time. She's married with a family of her own in Cardiff now. But I know she'd help me out if she could.'

'How come Carol didn't stay to look after your ma?'

'Her husband had work in Cardiff. She couldn't stay here. And I was unwed, being a bit younger than her, so it fell to me. All my plans for my glamorous future life cancelled, just like that.' Peggy laughed but it was hollow. 'But I don't mind. I couldn't leave Mam. I want to look after her.'

Josie nodded her understanding but she couldn't begin to know the sacrifice Peggy had made. She wished she could help her friend somehow. But then she could if she reformed the choir. If meeting Jerry hadn't been enough of a push, Peggy had cemented it all for Josie. She was going to do it. If it all ended in tears . . . well, she'd just have to make sure it didn't.

'You could do both, look after your ma and have your glamorous life,' she said with a sparkle in her eyes.

'How's that then?' Peggy asked suspiciously, eyeing her friend for clues to what she was getting at.

'I'm going to have a go at reforming the choir. I'd just decided I would before I saw you, but now I'm even more sure of it.'

Peggy squealed before clapping her hand to her mouth. 'Are you really?' she squeaked.

Josie nodded. 'I'm going to try anyway. But I need you to join and I'll need all the help I can get. I don't want to let anyone down.'

'Oh, Josie Williams, you are just what this village needs!

I will definitely join your choir if you'll have me. I can't believe I'll finally get to see something other than the rolling fields of Llandegwen. Pretty as they are. We will enter competitions, won't we?'

Josie beamed at her. 'Of course! If we can get enough people to join and if we can get to a good enough standard.' Her smile faltered slightly as she remembered Glenys confirming that there were rules and traditions. 'What if they – I don't even know who "they" are – won't let me do it? I don't know anything about the rules.'

'The village committee are the ones who decide on whether or not a new choir can be formed and who can lead it. Llandegwen is boringly traditional that way. But Glenys knows all about how they work and we'll both be cheering you on. It's worth a try, isn't it?'

Josie knew that her being an outsider in the village would make things difficult for her, maybe even impossible. But if she at least gave it a shot she wouldn't feel that she'd been the one to say no, it would be in the committee's hands from that point. Plus she knew the power music held in healing hearts, it had patched hers up many times over the last six years. And Glenys had told her how the village had really suffered since the war. There were fewer men to work in the mine, meaning the industry that had kept so many families going for years was struggling. And the men who had returned from the battlefields all carried the inevitable scars, both physical and emotional, of the horrors they had witnessed. No one had been untouched by the war, it had taken something from everyone, whether they were fighting on the front line or holding the fort back home in Llandegwen. A choir couldn't give them back all that they had lost, it wouldn't be a magical tonic to fix everything, but it might just be a big enough chink in the darkness to let in some light.

What she had seen and felt in the graveyard that afternoon had moved her in a way that meant she knew she had to try to convince the committee that she could do this. It was what the village needed. Maybe it was what she needed too. She just hoped it was worth the risk.

'You're right. I'll do my best to convince them,' Josie said with confidence.

Peggy clapped her hands excitedly. 'Oh, this is going to be brilliant! Anything I can do to help just let me know.'

'Well, you can start by telling me more about this committee and how I go about asking them if I can do this.'

'You have to put your case forward at the village meeting,' said Peggy. 'In front of the whole village,' she added tentatively.

Josie took a deep breath, eyes rolling and sarcasm lacing her tone as she said, 'No problem. It'll be a piece of cake.' It wouldn't be, but perhaps if she told herself enough times that it would she'd have some chance of succeeding. What had she got herself into?

Chapter Six

As it turned out, the next village meeting was to be that Monday evening, giving Josie just two days to prepare her case and to gather as much background knowledge of the committee members from Glenys as she could. She was determined to not make a fool of herself, and having something to focus on had given Josie the most wonderful jolt of energy. She just hoped she'd succeed in winning her case.

Glenys had told her that the committee was made up of five senior villagers including the vicar, the headmistress of the local school, a councillor and two men whose families had served on the committee for generations. Josie had worked out that the vicar, Mr Evans, was her way in. According to Glenys, Mr Evans loved to sing. He was so proud of his booming baritone voice that he unashamedly sang loudly and with great gusto over his congregation every Sunday. It was widely held that had he not had a greater passion for God than the stage he might have enjoyed a very different career treading the boards of the theatres in the West End of London. Josie hoped that if she could appeal to his love of music and the chance to sing publicly outside the confines of church, she would win him over. The others might prove trickier to convince. They were all, from what Glenys had told her, beacons of tradition and not known for their forward thinking.

There was no doubt that Josie had quite the mountain to climb in the task ahead of her but she would set out her credentials and speak from the heart. That was all she could do. This village used to love the music that the choir brought to them all, and it was this that she was determined to remind them of. Nonetheless, the excitement at the prospect of this new challenge soon turned to fluttery nerves as Monday evening fast approached and Josie prepared to stand up in front of the committee and many of the villagers, most of whom she'd probably said little more than a passing hello to in the week she'd been there.

Josie had submitted her request to be added to the agenda for the meeting that morning, as she was advised to do by Glenys. The process for this being taking a pencil to the piece of paper pinned up outside the village hall on Colliers Row, kept safe from wind and rain by a little wooden door. Josie thought it was like a little bird's house when she approached it. The deadline for adding to the agenda was ten o'clock that morning and as she neatly added her request at quarter to ten, she saw there were only two other points of business to be addressed. The first was a request from Marjorie Davies, the postmistress, that certain standards of handwriting be enforced on those leaving notices on the post office noticeboard. And the second was a plea from Mr Evans for ways in which the village could raise funds for some new hymn books, as, according to his note here, some were so badly falling apart that vital hymns were missing. Josie chuckled at the idea of enforcing handwriting standards and wondered at the kind of person this Marjorie Davies might be and how such a request would go down.

On her return to the cottage Josie relayed the short list of what was to be on that evening's agenda to Glenys and was slightly relieved when she said that unless something major was to be discussed there was usually a small turnout of villagers for these meetings. Just the usual diehard folk committed to their role in the community and determined to let nothing pass without their having the opportunity to have their say, or those who had nothing else to do and so went along for the chat. So it was quite a shock when Josie, Glenys, Harry – who Glenys had dragged along so clearly against his will to lend some extra support – and Sam walked up Colliers Row that evening to see the centre of the village swarming with people all heading into the hall.

'I thought you said not many people came to these meetings?' Josie questioned Glenys, a hint of panic and accusation in her voice.

'They don't, love. This is quite unusual.' Glenys looked baffled as they continued to make their way towards the village hall.

Once inside they quickly found Peggy two rows from the front of the stage where she had saved seats for their small group. She'd plonked herself in the middle of the row so that she could ensure she was able to debrief Josie and Glenys on the reason for the larger than normal crowd. Peggy leant across to Josie, who had sat at the end of the row so that she could get out and on to the stage to present her case with ease, and said, 'So word got out that you would be talking about starting the choir back up again tonight. Hence the full house.'

'But how? And why?' Josie was trying not to let the number of people taking every available seat rattle her nerves but wasn't exactly succeeding. 'Oh my goodness, there are so many people here some of them are even standing!'

'Well, Mrs Duffy came into the shop this afternoon and told me that she'd heard from Marjorie over at the post office that you were going to be requesting permission to set up the choir again. Marjorie knows everything, no one knows how, she just does. It's very annoying.'

'If Marjorie knows, then everyone in the villages knows. That woman is a mouth almighty,' Glenys grumbled.

'I suppose it's a good thing really, shows people care about the choir and are interested in it being set up again maybe?' Josie asked hopefully.

Glenys and Peggy exchanged glances before Glenys answered, 'Yes, love. That'll be it.'

Josie turned around to take in the full scene behind her. The hall was completely full. She was still telling herself this was a good thing when she caught sight of Anwen and her heart sank. Sitting around her were all of the other mothers from the school, all sitting with their respective families but close enough to one another that they appeared to be the intimidating gang that Josie was sure Anwen intended them to be. She caught Anwen's eye and was given that same smile that didn't quite reach her eyes – in fact it was more like a grimace – that Anwen had given her that first day they met. This was going to be hard enough without knowing there was someone in the crowd willing her to fall flat on her face. That could be the only reason Anwen was here and why she had rallied her troops to be here too. Josie turned back to face the front and drew in deep breaths as the committee took their seats which had been lined up on the stage to the right of the lectern.

It was Councillor Roberts who was chairing the village meeting that night and he was a man who seemed to take his role incredibly seriously, verging on too seriously. The phrase 'power hungry' had crossed Josie's mind as she listened to him outline what was to be discussed on that evening's agenda. First up was Marjorie and her complaint about the state of the notices that adorned her post office noticeboard.

'We should all take pride in how we present ourselves, including in something temporary like the notices you all put up or read on my helpful noticeboard,' the plump, rosy-cheeked woman of around fifty preached from the stage. 'Scrawls and smudged scribbles ruin the order and neatness of my post office and are unacceptable. How you expect anyone to want to look at such unsightly messes is beyond me. Jimmy Griffiths, you'd get far more takers for your window-cleaning services if people could actually read what you were offering.'

Josie looked across to her left to see a young man red in the face and shifting uncomfortably in his seat. Clearly this was the Jimmy Griffiths in question.

'OK, I think we've heard enough, Mrs Davies,' Councillor Roberts said before Marjorie could accuse anyone else in the crowd of crimes against handwriting. 'I'm sure we can all agree that notices that can be read are notices with more use than those that can't. I don't think we need to go further than that. Next is Mr Evans and the matter of hymn books.'

If he'd had a gavel he'd have banged it, Josie reckoned as the butterflies in her tummy were multiplying. Marjorie looked quite affronted to be cut off prematurely and forced off the stage where she had seemed originally quite at home.

Mr Evans took to the lectern to put forward his plea for funds to replace some of the hymn books that were missing said hymns. A cake sale was the suggested and agreed upon solution from which all monies taken would buy the church the replacements it required.

'And now to our final item on the agenda.' Councillor Roberts had to look at his notes for the name. 'Josie Williams, please.'

Glenys and Peggy gave her smiles of encouragement, while Sam and Harry were both staring at the floor, Sam with boredom and Harry blankly. Sam was also kicking at, but thankfully missing, the chair in front of him. *Here goes*, Josie thought as she stood up and walked towards the stage.

'Most of you won't know me so I'll introduce myself properly first.' Josie smiled at the crowd from behind the lectern, giving herself a moment to let the tremble in her voice settle. 'I'm Josie Williams and I'm new to your beautiful village. I was married to Matthew Williams, one of your own, and he always spoke so fondly of his home.' Josie caught a flash of fury cross Anwen's face as she said this and so she moved on quickly to the speech she had rehearsed before the nerves took hold and erased the words from her memory.

'It came to my attention recently that your village has a proud history of producing fine choristers. That your village choir used to compete in competitions all over Wales. I understand that because of the war the choir was disbanded and I would like to put myself forward, as someone who is passionate about music, to be the choirmaster. Or rather, choirmistress. I'd like to form a new choir.'

Before Josie could go on, one of the committee members – the older of the two men who had inherited their position through their family's standing in the village – asked, 'And what qualifies you to put yourself forward in this way, young lady?'

'Well, I have a musical background. My father taught me to play the piano when I was a little girl. I learnt to play classical pieces as well as hymns and popular songs. I was good enough to get regular work in the local churches and social gatherings where I lived in London.' She avoided the mention of pubs, remembering how Glenys had envisioned East End sing-a-longs when she'd told her about some of the performances they gave. She didn't want to risk anyone thinking she'd be tarnishing their Welsh choral traditions. 'I also sing, so I know how to look after and train the voice. But most of all, music is my passion. It has brought so much joy to my life—'

'But you're no Mr Rhys though, are you?' Anwen interrupted from the crowd. She stood, as immaculate as ever, in a floral tea dress beneath a wool coat that matched her outfit perfectly, her hair set in smooth, shiny curls. She had grabbed the attention of her audience with her clear and commanding voice. 'The poor man has only just been taken ill and you are already leaping in to replace him.'

'I'm not trying to replace anybody. Nor could I, I am sure.

I just think it's a shame to lose the tradition of singing that this village has held for so long and I would love to help to bring it back.'

'What do you know of our traditions? You aren't from here, you're not even from Wales.'

'Yes, exactly!' came a slightly feeble and clearly delivered under duress exclamation of support for Anwen from one of the other women Josie recognised from her posse.

It was as though something suddenly stilled within Josie and all nerves were gone now. She knew what Anwen was trying to do but it only strengthened her resolve to fight harder for what she wanted to achieve here. She wouldn't let this mean-spirited woman take away her chance to help the village to sing again.

'You're right, I'm not from around here. But I believe music is something that brings everyone together, no matter where they are from. It can lift your heart whoever you are, and bring light when it's dark no matter where you live. You can love music and singing whether you're from Llandegwen, London or the North Pole!'

'But—'

Before Anwen could finish picking another hole in Josie's argument, a strong deep voice from the back of the hall drowned her out. 'The girl speaks sense.'

Josie switched the focus of her gaze from Anwen to the tall, slim, middle-aged man with greying dark hair standing at the back of the hall who had spoken those words of support for her cause.

'God knows the last years have been woeful for us all. What harm can it do to let those of us who want to sing again?

I don't give a stuff where she's from. If she wants to do it, let her do it.'

Josie could see from the expressions of surprise on most faces in the crowd that the turn of events prompted by this man speaking were quite unexpected. Even Anwen was stunned enough to sit down.

'I agree, Fred. Good man, well said,' declared Mr Evans. 'The choir is a marvellous idea. I for one would love to have somewhere to go to sing other than the church. And who knows, maybe we could even compete again like we used to!'

The rest of the committee still looked unsure, however.

'Mrs Williams, if we were to agree to letting you set up a new choir in the village's name, what would happen if you suddenly decided to leave? As Mrs Lewis said, you're not from here. How long are you planning to stay?' asked the headmistress of Sam's new school, Miss Hughes.

It was a fair question, Josie thought. She looked at Glenys who nodded at her in encouragement, and then at Sam who had stopped trying to kick the chair in front of him and was now looking at her expectantly. She would speak from the heart, it was all she could do.

'If the war taught me anything, it is to live in the here and now. Plans can be destroyed by bombs, hopes can be snatched away by loss, hearts can be broken by letters containing words we never wanted to read. I know I'm not the only one who has felt these things. With all the best will in the world we can plan for one life and get another one we never expected. Everything I do, I do with my whole heart. That is the one promise I can and I will make to you. Singing has brought me so much happiness, even when I thought happiness could never be felt again. Please let me try to bring some of that happiness to those who want to sing again now.'

Josie's look was pleading as she said those last words to the committee. The hall was silent but for the odd creak of a wooden chair as a villager shuffled in their seat in anticipation. It was hard for Josie to read the room, she had no idea if her words had won enough, and importantly, the right people over. An anxious moment passed while the five committee members conferred before Councillor Roberts cleared his throat in order to deliver their verdict.

'We are all agreed. You may set up a new choir in Llandegwen. As it has been a privilege of previous choirs in the past, you may have use of this village hall for rehearsals. Miss Hughes will provide you with the schedule. There is no more business to be discussed, I declare this village meeting over.'

Josie could've jumped for joy, she was so happy she had convinced them that she forgot for a moment the risk she'd be taking in trying to restore the choir to its former glory; she forgot the potential consequences of failure. Mr Evans also seemed delighted as he clapped his hands and said, 'Well done, dear,' as the crowd began to rise and chairs scraped floors and chatter bubbled over to fill the silence.

Glenys and Peggy rushed to congratulate Josie as she stepped down from the stage, Sam at their heels.

'Oh, well done, love. Such beautiful words. You did so well.' Glenys was beaming at her.

'And did you see Anwen's face when Fred spoke up. He *never* speaks! Oh, it's all so exciting. When do we get cracking then?' Peggy's enthusiasm was infectious.

'Hold your horses. Give me a second to take it in!' Josie paused for a fraction. 'I reckon, as soon as possible, don't you?' She squeezed both their hands as they all revelled in her moment of victory.

But nothing made this moment sweeter than having her little boy put his arms around her waist, hugging her tight. She didn't know what was going on in his little head. She hadn't promised they'd stay in Llandegwen for ever, she didn't want to tempt Fate, and she knew Sam was still struggling to settle, but she hoped he'd eventually start to benefit from the move she made for them both. Perhaps tonight was the start of good things to come. It was definitely a step in the right direction, she thought as she took Sam's hand and followed the others out of the hall and into the chilly Welsh night.

Chapter Seven

The next day Josie woke early, still floating on the wave of the previous evening's success. She couldn't wait to get started and wanted to do so as soon as she could. Now that she had permission to form the choir her mind was already cooking up fun goals they could work towards. The competition in the Valleys that Peggy had mentioned was perfect for a new choir, but it was in a little under two months' time, which didn't leave her much room to pull everything together. They needed a minimum of ten members to qualify, so if she could rally that number of people that was the first step on the right path. And if she was lucky enough to recruit a strong soprano and baritone they could be on to a winner. To her surprise, Josie realised she was getting a little carried away with herself; she needed to organise the initial meeting first to see if anyone would even turn up, and if they did, then she'd have to see if they were good enough. She couldn't risk entering a competition if they were doomed to humiliate themselves.

She hoped she wasn't deluding herself in feeling that there

were people who seemed enthusiastic about the choir last night. There was that man Fred who had supported her, maybe he might like to sing. And she was sure Mr Evans would be keen, he'd pretty much said as much. She had Glenys and Peggy who had both pledged to join the choir – Glenys, she had discovered, had sung in the old choir, so she would definitely be an asset. Ever the positive thinker, she was certain there would be more.

That morning over breakfast Glenys had suggested they make some flyers announcing when and where the first choir rehearsal would be and pin them up around the village. Josie thought that was a great idea and while Glenys spent the rest of the morning baking she went into the village to get some paper and ink, telling Peggy of their plan while she was there. Peggy suggested pinning the flyers to the lamp posts that lit up the centre of the village along Colliers Row at night, as well as in the post office and outside the village hall.

Josie spent a very pleasant evening neatly sweeping ink across paper in a hopefully appealing and eye-catching manner, enjoying the fun of being creative and the excitement that hope at a new venture brings. Even Sam lent a hand, blowing on the ink to make it dry faster to avoid smudging, while Glenys kept the cups of tea coming. Harry, of course, continued to play the ghost of the house, silently retreating to his armchair by the fire in the sitting room, the lively chatter coming from the kitchen seeming to push him further away rather than to draw him in.

In return for her assisting Josie in pinning up the flyers around the village, Josie had promised to help Glenys first thing in the morning to make the order of pies she had to deliver to the bakery. They were to have their first rehearsal the following night at eight o'clock in the village hall, so she needed to tell everyone as soon as she could. It was with relief that Josie fell into bed early that night, a happy tiredness pulling her straight into sleep.

After a hectic start to the day – Josie had got so much flour in her hair that her golden strands looked like they'd whitened with age over the course of the morning – and armed with baskets of pies, flyers and pins, Josie and Glenys marched into the heart of the village. While Glenys delivered her pies to the bakery, Josie began to scout out the best lamp posts to display her flyers calling to all the budding singers out there. She'd become so caught up in her task that she hadn't felt the time passing and it was only when the church bells chimed the hour she realised that she was going to be late to pick up Sam from school. Hastily shoving the remaining flyers into Glenys's now empty basket, the older woman having since joined her to assist with the pinning, Josie dashed up Colliers Row towards the school at the other end of the village.

On arriving at the gate Josie's feelings of guilt at forgetting her son intensified to feelings of shame when she saw the playground completely empty but for her Sam who was looking at the same time both cross and forlorn, standing next to an unmistakably unhappy Miss Hughes.

'I'm so sorry, I know I'm late, I didn't realise the time and . . .' Josie's out-of-breath and rambling apology trailed off due to the fact that she didn't in fact have a good reason for her lateness. 'I'm sorry, it won't happen again.'

'See that it doesn't. But as it happens I was wanting to have a word with you, Miss Williams. Please come inside. Sam, you can play quietly out here while I speak with your mother.' And with that Miss Hughes turned on her heel and stalked off into the school. Josie gave a quick apologetic look to Sam before quickly following the headmistress into the school, presumably towards her office.

Miss Hughes led Josie down a long corridor with classrooms on either side, her heels sounding like a gavel echoing off the hard wood floor while Josie's made little clicks as she hurried to catch up with her. She was a very tall woman compared to Josie's fairly average stature, and so Josie felt as though she was tottering meekly behind the headmistress's powerful and long strides. They stopped when they reached an office at the very end of the corridor and Miss Hughes held the door open for Josie to enter.

'This is Mr Jenkins, Sam's teacher. Please take a seat, Mrs Williams,' Miss Hughes said from behind Josie as they entered the room and she moved to take her own seat behind her desk.

Josie glanced at the tall man who had risen to his feet rather formally when she and the headmistress had entered the room. She was taken aback slightly by how handsome he was. His presence distracted her for a second from the nerves she was feeling. Before she could stare at him for longer than was appropriate, Miss Hughes commanded her attention.

'We wanted to speak to you today to discuss Sam's behaviour,' Miss Hughes said briskly.

'His behaviour?' Josie's heart sank. She knew Sam wasn't a fan of going to school, but she had hoped his difficult behaviour in the mornings had been limited to his home life. She knew he hadn't made any friends, but had persuaded herself he just needed a little bit of time to settle in.

'Yes, he has been quite troublesome from day one, I'm sorry to say.' Her glare was so intimidating that Josie felt suddenly as though she were six years old again herself and about to get a telling-off. It was a most unpleasant flashback to her own school days. 'He doesn't take part in class, he generally refuses to answer questions when called upon in lessons and when he does deign to respond it is with a rudeness I am afraid is quite unacceptable. He won't play with the other children and today I caught him telling one of his classmates to "shut up" in the corridor.'

'Oh dear.' Josie was lost for words. How could she not have known Sam was behaving this way? He was never rude, and though he sometimes got a little overexcited and could definitely be a little bit cheeky, she always put him straight on right and wrong. She started to feel a bit panicky about how to handle the situation. It must've shown on her face as Mr Jenkins took pity on her and cut off his boss before she could list any more of Sam's faults.

'If I could just add something here, Miss Hughes,' began Mr Jenkins, his tone confident in a way that suggested he was at least her equal, rather than her inferior. 'I think Sam is just having a bit of trouble settling in, which is understandable given it's such a big change for him, and it's only been a little over a week.'

He'd said just what Josie had wanted to say, should have said. She gave Mr Jenkins a look that she hoped conveyed how grateful she was for his understanding.

'He has been struggling a bit with living in a new place. It's all a little strange for him.' Josie latched on to Mr Jenkins' defence and added to it.

'Yes, yes, but that's no excuse for rudeness. We do not tolerate rudeness at St Luke's, with all due respect, Mr Jenkins.' She looked cross at having to give credit to Mr Jenkins' words and it was clear she wished he hadn't said them at all. 'I don't know how you raise your children in London, Mrs Williams, but here in Llandegwen we teach them manners and expect them to behave appropriately. Either you teach your son the proper conduct we expect or I'm afraid you'll have to seek alternative routes of education for him. Do I make myself clear?'

Josie felt as though she'd been slapped. She had done everything she could to teach Sam how to behave, what more could she do? Was she a terrible mother? Looking at the evidence she felt such an intense sense of guilt and fear that she was. She'd dragged Sam away from his home, not being able to put a decent roof over his head by herself. She'd put herself and therefore him in the most dangerous position by the stupid mistake she made in London that had her essentially on the run. She hadn't looked at it that way before, she'd tried to frame it into a less sinister story in her mind, but that's what she was, on the run. She could never return to London or speak to anyone she knew there ever again. And that was awful enough but now Sam was so unhappy he was being really naughty and she'd been so concerned with her own problems in Llandegwen she hadn't even noticed.

On the brink of tears, Josie knew she had to leave the room before she fell apart in front of Miss Hughes, this woman who had judged her so harshly, and Sam's teacher. She had to keep some composure. She stood up quickly and gave a vague 'yes' in reply to the headmistress's chastising question, before fleeing the office. The tears had started to spill down her cheeks as she half ran half walked down the long corridor to exit the building.

'Mrs Williams!'

The male voice called her name just before Josie reached the door. She knew it was Mr Jenkins without having to turn around. Desperate for him not to find her crying she quickly, and unsuccessfully for she always flushed when she cried, wiped away the evidence from her face before he reached her.

'Thank you for waiting. I just wanted to say . . .' He seemed to notice her tear-streaked face for the first time and his manner became that of a man unused to a woman crying: uncomfortable. 'Are you all right?' Despite his horror at finding himself in such a situation, Josie thought she saw real concern in his eyes, which if she hadn't been so mortified by the situation she'd have found touching. As it was, she'd just been more or less told off by the headmistress and now she was crying in front of Sam's teacher. *Poor Sam, having such a mess for a mother*, she thought.

'Yes, thank you,' she sniffed before she was betrayed by her own emotions and fresh tears fell. 'I'm so sorry, I'm not usually such a mess. I'm usually much more composed than this.'

'No need to apologise. And I know. I saw your impressive speech at the village meeting the other night.' His tone was so dismissive that Josie almost missed the compliment buried beneath it. It surprised her and put a halt to her tears. She had no idea how to respond.

'Listen, what I actually wanted to say was I think Sam is a good lad. Miss Hughes can be a bit on the stern side, she has very high standards, which is good for the children, but I think she came down a little too hard in there. I wanted you to know, as Sam's teacher, I understand the situation. It's hard settling in somewhere new and what Miss Hughes failed to mention was that he's had a little bit of teasing over his accent. Just children being children, but I think that might explain the justifiable "shut up" from Sam Miss Hughes unfortunately overheard.'

It was a comfort to Josie that Sam's teacher understood their predicament and though she was relieved that he felt Sam's behaviour was justified, she was distressed by the thought of her little boy being teased.

'Thank you. For explaining. I should've known. I'll talk to him.' She could only manage short sentences as she processed all of the information she had just received.

'No problem. There's something else I wanted to suggest, actually. Sam has got quite a bit of energy for a lad his age and I wondered if he had a way to focus that energy, if that might help him settle more easily . . . ?' He seemed uncertain about whether or not to go on, probably worried he might make her cry again, Josie thought. But seeing her look at him expectantly he ploughed on. 'I run a little football club for the lads in the village. It's just a bit of fun for the young ones really, but I noticed Sam kicking his football about in the playground and he's pretty good. He's a little younger than most of the other boys who come to the club, but he's quite big for his age and as I say, he's good. I think it might be good for him. I thought I'd mention it in case it helps. I'd be happy to have him join the club and have a kick around with us. He might even make some friends.'

Josie's heart lifted at this. 'Sam loves football! Oh, that would be wonderful if he could do that. Thank you, Mr Jenkins. That's a perfect idea!'

He seemed to recoil slightly at Josie's overenthusiasm, not at all comfortable with the weight being put on his offer.

'It's really not a problem. I just think it would be good for him,' he said, backing away from her and looking over his shoulder, as if now he'd said what he'd intended he had more important things to be getting on with.

Josie didn't know what to make of him. On the one hand he had defended her and Sam and suggested something that could help her boy, and on the other he was clearly ill at ease with her emotional display.

She was staring at him again so she quickly snapped herself back into action and decided to quit this conversation while she was ahead. The sooner she was out of this school the better.

'OK. I'll mention it to Sam on the way home and we'll let you know. Goodbye then, Mr Jenkins.' Her tone had turned formal in an attempt to cancel out the emotion she'd displayed that he clearly disapproved of. She turned to leave and collect Sam from the playground.

'Tom.'

Josie stalled mid step and looked back over her shoulder.

'You can call me Tom.' It was an order rather than a friendly gesture, accompanied by a dismissive wave of his hand before he walked back up the corridor away from her.

I'll call you what I like, thank you, she thought to herself as she strutted out of the school to collect her son.

Chapter Eight

With all of the drama of the afternoon's events, Josie had barely had time to feel nervous about her first rehearsal as the new choirmistress. But now that the evening had arrived and she and Glenys were pulling on their coats ready to head off to the village hall, the butterflies had started to flutter in her tummy. Glenys must've sensed the nerves in her silence as she gave her an encouraging squeeze before they walked out into the drizzly damp night.

On the walk there Josie filled Glenys in on what had happened at the school that afternoon and she was quite livid.

'I have half a mind to tell that Miss Hughes exactly what I think of her!'

The thought of her tiny mother-in-law squaring up to the very tall headmistress entertained Josie all the way to the village hall.

They arrived ten minutes early in order to settle in and put out some chairs around the piano. Josie took a moment to sit at the instrument to get a feel for it. It was wonderful to feel the ivory keys beneath her fingers again. She hadn't played since she'd left London. It was only now that she had taken her place on the piano stool and fluttered her fingers across the keys that she realised how much she'd missed playing.

'Aren't you a talented one, love?' Glenys remarked with a smile after Josie had played the final notes of a piece her father had taught her. 'You'll be able to teach us so much. Mr Rhys was a fine choirmaster, but he couldn't play the piano like that, bless him.'

At that moment both Josie and Glenys's heads whipped around to the sound of the doors at the back of the hall opening. Peggy entered, brushing the drops of rain that must have started to fall in earnest from her coat as she did, her naturally curly hair wild-looking as a result of the damp night. Her eyes were dancing with excitement.

'Hello, girls! So, how are you feeling about your first night as choirmistress?'

'Nervous!' Josie replied, but she was smiling as she spoke.

Peggy looked around her at the empty hall.

'Am I early? I swear I heard the church bells ring out on my walk up. I thought I was going to be late.'

'Give it a few minutes, love. It's only just gone the hour. I'm sure people are on their way.' Glenys didn't look as confident as she sounded, Josie thought with a sinking feeling.

As the minutes ticked by Josie felt her heart deflating. The doors to the village hall had remained shut since Peggy's arrival, no other person had walked through them to join her choir. Josie had been staring at the doors, willing them to open while Peggy, probably with the intention of distracting them all, shared some bits of gossip that she'd picked up in the shop that day – 'Pamela said Marjorie was quite red-faced at being caught out holding the envelope up to the light to get a look at what it said. Whoever that letter was for can be sure that that nosy woman knows all about it!' – but Josie didn't hear a word. She was chastising herself for getting carried away with the romantic idea of bringing singing back to the village. Just because Glenys and Peggy thought she could do it didn't mean anyone else would care. How stupid of her to think that one impassioned speech at the village meeting would convince the villagers to join her. She was nobody to them, an outsider, it had been foolish to think she could make a difference. This was part of the reason she didn't want to do it in the first place. She was supposed to be making her life easier here, not harder.

'Nobody is coming,' she announced sadly.

Peggy stopped her chatter and Glenys sighed. They couldn't argue with her. The empty chairs in the hall and the hands on the clock pointing to a quarter past the hour were overwhelming evidence to support the case that the new choir had fallen at its first hurdle.

'I'm so sorry, love. I can't think what happened.'

'Maybe people didn't see the flyers?' Peggy was clutching at straws.

'We put them up all around the centre of the village, people would have seen them. They just didn't want to come.' Josie felt empty with disappointment.

The three women sat in silence for a moment.

'Well, that's that then. No point in us sitting here moping. Let's put the chairs away and head home. If I sit here any longer I might cry and I've done quite enough of that today already,' Josie said as she got up from the piano stool and began stacking the chairs she had so excitedly put out not even half an hour earlier. Glenys and Peggy looked at her with sympathy and a fair amount of guilt for a moment before they joined her in the task.

The clattering of the chairs against the wooden floor drowned out the sounds of the heavy doors suddenly opening and a very damp-looking young woman hastily entering the hall. Nobody noticed the pale, slim figure who stood there in a brown coat dripping from the rain, her headscarf plastered to her head, and clutching a now limp and quite torn flyer in her hand. At the same moment that the new arrival let out a confused 'Oh!', Josie had turned to see how many more chairs were in need of stacking, and in the process finally clocked that there was now a fourth person in the hall.

'Hello?' Josie asked, curiously.

'Um, hello . . . I . . . Am I too late? I thought the flyer said half past eight, but it was ripped when I found it and quite hard to read . . . I'm sorry, I'll . . . I'll go,' said the young woman, looking at the scene of disbandment in front of her, a spot of pink appearing on each of her pale cheeks. She turned to leave.

'Wait!' Josie called to her quickly. 'Are you here for the choir practice?'

'Yes,' the woman said shyly, holding out the limp, torn flyer that was now completely illegible thanks to the rain, as if it explained everything she couldn't.

Josie turned back to Peggy and Glenys and with a watery smile said, 'Someone came!' The two women returned her smile but they all knew that it didn't change anything. Three singers did not a choir make.

'Thank you so much for coming . . . ?'

'Bethan.' The woman gave her name uncertainly.

'Thank you for coming, Bethan. The rehearsal was meant to start at eight o'clock but as you can see, no one came so we've had to abandon ship, I'm afraid,' Josie explained sadly.

'Oh, I see. That's a shame. I'm sorry I got the wrong time. The flyer I found was torn, you see . . . Anyway, never mind. It would've been so nice to sing . . .' She turned to leave for the second time, but was once again called back, this time by Peggy.

'Hang on a minute, Bethan. Did you say the flyer you have was torn when you found it? Where did you find it?'

Josie and Glenys looked from one woman to the other, like spectators at a tennis match watching to see where the ball would fall.

'Yes, it was torn when I found it in the bin at the post office. I was putting up a new notice on the board for Jimmy Griffiths after Mrs Davies made him write his out again more neatly, but I dropped it in the bin below by mistake. I found the flyer when I fished it out. But there was a bit ripped away where the time was, so I got it wrong . . . I'm sorry.'

'You've nothing to be sorry for, love,' Glenys said before adding to Peggy and Josie, 'Isn't that strange that the one we put up in the post office got ripped up and put in the bin?'

Josie was already making her way over to the noticeboard next to the entrance to the small kitchen where she had pinned up a flyer earlier that day. She hadn't noticed before that it was no longer there. Instinctively she entered the kitchen and poked her head into the bin. There at the top were the remains of her flyer, crumpled and torn.

She stepped back into the hall, three pairs of eyes looking at her expectantly. 'The one I put up in here earlier is ripped and scrunched up in the bin in there too. I don't understand . . .'

'Could someone have done this on purpose?' Glenys was appalled at the thought.

'It would make sense. I was sure more people would come tonight. It would explain why they didn't,' reasoned Peggy.

'But why? Why would someone do this? *Who* would do this?' Josie was trying to get her head around it all.

'I've got a fair idea who might. It's just the sort of spiteful thing she'd do.' Peggy's eyes were flashing with fury.

Could Peggy really believe Anwen would do this? Did she really hate Josie that much that she'd do something so sneaky? Her sympathy for the scorned Anwen had subsided since the night of the village meeting and not for the first time she wondered how her lovely Matthew could have ever been involved with someone like her, even if they were just school kids at the time.

'Were the rest of the flyers torn down from the lamp posts? I didn't even look on the way here,' Josie said, frustrated with herself for once again being too caught up in her own mind to look at what was going on around her.

'Nor did I, love. And there'd be no use looking now. From the looks of Bethan here it's been spilling out of the heavens since we've been at the hall. We'd not be able to know if the flyers were so wet from the rain they fell to pieces or if they were torn. No, best not to think about that now and there's no use in making accusations and causing fuss.' Glenys gave

Peggy a look full of warning as she said this. 'What's done is done.' Peggy looked suitably chastised.

'So if nobody knew about the rehearsal tonight, do you think that means people might come if they did know?' Josie asked hopefully.

'Um . . . I really wanted to. And I heard Mr Evans tell Mrs Davies he wanted to when they were talking about it in the post office . . .' offered Bethan.

'I'm sure they would, love. How about tomorrow morning we go around the village and ask people ourselves? That way we know for sure that the message got through. We could have the first rehearsal tomorrow night if enough people are keen?' Here was Glenys once again offering to help Josie in her hour of need. The hope that had been extinguished before Bethan's arrival sparked to life again.

'That sounds marvellous, Glenys.' Josie's smile widened as Peggy and Bethan also offered to help to spread the word tomorrow from their respective jobs in the shop and the post office. By eight o'clock the next evening they were to have their first choir rehearsal, take two. Only this time, Josie hoped with all her heart, there would actually be some singers there.

After taking Sam to school on Thursday morning, Josie met Glenys outside the post office. The plan was to rally the troops for that night's rehearsal from the centre of the village. They would walk up and down Colliers Row and talk to those they passed. They had decided to drop into the post office first to speak with Bethan and confirm her attendance for that evening. She shyly but keenly nodded her head while attempting to express how much she was looking forward to it when Marjorie Davies appeared behind the counter alongside her assistant.

'And what would it be that's inspiring such an unusual degree of excitement in you, girl?' Marjorie demanded of Bethan, whose white cheeks flowered with pink embarrassment at the spotlight being thrown on her by her superior. Josie came to her rescue.

'It's our first choir rehearsal tonight, and I wanted to make sure that Bethan here was going to come. We need good members like her. I want the choir to be a huge success!'

'Well, in that case you should have come to me first. I have quite an exceptional voice,' Marjorie said without a hint of modesty. 'I was wondering how soon you might get started. Myself and Mr Evans were discussing it all the other day. He and I have the best voices in Llandegwen, though my voice is slightly better developed than his. If you had come to church you would already know this, of course.'

Josie stifled a giggle at the image of Marjorie and Mr Evans singing over everyone at church on a Sunday. 'Well, please do come tonight. We'll be in the village hall at eight. See you there too, Bethan.'

'Oh, I will be there. Make no mistake.' Marjorie's tone was commanding rather than agreeable, as she leant over the counter, almost pushing over poor Bethan in the process.

As they left the post office Josie could see Glenys had been biting her lip, the laughter in her eyes clear to see.

'Careful, Josie love, that woman will be running the show if you don't mind yourself. Quite an exceptional voice! What'll she say next?!'

* * *

After feeling initially apprehensive about approaching villagers with the intention of enticing them into joining the choir, Josie began to enjoy talking to the locals and getting to know those she'd not met before. The easy chat she had picked up while growing up in a pub gave her confidence and she was lifted by the enthusiasm of many of the people she'd spoken to. She'd had a lovely chat with Mrs Thomas who had promised to send her husband and son over to the village hall that evening. 'I haven't a note in my head but my men have beautiful voices. They're working down the mines today but as soon as they are home I will tell them they are to head over to you tonight. I thought you were marvellous at the town meeting, by the way.'

If Mrs Thomas kept her word, and Josie absolutely trusted she would, they would have two male singers tonight. With Glenys, Peggy, Bethan and Marjorie already onboard she just needed four more to have enough singers to enter the competition. Josie had her fingers crossed for Mr Evans making an appearance that night too. She'd dropped a note in at the rectory that afternoon in the hopes he might be free to join them.

Peggy, the true friend that she was proving to be, had mentioned the rehearsal to all of her customers that day. 'I was like a broken record, saying the same thing over and over, but if it does the trick who cares!' she informed Josie when she popped in on the way home from picking Sam up from school. She'd managed to catch Mr Jenkins, or Tom as he again insisted she call him, that afternoon as he opened the school doors for the children to spill out of at home time. She had wanted to let him know that Sam was keen to join his football club. She had kept her tone brisk, still conscious of the impression of an emotional wreck that she'd given him the previous day. She wanted to show him that she was usually quite poised. Not that she cared what he thought, of course.

'Have you found many members for your choir yet?' His question surprised Josie, he'd seemed so uninterested in any kind of conversation initially.

'Why, would you like to join?'

'Bloody hell, no.' He looked appalled at the mere suggestion and Josie felt stung. 'Someone like me singing would be ridiculous.'

'Singing isn't ridiculous,' she said hotly. Music was her passion and she didn't like the thought that he was belittling it. She'd reacted sharply, which was unlike her, but something about him made her immediately defensive. He had a pompous manner she wasn't used to, and she thought he was saying that one of the things she loved most was too silly for the likes of him, which upset her. Perhaps she was a little sensitive after the no-show the previous night.

'That's not what I meant . . .' He seemed annoyed, with himself, or her, Josie couldn't tell, but she felt she had first dibs on any position of anger given what he'd just said. 'I'm sure you got the people you needed.'

'Well, actually we got off to a bit of a rocky start,' Josie said reluctantly. 'Word didn't quite get around as well as I'd planned – long story – but I am hoping I have put that right today and I'll actually get some willing singers to turn up to the rehearsal tonight. Some people who don't think they are too important to sing. You know, people who don't find the idea of a choir ridiculous.' She gave him a pointed look before she turned her back on him in an attempt to match his haughtiness. He might have helped her out with Sam, but she wasn't going to let him put down her efforts with the choir. Anyone who thought singing was ridiculous was an idiot in her book.

She wasn't a woman to be crossed today but Anwen hadn't been given that message. After collecting Sam, Josie passed her at the school gates. Fully prepared to ignore her cold looks she was surprised to hear Anwen's snooty voice address her back.

'How's everything going with the choir?' Josie turned to find Anwen staring at her with a nasty glint in her eye and a sickly sweet smile. Her hand was on her hip, drawing attention to her perfectly tiny waist.

'Very well, thanks, Anwen,' Josie answered with the airy confidence of someone who had spent their day rallying troops and getting encouraging results.

Anwen gave Josie a questioning look, clearly confused by her answer. Josie smiled with satisfaction at this. If Anwen was responsible for sabotaging her flyers, then making a success of tonight would be the best revenge. The disappointment of the previous evening was still fresh enough in Josie's mind to restrain her from getting her hopes up too high. Nevertheless, the flame of hope for success tonight burned small and bright in her heart as she walked away from Anwen and back to Glenys's cottage, watching Sam running along ahead of her.

Chapter Nine

A strange feeling of déjà vu enveloped Josie as she entered the village hall that night and began once again to set out the chairs around the piano. The only difference being that where there had been excited chatter between herself and Glenys the night before, there was now a silence heavy with nervous anticipation.

When they had arranged the room to their satisfaction they both took their seats – Josie on the stool behind the piano, Glenys in the chair opposite her. Josie laid out her sheet music with an inordinate amount of care, desperate to fill the final minutes as the clock ticked towards eight. Glenys cleared her throat while Josie fussed about, the tension in the room almost unbearable. To say the wave of relief that washed over them when the heavy doors of the hall finally opened was palpable would have been an understatement. It was only heightened further by the fact that it was a young man neither of them had spoken to that day who walked through them. Word must have got around the village about tonight's rehearsal and this gave Josie the hope she was desperate for. She rushed to greet him.

'Hello! I don't think we've met before. I'm Josie Williams. Have you come to join the choir?' She asked this just to make sure the poor chap hadn't just wandered in here by mistake. She was still a little upset by the previous night's no-show, despite the hope that had been rekindled.

'Yes, if that's OK? Mr Jenkins told me you might still be looking for members?' Josie looked at him in surprise forcing him to add, 'I'm Gethin and I'm new at the school and I quite like to sing so he suggested I come tonight.' He adjusted his dark-rimmed glasses for something to do with his hands – he was clearly a little wrong-footed by Josie's bemused pause.

Tom had sent a singer her way – why on earth had he done that when he'd made it clear he thought the whole thing ridiculous? Her bemusement was starting to make things awkward so she plastered a smile on her face. 'Of course! I'm so glad you came. Please take a seat.'

Visibly relaxed by her warm welcome, Gethin moved to sit next to Glenys and introduced himself to her. As he did so Marjorie and Bethan walked into the hall together. Marjorie was so engrossed in explaining the importance of breathing in singing to Bethan as they approached the chairs around the piano that she didn't even acknowledge Josie. Bethan managed a meek half-smile of a greeting but she clearly didn't dare detach herself from Marjorie mid lecture. Their entrance was swiftly followed by Mr Evans who made a beeline for Josie.

'My dear, thank you for your kind note. I was so honoured to get a personal invitation tonight that had I had a prior engagement I would have immediately cancelled it. As it happens I didn't, but the point is I would have done so. I think this choir is a wonderful idea. And who have we got so far?' He looked around him at the small group who had taken seats around the piano and walked over to join them.

Mr Evans's entrance was followed by Peggy's and two men, generations enough apart and similar enough in appearance that they had to be father and son. They must be Mrs Thomas's family, Josie thought, delighted that the nice woman she had met that afternoon had kept her word. As she introduced herself to them, learning that Michael was indeed Mrs Thomas's husband and Owen their son, she got the feeling that they were perhaps there a little under duress. But they had come to sing, and that was what mattered. She'd just have to make it enjoyable enough for them that they would want to come back.

As Michael and Owen took to their seats, Josie looked up to see a very elegant woman somewhere in her forties dressed in a beautifully tailored navy blue wool pencil skirt and jacket walking through the hall doors. She was removing a matching hat from her perfectly set short dark curls as she made her way over to Josie.

'Good evening. Are you Josie Williams?' Her voice was soft but confident. And though her poise and tall elegance should have been intimidating, her eyes conveyed a kindness that immediately warmed Josie towards her.

'Yes, I am. Are you here for the choir?' Josie asked uncertainly.

'If that's all right, yes. I'm Catherine Morgan. It's a pleasure to meet you.'

'And you. And of course, I'm very pleased you have come. Would you like to take a seat?'

Catherine nodded happily and made her way towards Mr Evans who clearly knew her well and looked quite pleased to see her. The others seemed a little unsure of how to respond to the new arrival, but Catherine gave no sign of discomfort at their awkward reception and smiled and nodded hellos at them all with grace and ease. Josie wondered who she was. She'd have to ask Glenys more when they made their way home later.

She glanced at the clock on the wall. It was almost ten past the hour now and unlikely there would be any more singers joining them that evening. Josie had counted nine heads: one short of her target ten in order to qualify for the competition. Never mind, nine was better than none. Maybe if she made a success of it tonight other villagers might feel tempted to join. She made her way to the piano and stood in front of the group that was to be her choir.

'Hello, everyone. Thank you all very much for coming. I'm so thrilled to begin our first practice together. I thought to start with it might be nice for you all to just sing something together and loosen up your voices. See how we sound.'

She got a few nods of agreement from the group, giving her enough encouragement to go on, but there was still a layer of ice to be broken, she felt.

'I'm afraid I only have music for one Welsh song tonight – it was a song my husband Matthew taught me when we were together in London. He was actually singing it the night we met and I loved it so much I ended up marrying him because of it.' Her attempt at humour seemed to do the trick and the mood in the room took on a more relaxed air. 'But he said it was a song everyone knew well where he came from, so I'm hoping you will. In case he was fibbing about this you can stand behind me and read the lyrics on the sheet music over my shoulder.' There was a ripple of laughter at this. 'The song is "Myfanwy"?'

'Oh yes, I know it well, beautiful song,' boomed Mr Evans, clapping his hands together.

'As do I,' said Marjorie, wanting to assert her position as an experienced singer from the beginning.

'I might need a reminder of the words . . .' Bethan said quietly, tucking a lock of her black hair behind her ear.

'Me too. Glad I'm not the only one!' Gethin smiled at Bethan, prompting her cheeks to turn pink, her glance dropping to her feet.

Josie waved them over as she took her seat on the piano stool, the rest of the group rising to their feet ready to sing. In the beat of silence between Josie counting them in and her fingers hitting the keys, the doors to the village hall opened with a loud creaking sound. Nine heads turned to see who had come through the doors. Josie wondered who it was, she was unable to see for herself as she was seated, her view blocked by those stood behind her.

'Fred, good fellow! Have you come to join us?' Mr Evans was the first to break the silence.

Josie stood to find the tall, slim man with the greying dark hair who had spoken in her defence at the village meeting at the start of the week standing in the doorway, looking uncomfortable.

Fred cleared his throat before answering, 'Yes, I thought I might. If I'm not too late?'

He had a look of dejection about him that made Josie want

to rush to reassure and welcome him to their group. 'Not at all. Please come in and join us around the piano. We were just about to sing "Myfanwy". I have the words on my sheet music if you want to stand next to Bethan and Gethin here. If you need to.' She was smiling at him encouragingly.

'No, no, I know that song well,' he said as he walked towards them all, nodding hello to Michael and Catherine, the latter seeming genuinely pleased to see him there. 'I'm sorry I'm late. One of my sheep was missing and I had trouble getting him in in the dark.'

'Oh dear! You managed to get him home in the end, I hope?'

'I did indeed, thank you.' He was so serious, Josie thought.

'Well, thank goodness for that! And we were really only just about to get started, so your timing is perfect!' She had her tenth member and Josie was thrilled. As Fred took his place next to Catherine at the end of the line around the piano, Josie sat down on the stool once again, fingers poised to play. 'So let's give it your best voices now, everyone, and see how we get on! One, two, three, four . . .'

After she played the opening bars of music the group burst into song and Josie could only thank her lucky stars that she was facing in the opposite direction to them all so that none of them could see her face. They were singing of love and longing, but it didn't feel that way to Josie. She winced inwardly as the sound behind her resembled a combination of pots and pans falling out of a cupboard and how she imagined a one-man-band might sound if he fell over repeatedly. They were all out of time and they were all singing at extreme variations in volume. It was a shambles.

On reflection, perhaps getting them all to sing together right away wasn't the best idea she'd had. She'd clearly underestimated the diversity of their voices and there was evidently a lot of work to be done. However, to give them their credit, none of them had sung together before and many of them probably didn't get much of a chance to exercise their voices regularly. It was to be expected, Josie reminded herself, and she wasn't shy of a bit of a challenge. She just needed to organise them properly, according to their range and tone, and to give some of them guidance on developing their voice. She needed to show faith in them and to make it fun too. Wasn't that what she'd said in her speech to the committee? She wanted to bring the happiness singing and song could offer back to the village. So that's what she would do, one step at a time.

As she played the closing notes, composing her expression into something more supportive and encouraging than her current wince, she prepared to turn around to face the group. However, almost as soon as the song was finished laughter erupted from the singers.

'Oh dear!' Catherine put her hand to her mouth to stifle her giggles.

'We're not very good, are we?' Peggy's voice was high-pitched with mirth.

'Strangled cats, that's what we sound like.' Owen nudged his father who joined in with the laughter.

'Speak for yourselves, *I* sounded perfectly fine,' Marjorie said crossly, only making the rest of them laugh harder.

Josie was bemused but their good humour was contagious. Laughing too she asked, 'But did it feel good, to sing?'

'Oh yes, dear. Singing feels glorious. Even if we didn't do the best job of it,' Mr Evans said. Peggy and Bethan were drying their eyes, while Glenys looked as though she'd given herself a stitch from giggling. Even Fred's sad eyes had a glint of lightness to them, which was all the encouragement Josie needed to be determined to help them all to sing together better. If one song could put smiles on almost all of their faces, just think what singing regularly could do. And there were certainly some strong voices among them – two or three boomed out louder than the others – but they had drowned out the softer singers, making it difficult for Josie to get a grasp on the range. She needed to hear them all sing individually to really get a sense of what she was working with here.

'Well, the first time was never going to be perfect. Let's just look on it as clearing away the cobwebs. Give yourselves a pat on the back for that. Now I think it would be a good idea for me to hear you all sing on your own, just so that I can hear your voices properly and then I can work on how to place everyone.'

Josie saw a look of panic on Bethan's face at this idea. She was clearly very shy and being in the spotlight, even if everyone else had to do it too, wouldn't be easy for her. She'd have to think of a way of easing her worry. Hearing the more confident singers first would be a good start. Perhaps as everyone relaxed Bethan might too.

'Who would like to go first? Mr Evans?' He leapt up immediately, delighted at the idea, as she knew he would be. 'I'd like you to sing some scales. I'll give you the key. Ready?' She played the first note to start him off and then Mr Evans boomed out the scale in his thundering baritone voice. He really was very good, Josie thought. But clearly he was used to being able to sing as loud as he wished in his church services. She'd need to work with him on controlling his volume so that he didn't drown out the other singers.

'Marvellous, thank you, Mr Evans. You have a very powerful voice, I'm impressed.'

'Thank you, my dear. I always fancied myself as a bit of a Bing Crosby but with more oomph, you know, and a dog collar.' He was quite serious and Josie had to bite her lip to stop herself from giggling.

'Marjorie, would you like to step up next?'

The buttons on the postmistress's dress were already slightly straining to contain her plump frame, but they looked set to burst when an operatic shrill rushed from her lungs at a volume so high Josie thought she might be heard all the way out at the coal mine.

'That was wonderful, Marjorie. I wonder though if we could try it again with a bit less power?' Josie whispered her next words, instinctively realising that Marjorie probably needed a little more diplomacy than the others when it came to constructive criticism. 'Just because we need to be able to hear everyone else too and your voice is so strong you'd overshadow everyone and that wouldn't be fair, would it?'

'I suppose not,' Marjorie agreed, though she didn't look entirely convinced by the idea of her overshadowing everyone being a bad thing at all.

She actually had a lovely voice when she controlled it. The shrillness was lost and a purity took its place. This was really encouraging, Josie felt. The others each took their turn to stand and sing next to the piano and the concern Josie had felt at the seemingly mammoth task ahead of her of whipping these singers into shape eased somewhat when she heard their solo voices. They could all sing; a few were a little rough around the edges – Owen and Gethin needed to work on their breathing – and Josie was a little concerned about Bethan who she could barely hear above the piano, even when she played softly. The young woman's shyness was making it difficult for Josie to place her voice, given she couldn't really hear it. To spare her blushes further, Josie hadn't made a big deal of her whispered notes. Instead, she vowed to find a way to bring Bethan out of her shell. She clearly loved to sing, that's why she was there, Josie just had to find a way to give her the confidence to really embrace the music and sing from her heart.

It was Fred who really moved Josie that night though. His voice was also quiet, in fact his entire presence was quiet. If it hadn't been for Catherine giving him a reassuring nod as he joined Josie at the piano and the words of support she gave him when he had finished singing his scales, he might have been a ghost, so detached from the group he was. But his soft tenor voice was like silk and he made even boring scales sound full of meaning. She knew nothing about him, other than that he seemed to be well respected by Mr Evans and Catherine.

She had so many questions to ask Glenys later that night. The more she knew about her new choir the better able she might be to help them find their strongest voices. She had to admit that she was also just a bit curious. Maybe village life and the desire to know everyone else's business were rubbing off on her.

After everyone had sung their scales there was just enough

time to discuss when they were to meet next and what they might sing.

'I can ask Mr Rhys if he wouldn't mind us using his old choir songbooks on my next visit to the poor old fellow. I'm sure it would cheer him to know they are being dusted off and put to good use again,' Mr Evans said.

'That would be brilliant, Mr Evans, thank you. Then perhaps we can choose a few songs to start us off and work on those.' Josie had been worried about her lack of music for the choir. She had brought the small number of music sheets she had from London, but unsurprisingly they didn't include any Welsh choral music, other than the one piece Matthew had left her. It was the song he had been singing the night they met in her ma and pa's pub, the song that made her fall in love with him. He had given it to her as a wedding present and she had cherished it. She wondered if he knew it might come in handy one day. The thought made her smile.

'What about the competition, Josie?' Peggy asked. Josie hadn't mentioned the competition yet. She didn't want to overwhelm some of the less confident members with something so serious and so quickly. She was also selfishly still quite nervous about putting herself so much on the line with the choir. Choral competitions were a serious business in Wales and she hadn't quite found her groove yet in Llandegwen. She didn't want to push things too far too soon. She could still lose the only home she had on offer if it all went wrong. But clearly her friend was desperate to go, she knew that was a large part of Peggy wanting to join the choir. Josie felt guilty at the thought that her own selfish fears might be holding the choir back. It would be good for them to have a competition to work towards, and after hearing each singer individually she had faith in them being good enough to compete if they worked hard enough. It wouldn't be easy but it would be just what they needed for the choir to be taken seriously. In for a penny, in for a pound, wasn't that how the saying went?

'What competition is that?' questioned the ever-competitive Marjorie.

'It's the Welsh Valleys Choral Competition. It takes place in Bridgend end of next month.'

'That sounds exciting,' Bethan said timidly.

'It would be, we'd have so much fun,' Peggy promised Bethan.

'Well, I would like to have a goal in mind to work towards and it's about time this village started competing again. We used to do very well before the war,' Marjorie added.

'But we weren't very good.' Michael was doubtful.

'Strangled cats, remember?' Owen added.

'If the competition is at the end of April, it doesn't give us much time to prepare. Perhaps we should see how we get on first?' Catherine's natural confidence had been challenged a little by this idea.

'But the closing date is the end of next week. We haven't got time to wait. We need to get our application off as soon as we can to be sure it's accepted,' Peggy informed them all.

'It was clear from tonight's rehearsal that we were excellent, some of us more than others, of course.' Marjorie smoothed her mousy brown hair as she said this, clearly indicating that she felt that she was one of the "some". 'We will of course be ready.'

'What if we practised a few nights a week? Three maybe, if

we could all manage it?' Glenys looked at the rest of the group as she asked this and was given nods of assent all round, but some of the group still looked a little anxious about the idea of competing so soon, namely the Thomas men and Catherine. Even Bethan had started to grasp the enormity of the challenge. It was time for Josie to be the leader she had promised them she would be. She had to get them to believe in themselves enough to enter the competition.

'Glenys is right. If we work hard and practise three times a week we can absolutely do this! You all have wonderful voices and I have total belief in us all doing Llandegwen proud. I was going to mention the competition next time, but I hadn't realised the closing date was so soon. It'll be hard work but I really think we can do it. What do you say?'

Her question was met with silence, until Fred, who had said nothing till now, became the unlikely figure to give the choir the final push they needed to accept the challenge in front of them.

'I say we do it. What have we got to lose, eh?'

Josie beamed, Peggy clapped and the room filled with nervous laughter.

'Well, that's settled then,' said Mr Evans with a smile as he leant back in his chair.

Chapter Ten

'Well, that went well, didn't it?'

'Oh, Glenys, I was just happy that people showed up at all, everything else was a bonus. Including your own lovely voice! You really played that down.' Josie nudged Glenys playfully as the older woman flushed at the compliment.

Glenys had enjoyed herself and as Josie reflected on the night on their walk home together she realised she had too. Her relief at the mere fact that people had shown up at all had been quickly replaced by excitement at having some really good voices in the group. Yes, they had got off to a tricky start when they first sang together, but she could hear their potential when they sang solo, and she felt that they had heard it too. It was going to be so wonderful helping them to sing their best. She'd been so reluctant to do it at first that she'd forgotten how much joy she got out of music and how much she missed having a purpose. She had needed something to do to feel like she was part of the village, that she had a role there. She also needed something to focus on to take her mind off the huge change she'd made in her life in coming to Llandegwen, the dark mess she'd run away from in London, and the ache she felt in her heart at having no family of her own close by, except for Sam.

She felt guilty for even thinking that, given how generous and supportive and generally wonderful Glenys had been to her. She was everything family should be, but it wasn't like it was with her own flesh and blood. Now that she thought about it, when was the last time she'd heard from her own flesh-and-blood brother? Was it months since she'd last had word from Billy? Last she'd heard he had taken a job driving buses across America. He'd told her he wouldn't be able to write to her for a while but that she should get in touch with his old friend Ronnie, who was doing well for himself in the East End these days. That was his solution to her predicament when she wrote to him telling him of her struggles to put a roof over her head. He'd been sympathetic but he hadn't quite made the fortune he'd hoped to make in New York and so he couldn't do much to help out. She could tell he was worried about her by his rushed hand and clumsy sentences though, especially if he wouldn't be able to write to her till he'd got himself sorted, and who knew how long that would take? But now it had already taken too long and it was too late. He wouldn't know where to find her. She wondered if he'd ask Ronnie where she was, and the thought made her feel sick. What would Ronnie tell him? Both lies and the truth would hurt Billy – he'd clearly been away so long he'd had no idea what his old friend had become. In a way she hoped she'd never hear from her brother again. As sad as that was, at least it meant they'd both be safe.

She thought once more of Glenys sending her the train fare

to Wales and in turn a way out of the nightmare she'd found herself in and she felt another rush of warmth for this older woman. She was grateful to Matthew for so many things – giving her the chance to know how it felt to be loved by a good man, and Sam, of course – but right now his mother was right up there with the gifts he had given her.

It was funny, Josie had thought being in Llandegwen would make her feel closer to Matthew, but sometimes she had to look at the photograph of him in his soldier's uniform on the shelf next to the fire in Glenys and Harry's living room to remind herself of the lines of his face. His image had been fading from her mind for a while now, but she thought being in Llandegwen would bring it back to her in full colour again. She felt a little guilty and confused that it hadn't. Josie's mind was overwhelmed by conflicting thoughts these days, which was exactly why the choir was so good for her. It would focus her mind on one, brighter thing.

'So what's the story with Catherine? You all seemed quite surprised to see her when she arrived.' Josie's mind had returned to the questions she'd saved up to ask Glenys after choir practice that night.

'I have to say you could've knocked me down with a feather when she walked in. She's the mayor's wife. I've only ever seen her in the village doing the odd errand. She's always very polite, says hello and everything, but no one really knows anything about her.'

According to Glenys, Mayor Morgan didn't really get involved in Llandegwen social affairs. He was mayor of Castleforth and the surrounding villages, Llandegwen included, but he carried out his business in the town. Village life didn't seem to interest the Morgans much. Until now, it would appear. They lived in a grand house on the outskirts of Llandegwen, up near Fred's farm. The locals found their choice to live in the village curious, given they rarely socialised there – presumably there were much grander engagements to attend in the town. Which is why it was so strange to them all that Catherine would want to join the choir.

'I don't even know how she'd have got wind about the choir. Perhaps Mr Evans mentioned it to her. He would be the only one of us who sees her, what with parish matters often taking him to the town hall. Oh, and there's Fred, of course, I think he might know her a bit better than the rest of us with them being sort of neighbours. But then Fred keeps himself to himself, so who knows.'

'I wondered about Fred too. He seemed like a bit of an outsider. I thought that the night of the committee meeting too. He seems to hover almost on the edge of things and everyone looks quite surprised when he speak up.'

'You have got the measure of things there, Josie love,' Glenys chuckled. 'You might not be from these parts but you've worked Fred out right away.'

'But why is he like that?' Josie tucked a wisp of her blond hair that had fluttered across her face back into the pin it had escaped from.

'He was always a quiet man but he was friendly too, up for a bit of a chat in the village when he made his deliveries from the farm. A gentle soul. His family have lived on that farm going back generations. They were always involved in village matters. Fred should be on the committee but he didn't want his place.'

'Why not?'

Glenys thought about it. 'I'm not really sure, love. All I know is that after his wife died we saw less of him. She was a lovely woman, died giving birth to their boy. It was ever so sad.' Glenys pulled her coat around her a little tighter. 'He was left to look after the poor lad by himself. He had offers of help from lots of folk here, but refused them all. He did a good job though. David grew up to be a good lad – he became a soldier like our Matthew and died like him too. That's something me and Fred have in common. But like I say, he keeps himself to himself. I certainly didn't think he'd be one for the choir.'

Josie was even more intrigued by Fred after hearing Glenys tell his story. She now understood some of the sorrow she saw in his eyes and had heard in his voice when he sang his scales as if his heart depended on it. He had suffered great loss, that was obvious from what Glenys had said, but she didn't want him to keep himself separate from the group. Choirs were all about unity, singing together in perfect harmony. She'd have to find a way of drawing him into the group.

When they arrived back at the little cottage a short time later, Glenys began regaling Harry with the events of the evening while Josie went upstairs to check on Sam. As she stood on the lower steps she glanced over at the couple she was sharing a home with and saw Harry smile and nod as he listened to his wife, wide-eyed with excitement, telling him who was there and the competition they were to enter. His easy manner with his wife when they were alone contrasted so starkly with the awkward and silent man Josie usually saw that it proved even further to her that it was her and Sam's presence that displeased him. She shook her head and carried on up the stairs.

Standing on the landing she gently opened the door to the bedroom she shared with her son. His little body immediately twisted round to face her.

'Sam, you're still awake!'

'I couldn't sleep, Mummy.'

'Oh my angel, why not?' She padded softly over to his bed and knelt down to face him, stroking his dark hair.

'I needed you to sing to me.'

'If I sing to you now, will that help?'

'I think so,' he said with great seriousness. His expression made her heart melt. This was the sweet boy she knew him to be. She just wished the school and the rest of the village could see it too. She so wanted him to be happy, and as she made efforts to carve out her own contentment in the village, she'd need to work harder to help Sam find his. She kissed his head as he dropped off to sleep to the sound of her voice.

It wasn't until Saturday morning, when Josie took him to his first football practice, that Sam had told her how his grandfather had spent the hour or so that she and Glenys had been at choir practice telling him about Matthew as a boy.

'He said I look just like Pa did when he was my age. Is that true, Mummy?' Sam was always keen to hear stories about his father. His constant curiosity, though completely natural, was also a painful reminder to Josie that her boy would grow up without a father.

'I'm sure it is, my angel. I didn't know him when he was a

boy but your grandpa did. And you definitely have the same eyes as he did.'

'You always say that.'

'That's because it's true.' Josie gave him a squeeze as she said this, which he pretended to hate, but Josie knew he still loved. She wondered how many more years she'd have of those cuddles. 'Did you have fun with your grandpa then?' She was genuinely curious. She hadn't expected Harry to entertain Sam at all while she and Glenys were out of the house.

'Yeah, I suppose. I liked hearing about Pa. But Grandpa got a bit sad when he talked about him.'

'He must miss him, Sam. Like we do.' As Sam nodded his head at this Josie wondered once again about the puzzle that was Harry Williams. It was good of him to talk to Sam about Matthew. Maybe there was some hope for them getting along after all.

'It would probably help if you left.'

'Excuse me?' Josie paused wringing her hands while she anxiously watched Sam running up the field in pursuit of the football to check she'd just heard Tom correctly. He had walked away from the boys towards her but she'd been so focused on Sam she hadn't noticed till he'd spoken to her.

'You're putting him off, standing there with that look on your face. It would be better if you left him to it.'

Josie was a little taken aback by his bluntness. She hadn't been aware she had any kind of look on her face and she wasn't used to people telling her what to do when it came to her son. She felt her defences rising. Josie was just about to tell him she knew what her son needed and she'd rather stay, but as she opened her mouth she glanced at Sam and caught him looking uncomfortably from her to the other boys. She knew that look, it was the one he always gave her when she waited for him at the top of the street in London as he played with his friends. He wanted her to go.

Josie swallowed the words she had been about to utter and grudgingly, her pride not relishing the moment, turned back to Tom. In the few seconds that had passed he'd already walked away, back towards the boys and was now blowing his whistle to get their attention. He hadn't waited for her response, which Josie took to mean he'd been ordering her to leave, not asking. She bristled at this realisation but given he was right and she didn't want to ruin this for Sam, she reluctantly retreated from the field. As she did so, she inwardly fumed at the way Tom had spoken to her. She didn't want to acknowledge that she might have perhaps been more cross about the fact that he was right in what he'd said, rather than with how he said it. It was easier to be indignant with someone than to admit they had a point.

Stomping off her vexation, Josie headed back into the village. Given she now had time to kill, she thought she might call into the shop to let Peggy know that she'd sent off the letter of registration that they had written together to the Welsh Valleys Choral Competition the previous day. They had had to submit their number of choristers, the name of their choir and which category they would be competing in. As theirs was a mixed choir with only ten members there was just one category open to them, but having just the one was more than enough for them to focus on for now, Josie felt. They would be sent the rules and details of the event once their registration had been accepted, but several members of the choir knew from years back that you had to sing three songs in order to be judged. Josie was going to speak to the group at that night's rehearsal about which three songs they should choose. She was hoping Mr Evans would have got permission from old Mr Rhys to use his songbooks by then.

When she got to the shop she found that the door hadn't been closed properly by the last person who had passed through it and so it didn't announce her arrival with its customary ding of the bell. Her entrance continued to go unnoticed as she moved behind the baskets filled with vegetables which were stacked on two shelves, providing a barrier between the door and the counter. The highest shelf reached head height on Josie and therefore concealed her movements to a large degree. Which was how she was able to hear Anwen telling two other patrons just what she thought of the new choir.

'I mean, it's just so embarrassing. It's one thing for the committee to indulge her silly little sing-songs and pretend it's a choir within the village, but it's quite another to let her humiliate Llandegwen publicly at a competition. For all we know she'll have them singing "Knees Up Mother Brown" or something equally as brassy as her.' Josie could only see the back of Anwen's head but it was enough to know that she had shuddered as she'd said this.

'Bethan said that she had them sing "Myfanwy", so I don't think she'll—'

'But it's not just the songs, though, is it?' Anwen cut the poor woman off. 'It's who's in the choir too. That oddball Fred, for example. And that tragic spinster Peggy. She's so desperate for any kind of social engagement, being stuck with that crazy old mother of hers.'

'Shhh, Peggy might hear you!' Josie recognised this woman as Joan, another of the mothers from the school. She had at least had the decency to look mortified at the idea that Peggy might overhear the unkind words being spoken about her in her own shop. Josie flamed at the idea of her kind friend being disrespected in such a way. She was about to step into full view and say as much but held back as the women continued their discussion, half of Anwen's face now visible to Josie.

'Don't be so dramatic, Joan. I know that stockroom is right out the back, that's why I sent the woman there. And anyway, I'm only speaking the truth, they are all oddballs in that ridiculous choir. No self-respecting person would join and I think the village really should intervene in this competition nonsense.'

'But the vicar is in the choir and he's on the committee . . .' Joan trailed off as Anwen glared at her.

'I actually heard that Catherine Morgan joined. She wouldn't be part of anything improper, so I think you might be wrong there, Anwen.' Josie didn't recognise the second woman who hadn't spoken till now, but she was happy to see there was at least someone who was prepared to question the queen bee. She was even happier when the news of Catherine being a member of her choir visibly stunned Anwen.

'The mayor's wife? Are you sure?'

'Quite sure. Marjorie Davies was crowing about how they had some class in the choir, and it wasn't just her usual boasting, Bethan confirmed it.'

Anwen's face turned beetroot with rage as she fussed with

her basket, making it clear she was intending to leave. 'Tell Peggy she was too slow, I have to go. Goodbye, ladies.' And with that she stalked towards the exit, lost in her own fury, not looking where she was going, and slammed straight into Josie. It was clear from Anwen's expression, which resembled a mix of surprise and horror, that she was unsure of how long Josie had been standing there, and therefore how much she might have overheard. For a moment Anwen was a deer in the headlights but she quickly recovered herself, and deciding attack was the best form of defence, she barked at Josie, 'Didn't anyone ever tell you that it's rude to lurk in doorways? No wonder your son has no manners.' And with that she shoved past and left the shop, slamming the door behind her with such force that it shook in the frame and the bell jangled almost hysterically.

For a moment no one said anything, the silence only broken by Peggy, oblivious to everything that had just occurred, returning to her place behind the counter clutching a tin of something Josie couldn't quite make out.

'Where's Anwen? Has she left after sending me digging out the back for her precious evaporated milk?'

'I'd better go too. Hello, Josie,' Joan said meekly as she scurried from the shop, clearly uncomfortable with facing the music Anwen had orchestrated. The other woman, whose name Josie still hadn't learnt, sauntered out behind Joan with a smirk on her face, giving Josie a conspiratorial wink as she passed her.

Peggy was still behind the counter holding the tin looking baffled as Josie made her way towards her.

'What was all that about?'

'Oh, just Anwen being a cow, and then being put back in her box,' Josie said with amusement, her eyes glinting. When it was clear that she would say no more, Peggy rolled her eyes and shook her head. The scene Josie had witnessed had been too perfect to describe.

'I won't ask then.'

Josie noticed for the first time that her friend looked tired. 'How are things with you?'

'Oh, you know.' Peggy seemed as though she would stay silent, but Josie's concerned look encouraged her to open up. 'Mam is having one of her bad days. I was late opening the shop, she was so desperate for me not to leave her up there on her own. It's silly as I'm only down here, it's not like I've gone anywhere.' Peggy massaged her temples to alleviate some of the tension behind her eyes.

'Is there anything I can do?'

'Yes, you can stand here and keep me company for a bit. Entertain me with your sparkling London-girl conversation.'

Josie laughed. As tired as Peggy clearly was with carrying the burden of her mother's problems on her own shoulders, she was always quick to find energy for fun. Josie admired her friend so much for doing so. She'd remind herself of that the next time she let the clouds in her life weigh her down.

'OK. Let's see . . . do you know Tom Jenkins? The teacher at the school?'

'Yes, I do. Well, I don't know him, know him. But I know as much about him as everyone else here does. Why?'

'He's Sam's teacher and he was really helpful when Miss Hughes had a go at me for Sam's behaviour. He actually stood up for Sam in front of her. And he's let him join his football club even though he's a little too young. But then he was really rude about the choir. He called it ridiculous, as if it was beneath him or something. And just now he pretty much told me to go away because I was putting Sam off at his football club. I just don't know what to make of him. On the one hand he's been so nice but on the other he's been a pompous sod, quite frankly.'

Peggy looked thoughtful. 'Well, the pompous thing is because of who he is, but I'm surprised he was rude about the choir. He doesn't normally get involved in any village events.'

'What do you mean by who he is?'

'He's a Jenkins.' Peggy shrugged as if that explained everything. Josie looked at her expectantly until Peggy realised she needed more information. 'The Jenkinses own three of the small collieries in this part of the Valleys, including the one down the road. Have done for generations. They are filthy rich and very powerful. Hard not to be pompous when you come from that kind of family.'

'But he's a teacher?' Josie was very confused.

'There's a reason for that.' Peggy's tone had turned gossipy now that it had dawned on her that she had a new audience for this piece of information, so used was she to the fact that everyone in this village already knew everyone else's business. She leant over the counter conspiratorially and Josie did the same from the other side, eager to know the story. 'He's been disinherited from the family's fortune. Exiled.' Peggy's eyes widened as she said this, to give the statement its full dramatic effect.

'Why?' Josie was riveted.

'Years back, before the war, there was a really bad accident in the mine outside Llandegwen. One of the boys lost both his legs when a beam collapsed on them. Apparently everyone had been saying the structure was dangerous for weeks and needed looking at, but they were ignored. On top of that the boy was too young to be working in the mine, he was illegal. So to cover it all up the Jenkinses pretended that it never happened, that the lad was never employed by them. Wiped his name from all the records. But that meant the family didn't get any compensation and weren't able to give their son the proper care he needed. I think he ended up in a home somewhere. It was so sad. I was just a kid at the time, but the whole village knew what they'd done. No one could say anything because they needed their jobs but Llandegwen made it clear the Jenkinses weren't welcome here.

'Tom would've been a kid back then too, and he and his brothers got picked on a lot for what his family did. So he's always kept himself to himself. Everyone was shocked when he moved to the village and got a job at the school, but then word got round that he'd been given the cold shoulder by his family. Apparently he wanted nothing to do with the collieries or their money because of what his family had done to that poor boy's family. He wanted to work in the village to give something back, he said. He didn't want to be tarnished by his family name. But it's not as easy as that and people are still suspicious about him snitching on them to their bosses at the coal mine. So he's still treated like he's got the Jenkins power. He could go back to their fold at any time, as far as many people here are concerned. I don't know, though, he's a bit self-important and he keeps to himself, but he has been teaching for years now and he lives in a tiny cottage, nowhere fancy, so it can't all be an act.'

Josie took this all in. So when Tom had said 'someone like me' he'd meant someone of his class. In Josie's book that was a pretty snobbish thing to say, even if he was living a more frugal life these days. She felt that she had more of the measure of the man now that she was aware of where he came from, family fortune or no family fortune.

'Did he ever marry?'

'No, he's a defiant bachelor. Many women have tried and failed to snag him. Money and that ridiculously handsome face of his have made him the number one target for the ladies in villages and towns for miles. He's kept them all at a safe distance though, which is another reason I think he's genuine in wanting to give back to the village after what his family did. One of Anwen's snotty friends courted him for a while after the war, but when it ended she said it was because he wouldn't give up teaching to get his inheritance. I think there's more to him than most people think.'

'Maybe. But none of that excuses being rude though. He can be both honourable and a snob, I suppose.'

'No one's perfect, are they?'

'Speak for yourself, madam,' Josie joked as she said goodbye to her friend who she was pleased to see was lighter in spirit than before.

Chapter Eleven

With a spring in her step at seeing Anwen's cool feathers ruffled and Peggy's mood lifted, Josie returned to the field next to the school to collect Sam. She was anxious about him playing football with older boys and worried that he might have similar problems fitting in here as he was having at school. But she needn't have given it a thought. Sam didn't even notice she had returned, so engrossed was he in the game he was playing. She was so happy to see his adorable look of concentration as he held his own on the pitch with the other boys. And when Tom blew his whistle and instructed the boys to return their coloured sashes to the cardboard box they had found them in – half the sashes stitched with a patch of blue cotton and the other half stitched with the same in green to signify teams – Josie was pleased to see Sam do what he was told without hesitation. As she watched Sam chatting to the other boys, Tom wandered over to her.

'He did very well today,' he said, glancing back over his

shoulder towards Sam. 'He even gave some of the bigger lads the runaround. He's fast.'

Josie could sense that Tom was uncomfortable in her presence and it was requiring some effort for him to speak to her. *Maybe he feels bad about telling me to get lost earlier*, she thought, mulling over everything she'd just learnt about him from Peggy.

'Really? That's a relief. Looks like he's getting on with the other boys too?' Josie hoped she hadn't misread this bit. She really wanted Sam to make friends.

'Yes, he's fitted in really well. Should help him in the playground back at school next week. He was like a different lad out here on the pitch to the one I usually have in my classroom.'

This was an enormous relief to Josie and she was wrestling with how to show her gratitude without letting him think she'd forgotten his rudeness earlier. 'Well, thank you for including him. It means a lot.'

'It was a pleasure to help,' he said seriously, running his hand through his sandy brown hair awkwardly.

Suddenly it seemed that neither knew what to say next. Josie desperately wanted to extricate herself from the conversation, and just as she was about to Tom found his words. 'So, how did your first rehearsal go? With the choir? Did Gethin show up?'

The last thing Josie expected was for him to bring the choir up again. She hoped he wasn't going to belittle it again. She wasn't going to pretend she'd forgotten what he'd said, even if he could.

'He did. I was surprised you sent him our way, given you

think the whole thing . . . what was the word you used? Ridiculous?' She looked him right in the eye, pale hand on her hip.

'I didn't say it was ridiculous. That's not what I meant.' He rolled his eyes in a dismissive way that was almost impatient. *How arrogant*, Josie thought.

'What did you mean then?'

'I meant, it's ridiculous for some people because—'

'Because they're above such things?' Josie cut him off, losing her patience with this privileged prince of the coalmines. 'Because they're too good for our little choir?'

He stared at her, his look a mixture of anger and disappointment. It unsettled Josie slightly, made her falter up there on top of her moral high ground just ever so slightly.

'If that's the opinion you have of me from one conversation, then I don't think there's much point in me trying to convince you otherwise. Have a good day, Josie.' And with that he walked away, leaving Josie with the unpleasant feeling of being somehow in the wrong.

She shook it off. He had been rude about something that was important to her and she wasn't going to let him get away with it, even if he had been helpful with Sam. Now that she knew what she did about him, his haughty manner and well-spoken voice, not to mention his very handsome face – annoying as that was to notice – meant that Tom Jenkins was a man unused to being challenged. He even undermined his employer, Miss Hughes, at the school the other day, albeit in Sam's defence. Well, Josie wasn't a woman to be dismissed.

She quickly found Sam and told him it was time to leave. He was the perfect antidote to such an unpleasant conversation, with his stream of chatter, void of pauses for breath, about some boy called Bobby who had given him the nickname Flash.

'It's because I was so fast, Mummy!'

'So I heard, Sammy,' she said, ruffling his hair, putting all thoughts of Tom Jenkins to the back of her mind.

It was customary for whoever was last to use the village hall of an evening to lock up the heavy doors and return the keys through the letter box of the house belonging to Mrs Moss. It was Mrs Moss who opened the hall each morning in preparation for the day's events, ensuring the kitchen was fully equipped for whichever groups would be using it. This had been explained to Josie by Miss Hughes when she had been granted permission by the committee to form her choir. After the success of her first rehearsal Josie had written the Llandegwen choir's name into the eight o'clock slots on Mondays, Wednesdays and Thursdays, in pencil on the roughly drawn out weekly schedule pinned up on the noticeboard outside the little kitchen. The evenings were generally clear so it had been no trouble getting the extra slots they needed to put in enough practice to be ready for the Welsh Valleys Choral Competition at the end of April. Josie had yet to meet Mrs Moss, so it had felt strange posting the keys through her letter box that first night. She lived in a house on Colliers Row, a stone's throw from the post office and one of the first houses one came across as they left the centre of the village. Her house was perfectly placed so as not to be out of anyone's way. Perhaps that was how Mrs Moss got the job.

Josie had been thinking of the elusive – as that was thus far the only way that Josie could describe her – Mrs Moss as she poked her head into the tiny kitchen attached to the village hall that Monday night. She wanted to see if the choir might be able to have a cup of tea at the start of practice while they discussed which songs they would work on for the competition. She thought making the discussion feel more like a chat over a cuppa might relax everyone and encourage those who were quieter to contribute too. She was pleased to see that Mrs Moss was as good at her job as housekeeper for the village hall as she had hoped she would be – there was tea, a big shiny silver teapot big enough to serve a large group, and even a small drop of milk kept in the cool shadow of the stone shelves.

She heard the doors to the hall creak open and walked back out into the hall to greet whoever had turned up first. It was Bethan who was looking around the empty hall uncertainly until she spotted Josie emerging from the kitchen.

'You're the first to arrive! I was just thinking about making some tea for the group. I want us to talk about which songs we should sing tonight and I thought tea would go well with the discussion. Might you help me?'

'Yes, absolutely.' Bethan had been hanging up her coat while Josie was speaking to her, and now she smoothed the skirt of her sage green cotton dress as she hurried towards the kitchen to be of use.

While the two women were boiling water and gathering cups and saucers Gethin had arrived and popped his head around the entrance to the kitchen.

'Hello there! Is there anything I can do to help?'

'Oh, Gethin, great. You can help us carry everything when we're done,' Josie ordered.

'Right you are. Hi there, Bethan. Are you well?'

Bethan seemed to almost jump in surprise at being addressed directly. She had been trying to blend into the tea-making background. As she turned now to answer Gethin, Josie could see that her cheeks had turned a rosy pink. If Gethin noticed Bethan's embarrassment he didn't show it and continued to talk easily to her about a student in his class who had wanted to know how long it would take for a letter from Llandegwen to be delivered to Bristol. Though Bethan still seemed surprised that he was talking to her, she also appeared to be pleased by his attention and Josie watched as her shoulders relaxed ever so slightly in the young man's company. Maybe Gethin was the key to getting Bethan to loosen up and sing with confidence. He was certainly having an effect on her now and he seemed keen to make her laugh. Josie was no Cupid but she knew a spark when she saw one. It couldn't hurt to give that spark a little oxygen to flame, now could it?

'Actually, you two, I should probably set up the chairs and greet people when they come in. Can I leave you both to sort the tea while I do that?'

Bethan nodded yes, her expression showing she'd forgotten Josie was still there at all, while Gethin offered a cheery, 'Of course!'

Josie was smiling to herself as she left the pair in the kitchen and walked out into the hall to be met by Mr Evans and Catherine coming through the large doors. Mr Evans was carrying a box of songbooks and Josie clapped her hands together enthusiastically at the sight.

'Oh wonderful, are those Mr Rhys's songbooks?'

'They are indeed, my dear. The poor old fellow was so glad

to hear they were to be put to good use again. He had a few thoughts for us on which songs to choose and I said I'd throw them into the hat tonight on his behalf.'

'I'd definitely be glad of some advice from him. Please do tell him thank you from me the next time you see him. I hope his health isn't causing him too much bother.'

The vicar gave Josie and Catherine a rundown of the state of Mr Rhys's health as they began putting out the chairs. Catherine was so sympathetic about the old man that Josie presumed she knew him.

'Oh no, I've never met him. But it's just such an awful thing, illness in old age, isn't it? He must feel so helpless. And yet he's kind enough to give our choir his support. I feel he must be a good man,' Catherine said with the utmost sincerity.

Josie looked at the glamorous older woman, so clearly privileged and important – so important that her presence in the choir shut Anwen up and visibly surprised the other members of the choir that first night – but yet able to empathise with a man she didn't know, a man whose life was probably so far removed from her own. It made Josie warm to the mayor's wife even more. She was still curious about why she had joined their little choir though. It was something Josie was dying to know and hoped she might one day be able to ask, once she got to know the woman better. Whatever Catherine's reason, Josie was glad to have her. She was a nice person to have around and she had a way of putting others at ease that was great for the choir. And as if to illustrate Josie's point, she gave Fred the warmest of welcomes as he came through the doors moments later. He still looked very serious but he visibly relaxed at her greeting and he joined them by the piano more readily as a result.

Next to arrive were the Thomas men who were deep in conversation about a disagreement that had taken place between two of their fellow miners that day in the pit. Josie just caught the tail end of their conversation where Owen seemed to be defending the man called Bob.

'He only reacted that way because of what happened to him in France.'

'He's not the only one who fought in the war though, son. You and I did too. There are rules. We're on the same side in the pit.'

Owen looked frustrated with his father but Michael didn't seem to register this. Instead he put a smile on his face and greeted the others, the conversation he was having with his son now over. Before Josie could wonder who Bill was and what they all might have seen in the war, Marjorie, Glenys and Peggy entered the hall. Glenys had said she would follow Josie on when she had left the cottage that evening, as she needed to set up the kitchen for some early morning baking the next day. Josie had been happy to have the time to herself to walk into the centre of the village and start setting up the hall, but she was relieved to see the tiny woman here now. Glenys was her champion and goodness knows she felt like she needed one of those at the moment. They had a giant mountain to climb and though Josie was excited by the challenge, she had to admit she was more than a little daunted by it too.

'Evening, everyone,' Josie said with a raised voice as the last arrivals took their seats, which she had arranged in a semicircle around the piano so that they could all face one another when they talked about the songs they would sing. 'Ah marvellous, here's Bethan and Gethin with some tea for us all. Thank you very much, you two.'

The pair had emerged from the kitchen with a tray each, carrying cups of tea on saucers. Bethan was still pink-cheeked but beaming as she handed out tea to the rest of the choir.

'I thought we could have a cuppa while we had a chat about what songs we might like to sing for the competition. We've not had the rules through yet, but if we go with what's been required in the past we need three songs. Mr Rhys has kindly given us his songbooks so we can look through them for ideas, unless any of you have come with suggestions?' Josie looked at her choir expectantly from her stool in front of the piano.

'I know we made a dog's dinner of it last week but maybe with some practice, I think we should sing "Myfanwy",' Michael offered. 'We always used to sing it, in the old choir like, and it's a favourite of mine. Anyway, that's my two pennies' worth.'

'It is a beautiful song and very popular,' Glenys agreed. There were nods of approval from some and mumbled yeses from others.

'Well, you all know why I love that song, so I think that's a great suggestion. Thank you, Michael,' said Josie.

'We just have to make sure we don't sound like a bag of cats next time we sing it.' Everyone laughed at Owen's vivid reminder of their last rendition of the song.

'Don't worry about that. I'll have you breaking hearts all over Wales with that song once I'm done with you all,' Josie said with a confidence she was starting to feel.

'As long as we don't break the glass in everyone's windows, I'll be happy,' Michael joked.

The good humour of Owen and Michael Thomas had rubbed off on everyone in the room apart from Marjorie who, while the rest of the choir were laughing and relaxing in one another's company, sat there with the face of someone sucking on a lemon. She took everything so seriously, it seemed, and she really didn't like being described as one of the cats in the bag Owen was referring to. Josie could see her crossness mounting and so decided to pre-empt it by moving the conversation on.

'OK, we're all agreed on "Myfanwy". Any other ideas?'

'What about "Suo Gân"? It's a lullaby,' Catherine offered.

'Oh yes, my mam always used to sing it to me when I was little,' Peggy added.

'Indeed, it's a wonderful song to sing as a choir. We'd need a strong soprano to sing the solo though,' Mr Evans chipped in.

Marjorie perked up at this. 'I would happily put myself forward for that role.'

'Of course you would,' Peggy muttered to Glenys, rolling her eyes.

Marjorie shot her a look. 'Well, I don't see you putting yourself forward, missy.'

Josie had moved over to the box of songbooks that the vicar had placed next to the piano and picked one out. She flipped through it until she found the song in question. Placing the music on the piano stand she began to play the opening bars, cutting off any further bickering between the postmistress and her friend. Silence fell in the room but for the odd chink of a cup knocking against its saucer. Catherine's soft voice swept into the room as she stood to sing the words. She had her eyes closed but it seemed to Josie as if she were singing to someone in particular. Josie didn't know the meaning of the Welsh lyrics but they were clearly coming from Catherine's heart. She continued to play as Glenys, Marjorie and Peggy joined her in the next verse. It really was a beautiful song, Josie thought, and she could hear as she listened to the voices of these women that the harmonies they could create as a mixed choir would make this a perfect choice for them to sing at the competition. Josie was excited. After she played the final notes there was a moment of silence while everyone's minds returned to the room, so transported had they all been by the music. The women who had stood to sing looked at one another and laughed a little self-consciously before sitting themselves back down.

Josie had turned back around to face the group. 'I think we have our second song there, don't you?' She was beaming at them and they all nodded their agreement, eager to get to work. This is just what Josie had hoped for when she started the choir. The music was already starting to put smiles on faces and to stir up feelings of better times. And Josie was feeling more confident that she wouldn't fail. As the discussion moved on to what would be the third and final song they would work on everyone had something to say on the matter, suggestions bubbled over into the room, there was a fizz of excitement sparked by the potential they had sensed as the women sang 'Suo Gân'. Several songs had been thrown into the ring, including one from Mr Rhys via the vicar. However it was Fred's suggestion that they sing the hymn 'Calon Lan' that won in the end.

They had just enough time at the end of the hour to do some vocal exercises, pledging to get to work in earnest on Wednesday at the next rehearsal. Josie took a moment to take in the animated chatter that buzzed around the hall after the practice had ended. No one was rushing to get their coats and leave, they were all taking their time talking in pairs or threesomes about the evening's events and the songs they were to sing. The sight made Josie's heart soar. She had asked Gethin and Bethan if they would mind clearing away the tea things and making sure the kitchen was as they found it, while she collected the songbooks and put away the chairs. They were eager to help and Bethan chatted away to Gethin as they got on with their task.

As the pair walked towards the little kitchen and out of earshot, Glenys, who had hung back to keep Josie company, nodded towards the kitchen and said, 'I don't think I've ever seen that girl talk so much before.'

'Perhaps the rest of us just aren't as charming as the young Mr Gethin there,' Josie replied with a glint in her eye.

Glenys eyed Josie suspiciously. 'Am I right in thinking you might be playing Cupid here, love?'

'I don't know what you mean, Glenys.' Josie was all innocence. 'They did such a good job making the tea together I thought they might like to wash up together too.'

'Oh, you're a clever one!' The two women laughed and then exchanged knowing looks as the young pair exited the kitchen and made to put on their coats, bidding Josie and Glenys goodnight. Gethin held the door open for Bethan and she smiled at him shyly as they left the hall. As Josie watched the door close behind them she felt her plan might just work.

Gethin clearly had a way of coaxing Bethan out of her shell a little, and even if they didn't fall madly in love in the way that Josie's over-enthusiastic romantic mind had envisaged, their blossoming friendship might just allow Bethan to blossom as a singer too. Nevertheless, she had a funny feeling about those two.

Josie popped the keys through Mrs Moss's letter box, once again thinking how strange it was to have this exchange with someone she'd never met. She and Glenys had been digesting the events of the choir practice on their walk home. Josie had remarked on how she had noticed that Catherine sang the lullaby as though she were singing it to someone special, and she had wondered what the lyrics meant.

'I don't know about that, love. The song is about a mother singing her child to sleep, the words are very soothing. It's well known that Catherine never had children though. I'd say it was more likely a childhood memory she was thinking of.'

'That could make sense.' Josie nodded as they walked. She supposed she might never know.

Chapter Twelve

After a morning spent helping – though it was more like observing, as Josie still hadn't managed to be hugely useful to Glenys in the kitchen – Glenys bake her order of pies for the bakery that day, she accompanied her into the heart of the village to deliver them before the lunchtime rush. Mr Driscoll, the baker, greeted them warmly as they entered his shop. He was a portly, rosy-cheeked man who always seemed to be in a jolly mood. In the handful of times Josie had been in his shop she always felt as she opened the door that she was walking into warm sunshine. Part of that warmth came from the heat emanating from the bread ovens and the delicious smells of freshly baked dough that wafted out of them. But the other part came from the friendly baker himself.

This Tuesday he was joined by Mrs Duffy, who Josie had been embarrassed to see each time she passed her on Colliers Row ever since Sam had kicked his mucky football against her newly painted red gate. Josie's cheeks coloured as she realised she couldn't just give her a polite hello and hasten past her now. Anwen's words about bad manners still rang in her ears as they all exchanged polite greetings.

'I have to tell you, Josie, Mr Duffy passed the village hall on his way back from the Plough last night and he said he heard some lovely female voices coming through the windows. Songbirds, he said. I'm guessing that was your choir he heard?'

'Oh yes, it must have been,' Josie said, still feeling awkward, not knowing if this woman disapproved of her.

'Well, that's high praise coming from him. He's not one for compliments.' Mrs Duffy pursed her lips at Josie before breaking into a smile. 'Well done, girl. After what people have been saying about your choir I'm glad you're proving them wrong.'

'What have people been saying?' Glenys was both outraged that anyone could have anything bad to say and resolutely protective of Josie.

'Now I don't want to be telling tales, but Anwen Lewis took issue with the choir competing in the Valleys. She thought you might not be good enough' – Mrs Duffy waved her hand dismissively at this notion – 'but she hadn't heard you sing, had she? If my husband says you were good, then you must be good.'

Josie and Glenys looked at one another. 'That little madam!' Glenys was furious. 'You don't look surprised to hear this?' she questioned Josie.

'I heard as much from the horse's mouth last weekend. I think she might have changed her tune once she realised who one or two of our members were though.'

'Yes, you've done well to get the vicar and Catherine Morgan to join. Nobody can question you with them so heavily involved,' Mrs Duffy said with a nod that suggested that that was the end of that. 'Good luck now, Josie. I hope you'll give us a little concert before you go off competing.' She said her goodbyes to Glenys and Mr Driscoll before turning back to Josie as she opened the door to leave. 'I hope that lad of yours is behaving himself now.' And with a good-natured wink she was gone.

Josie breathed a sigh of relief. Mrs Duffy hadn't forgotten the gate incident but she hadn't held it against her and was giving her choir her support. At least that was something.

To say that the next two nights of choir practice were a challenge for Josie would be an understatement. After choosing the songs they would work on she decided to concentrate on the gentle lullaby 'Suo Gân' first, given it was the song that had fired up such optimism the other night. Her first task was to name her female soloist. Marjorie had of course put herself forward but Josie feared the other women were too modest to do the same, and so she requested that they all sing two lines each, one after the other, so that she could hear who might have the strongest voice to sing over the background harmonies. To her disappointment Bethan was still barely singing above a whisper. Josie had to strain her ears to hear the soft notes that managed to escape from her mouth.

It was even more disappointing as Bethan's friendship with Gethin seemed to be going strong. They sat together on both nights and Gethin seemed keen to talk to her whenever he got the chance. But it wasn't making the difference Josie had hoped that it would. She wanted Bethan to come out of her shell for her own sake but also she needed her voice to be heard in order that the deeper male voices didn't overbear the female voices, now that the balance of numbers was tipped in their favour. Without Bethan's audible vocals, they were essentially four to five. It was still early days though, Josie reminded herself. Bethan wasn't going to burst out of her cocoon a butterfly overnight. She'd just have to work a little harder with her, so she made sure to give her lots of praise whenever she could. For now though that left Josie with four women to choose from.

As it turned out Marjorie did have the strongest voice out of them all and no one complained when Josie declared her their soloist. But in true Marjorie Davies style, she'd left her humility at home that night as she regaled them all with stories of her own talent and its origins.

'It was always going to fall to me, no offence, ladies. But you should take comfort in the knowledge that I come from a long line of choristers. My father and my grandfather sang in the Llandegwen choir when they were their most successful. And of course my mother had a beautiful voice, I think I get my tone from her . . .' Marjorie was standing, addressing her audience without really looking at them, which was just as well as if she had, she'd have seen them either looking at the floor or staring at the ceiling in boredom. Catherine, to her credit, was biting her lip, trying not to laugh. She obviously found Marjorie's habit of presenting herself as someone of importance comical rather than offensive. Which was a relief to Josie. Peggy, on the other hand, looked like she wanted to give Marjorie a thump. Josie hoped her friend understood why she had had to choose Marjorie over her. She had the strongest voice. Even if she was far too aware of it herself.

'. . . my daughter also sings like an angel. If she wasn't so busy with my darling grandchildren she would be an asset to this choir. But she's such a dedicated mother—'

'Right then,' Josie broke in before Peggy lost her temper and everyone else fell asleep. 'Now we have our soloist, shall we work on some harmonies?'

And therein lay the next challenge. Where Josie struggled to get a sound out of Bethan, she fought even harder to find a way to get Mr Evans to dial down his volume levels. He seemed to be completely unaware of how loudly his voice boomed out above the others. A harmony could only work if everyone sang, well, in harmony obviously, but also at the same volume. At this rate they'd find it tricky to hear Marjorie's solo above him. He was so oblivious though, he was just having too much fun. Each time Josie made them give it another go he looked at her eagerly, waiting to be told he'd got it right that time. To his credit he took everything she said in great humour.

'Right you are, my dear. This time I'll get it, I'm sure. I bet Bing Crosby had the same trouble, not that he was in a choir but imagine if he was!' Josie smiled at him encouragingly and knew he was trying his best. She might have to do some one-to-one work with him. Maybe if he didn't have other voices to compete with he'd naturally lower his volume and that way he'd feel the difference and be able to control his voice better. She resolved to try that next time they had choir practice.

On the Thursday night Fred volunteered to help Josie lock up. Glenys had to dash off to make Harry his lunch for the next day as he was leaving early for the mine the next morning. He'd given up working in the coal mine years before but now and then he went back over there to give the younger men who were not yet old enough to go underground advice on working in the pits. Harry could no longer go into the pit himself after suffering an injury. A pit wall collapsed on his right leg, crushing his ankle and shin. It took such a long time to heal, it even stopped him from fighting in the war, but most difficult of all for Harry, it made it too dangerous for him to carry out the work he used to do. You had to be in full strength to work down there, Glenys had told Josie. If your body was in any way damaged you were done for.

'It broke his heart to have to give it up,' Glenys had explained to Josie one morning when they were baking. 'He's a grafter, my Harry, to the bone. Having to stop doing what he'd always done hit him hard. It's good that he gets to go back there now and then to teach the young lads the ways of the mines before they get down there themselves. It's something, isn't it?'

Josie had wondered if this disappointment in life was what shaped his sullen nature, but then she remembered the different man she'd seen when she'd witnessed him alone with Glenys. Try as she might to make Harry's behaviour less personal to her and Sam, there was no denying what she'd seen standing on the stairs that night as he'd looked at his wife with adoration and a softness she hadn't seen before or since.

Without Glenys to help her that evening she was very grateful to Fred for his offer to help Josie to collect the songbooks and put away the chairs after everyone had left. She also realised this was her chance to get to know the man a little better. He was still keeping himself on the sidelines of the group, though Josie saw Catherine's attempts to include him in conversations whenever she could. But he had contributed when it mattered and he sang with such determination that Josie sensed the choir was important to him. She hoped in time, much like with Bethan, it would give him a little more confidence.

'What do you think of our choir so far, Fred?' Josie broke their easy silence.

'We're not too bad. Nothing a bit of hard work won't fix.'

She asked him a few more questions about the choir as they piled up the wooden chairs to take them to the little storeroom where they lived until they were needed, but she wasn't really getting much out of Fred that way. She was wracking her brains to think of ways to get him to open up and speak more than a few words at a time and so she tentatively changed track as they were putting on their coats to leave.

'Do you know, I've always wondered, what's life like living on a farm? It's just I grew up in a big city, not even a tree on my street. I just can't imagine it.' She looked at Fred hopefully as he thought for a moment.

'There're plenty of trees. And fields and animals to be tended to. It all keeps me busy enough.' Josie nodded and sighed inwardly, thinking this was all she was going to get from him. But just as she opened the hall doors and moved to leave he said, 'I'm on my own up there, on the farm, no one to talk to . . . except the animals, I suppose.' He laughed a little sadly at this.

'That must be hard sometimes?'

'I was never one for social things. My wife liked that sort of thing. She was enough company for me. And then I had my lad to keep me entertained. He was a talker like his mother.' Fred smiled fondly at the memory of his family and Josie's heart ached for him. Knowing he'd lost them both and hearing how much he missed them as he spoke of them now really moved her and she wanted to know more about the people Fred had loved.

'Might you tell me about them while we walk home?'

His dark eyes were watery with unshed tears as he looked at Josie and said, 'I'd like that.'

They stepped out into the chilly spring night and Josie locked the door behind them, putting the keys in her coat pocket ready to drop them through Mrs Moss's letter box when they passed her house.

'What was your wife like?'

He appeared lost in a memory for a moment before he said, 'She was the loveliest person I ever met.'

They broke into a slow easy stride as Fred opened up to Josie about his Mary. He'd met her when she moved to the village to take care of her sick grandmother. She loved animals and used to take walks up to the farm where Fred worked as a young man alongside his father. Fred described how she'd often ask him to walk with her when he had finished his jobs. He was usually shy around girls but she was so easy to talk to. He fell for her in those first days of their walks together and was amazed and delighted that she fell for him too.

'I never knew what she saw in me. She would light up a room when she entered it. She was kind to everyone she met, especially me. There will never be another one like her for me.'

'Do you miss her?'

'Every day. But she gave me our son before she died. The greatest gift she could ever give me.'

'It's the same for me with my Sam. I lost my husband Matthew in the war. But he gave me Sam before he went.'

'You understand then.' They stopped and the look they exchanged was heavy with the meaning of a shared experience.

'I do,' Josie said, feeling afresh those conflicting emotions of loss for the one you gave your heart to and joy for the little piece of them that they left behind in your child. But Fred had lost this too. The thought of not having her Sam any more, well, she couldn't even bear to imagine it. Fred's pain must be immense.

'It must get lonely at times all the way up there on the farm?'

'It was the way I liked it, especially when David was gone. Gave me some quiet to settle my thoughts. But then it just became a habit, I suppose.'

Josie nodded, she could see how having the peace and quiet of life on a farm could be helpful at first.

'What made you join the choir?'

'Catherine Morgan told me I should do it. She lives in the big house up by my farm and drops in for tea now and then. I told her about the committee meeting and all that, and then she was on at me that we should both join. I've never sung outside my farm before but Catherine said it might help if I sang with others. Give me something else to think about other than the farm.'

Josie smiled at this. Fred's motive for joining the choir was not a million miles off her own reason for setting it up. It was something to focus on. She hoped it was helping him in the way it was starting to help her.

'And has it? Helped, I mean.'

Fred stopped for a moment and gave Josie's question some real thought. He faced her then and with a voice full of sincerity said, 'It's starting to. It's starting to.'

Josie felt a little choked with emotion at this. She'd wanted to bring music back to the village, to give those who wanted to sing a place to do it, to restore some of the hope that the war had taken away. And not just for them, she realised now, for herself too. Now that Fred was standing here telling her that already the choir was making a difference to his life, well, Josie was even more fired up to make a real success of it all. She owed that to Fred and everyone else who had believed in her idea. And she owed it to herself too.

They continued to walk together in comfortable silence until Josie dropped the keys through Mrs Moss's letter box and bid Fred goodnight at the turn-off she needed to take from Colliers Row on to the road that would take her home. After a few steps she looked back at Fred's tall frame as he walked off into the darkness. She thought, with a smile, that his shoulders looked just that little bit lighter.

Chapter Thirteen

Before she was due to collect Sam from school that Friday afternoon, Josie decided to see if Mr Evans might be free for an extra practice after teatime that evening. She had no plans of her own, other than sitting in front of the fire with Glenys, Harry and Sam as usual, but she was full of energy after the previous night's practice. Seeing how much everyone was starting to relax and enjoy the singing was wonderful, and her talk with Fred as they walked home that night had really motivated her. If the choir could help someone like Fred, who had withdrawn from life for so long, find something to hope for, something that could bring him some happiness, then it could do the same for others. It could do the same for her. It was already putting a big smile on her face, despite the rocky start. They still had lots of work to do but the enthusiasm was there already and that was half the battle.

Mr Evans had seemed keen when she'd mentioned the idea of some private tuition during practice the previous evening. And so she arrived at the rectory that afternoon in high spirits at the thought of getting to work. His housekeeper greeted her with a look that was a mixture of surprise and suspicion as Josie explained the purpose of her visit.

'If you could wait there, just a moment . . .' She blinked at Josie before scurrying off to find the vicar who appeared moments later looking delighted to see her. He would meet her at the church that evening at half past seven. There was a piano there and it would provide a good substitute venue given the village hall was to be occupied that evening by the Llandegwen village business owners' meeting. It was a relief to have such an enthusiastic student, Josie thought as she wandered off about her business for the rest of the day.

Josie hadn't set foot in the church before that Friday evening. She wasn't one for God or prayers. She'd not been raised that way and going to services every Sunday was just not something she ever thought about making a part of her life. Not that she begrudged it of anyone else, in fact she thought it must be nice to have somewhere to go to when you felt a bit hopeless and to have something to believe in when times got hard. Maybe if she'd had such a sanctuary she wouldn't have got herself into such an awful mess in London. It just wasn't for her, she supposed. It was a great relief to her that the vicar was the kind of man who understood those who did not share his beliefs as much as those who did. He treated everyone the same and he never preached outside the pulpit. Mr Evans seemed to judge no one and welcome everyone, whether they attended his services or not. And so it was that Josie entered his church that evening without any worries of trespassing or entering a place where she didn't belong.

St Luke's – the same saint that gave his name to the local school – was empty as Josie entered through one of the big, heavy wooden doors. The sound of the door clunking shut behind her echoed loudly as the sound seemed to bounce off the stone walls until it disappeared into the high wooden beams holding up the roof. It was a simple and small church. The floor was dark stone, the walls a pale grey sandstone brick. The latticed windows, though black with the darkness of night now, would let in rays of daylight when the sun came up. The larger more detailed window above the raised altar was the only one to contain one panel of stained glass. Josie imagined it might create a little rainbow of colour across the plain white linen cloth that covered the altar if the sun shone down on it at just the right angle. She was about to take a seat on one of the wooden pews while she waited for Mr Evans when he came bustling out of the vestibule, his usual jolly mood lighting up his face as well as the room.

'Hello there, Josie. I hope you've not been waiting long?'

'Oh no, I just got here. It was nice to have a moment to look around the church actually.'

'It's small but rather lovely, I like to think,' he said as he looked around the building himself to confirm his opinion.

'Yes it is.' Josie smiled.

'Did you find the piano?' Mr Evans started to make his way to the space to the right of the altar that separated it from the first pew where the instrument had been covered by a red velvet cloth. Josie didn't know how she'd managed to miss it given there wasn't much else in terms of furniture in the church to hide it.

'I must have been so distracted by the rest of the building

that I failed to notice it.' She attempted to explain her total lack of attention to detail.

Mr Evans chuckled as he removed the cover and encouraged Josie to take a seat on the stool.

'Thank you for taking the extra time, Mr Evans, I know you must be quite busy.'

'It is I who should be thanking you, my dear. It is kind of you to give me the extra help.' Josie batted this away but the vicar was quite serious as he said, 'It is a very kind thing you are doing for the village too. I hope you know that. I know it must be hard to be new to a place, and to have to start your life over again. But you are doing a great job of it all and I can see you've already made a difference to some of the people here who really needed a lift.'

Josie flushed at his unexpected compliment. 'Oh I don't think it's that kind of me. I'm getting so much out of running this choir too, I fear my motive might have been more of a selfish one.'

'I've not known you long, Josie, but I can tell that your motives weren't all for your own benefit. You like to help others. I mean, look at you sitting here tonight helping me with extra singing practice! Give yourself some credit, my dear. You are doing a good thing.'

He looked at her with such sincerity that Josie felt a little choked by his words. She could only manage to nod at him. Having Mr Evans believe in her was quite reaffirming somehow.

'Shall we start with some scales to warm up? Then we can work together on some tricks to help you control that marvellous voice of yours.'

Mr Evans clapped his hands together with gusto and said, 'Whatever you say, dear choirmistress, where you lead I will follow!'

Once they got started they worked solidly, barely pausing. Mr Evans, to his credit, listened to every word Josie spoke to him and gave her direction his full concentration. By the time the church bells tolled nine o'clock they had hardly felt the time pass them by, so absolutely focused had they been on their task.

'My goodness, is that really the time? I must not keep you any longer.'

'I had no idea it was this late! I hope I haven't pushed you too hard? I think we've cracked it though.' Josie smiled at the vicar encouragingly. 'I really mean it, you've done brilliantly and your voice sounds so lovely when it's that bit softer.' As she had hoped, once Mr Evans could hear just his own voice and the piano, he was less inclined to shout out the notes. And when he could hear the difference himself, he was able to hear the rise and fall in volume. She had sung with him too, lowering her own voice to entice him to lower his so that the two complemented one another rather than one drowning the other out. 'You have such a lovely voice, my dear, I wanted to hear it more than my own,' he'd said as she congratulated him on mastering what she was teaching him. It was so satisfying to have worked so hard and to have achieved just what she'd wanted to. Josie couldn't wait for the next choir practice where the new and improved Mr Evans could showcase his more controlled voice. He seemed excited too. He was quite thrilled that he'd finally got the hang of what Josie had been trying to get him to do at the previous choir practices.

'Well, it's all down to you, my dear. You are a fine teacher and a very patient one. I just hope that I don't let you down on Monday. I promise to practice!'

'You won't let me down. I already know that.' She patted him supportively on the shoulder as she got up from the piano and moved to put on her coat. 'I will see you on Monday.'

'I'll be there with bells on,' Mr Evans promised, as Josie gave him a cheery wave and walked down the aisle and out of the heavy church doors.

The night was quiet and Josie felt a little chill in the air; a hangover from winter where spring had not yet warmed up the evenings. She pulled the collar of her wool coat further up her neck and closer to her chin to fend off the nip in the air as she walked up the narrow Church Lane that led on to Colliers Row. She was lost in thought about what she needed to do next to get the choir into good enough shape for the competition. She'd only taken a few steps on to the main street of Llandegwen when she heard footsteps behind her. Her heart turned to lead, her breath froze in her lungs and the first thought that leapt into her head was had he found her? But she'd been so careful. Immediately her mind started to race through all of the ways she might be able to run when the voice attached to the footsteps said, 'We're the only two people out at this time of night, are we really going to pretend the other isn't there?'

Relief washed over her. It wasn't him. She turned to face Tom Jenkins, unable to find her words just yet but needing to see for sure that it was Sam's teacher and not her past catching up with her.

'You look like you've seen a ghost. Is it really that much of a horror to see me?' He looked concerned but also a little hurt that the sight of him could turn her already pale skin so frighteningly white.

'No . . . I just . . . you startled me. I didn't expect to bump into anyone, that's all.' Strangely his presence there, his broad frame and strong arms, made her feel safe, and it was more than the fact that she was relieved that he wasn't the person she feared most.

'Forgive me for asking, it's just I know you don't think all that much of me. For some reason I have a bit of a problem saying what I mean to you.'

Josie was still trying to get her breathing to return to normal but even so she had no idea what to say to that. Tom looked at her curiously and moved closer to her, putting one of his strong hands on her shoulder.

'Are you sure you're all right?'

'Yes, sorry, I'm fine. I'm just being silly. Alone in a strange place, late at night and all that!' She laughed but there was no humour in it.

Tom continued to study her face. 'Would you like me to walk you home? I'm heading that way anyway.'

She was going to decline his offer but she realised that she suddenly didn't want to be alone. Her heart rate hadn't entirely returned to normal just yet.

'Thank you, that's very kind of you.'

He nodded in his stiff, formal way that indicated he was taking her gratitude as a given, Josie thought to herself as she fell into step beside him. She wasn't sure if he was aware that his simple agreement that his gesture was indeed kind came across as a little arrogant. And she wasn't sure why it bothered her so much either. Perhaps she had an inferiority complex to match his superior one. She had to supress a smile at this thought.

'So what has you out on the streets of Llandegwen at the scandalous time of nine at night?'

Josie looked up at him, was he making a joke? 'I was helping one of my choristers with a bit of extra practice.'

'That's very noble of you. You really are taking this choir thing very seriously, aren't you?'

'Yes, I am. And as you can probably tell, I don't do very well when others don't. I've already had to listen to some other people's scathing views on what I'm doing so forgive me if I'm a little sensitive on the subject.' She hated how prim she sounded as she said this but after the fright she'd got when she'd heard those footsteps behind her, she was feeling a little fragile.

Tom let out an exasperated sigh. 'Are you ever going to let me tell you what I actually meant by that, granted badly expressed, comment?'

She hesitated. She hadn't really wanted to get into it again, but he was walking her home after all and she didn't want to seem like a spoilt brat. She nodded at him to go on.

'What I was trying to say was that it would be ridiculous for someone like me to join your choir because I don't have a note in my head. I'm quite possibly one of the worst singers you'll ever hear. Trust me, you don't want me in your choir. And for the record, for those who can sing, I think it's a great idea.'

Josie looked up at him suspiciously, trying to work out if he was serious or not. 'Really?'

He laughed. 'You're very quick to judge, aren't you?'

Josie was quite put out by this. She didn't think she was at all judgemental. She was hardly in a position to be, given what she'd done recently. Tom must've seen her knotting her brow as she tried to decide whether or not to take offense so he swiftly changed the subject.

'You didn't ask me why I'm out on the streets at this hour. I was having a pint in the Plough and witnessed a bit of drama in there.'

Josie decided to let the judgemental comment go, she was more curious about what constituted drama in a Llandegwen pub. She also figured talking about something else might make the walk home pass more quickly.

'Really? What happened?'

'Phil Davies had a bit too much to drink. That's not unusual in itself, but I think he'd been in there all afternoon. He was all wound up about something, antagonising everyone and anyone who was just trying to have a quiet pint. He had to be thrown out in the end. Not the first time it's happened, but still.'

'Is he related to Marjorie?' Josie hadn't come across Phil Davies yet, but the surname made her ask the question. Though she couldn't imagine how someone as prim and proper as Marjorie could be part of the same family as the person who fitted this Phil's description.

'He's her husband. I always feel a bit sorry for Marjorie. She rubs a lot of people up the wrong way but it can't be easy living with a man like him.' His brow furrowed with concern for the postmistress as he looked ahead into the distance.

Josie was completely thrown by this information. Marjorie was so bossy and self-aggrandising, Josie had imagined her husband to be a meek sort of a man. She couldn't imagine anyone giving Marjorie Davies any trouble. Now that she thought about it, Marjorie had yet to mention her husband. She'd boasted about her perfect son and daughter a few times, but she'd never mentioned Mr Davies. Maybe Josie had been too quick to judge the older woman, there was clearly more to her life than she had shown Josie. Tom's judgemental comment rankled even more now.

'I had no idea.'

'I don't think many people do. He's usually harmless in the Plough, just drinks his pints and staggers home. It's just I've seen that aggressive side of him a few times now and it makes me think. I'm sure it's nothing really, but even so, living with a man who's drunk most nights of the week can't be fun. She's a proud woman, though. I wouldn't ever say anything to her.' He was warning her not to either.

'Oh no, neither would I.' Not that she needed him to tell her that. 'I don't know her well enough yet to say anything about her really. I just feel a little bad for thinking she was just a busybody.'

'Everybody assumes that's all she is, and she does like to know everyone's business. But maybe her life isn't as easy as everyone thinks. Maybe people should assume less and observe closer.' He spoke in the way Josie imagined he might to a pupil he was trying to show the error of their ways.

She knew he was talking generally but what he was saying applied to her and she hated that he'd held up a mirror to a side of her nature she'd not seen before. Another flaw in her character she'd have to live with. She also knew from what Peggy had told her about his family that his words were a little forceful on this subject because they applied to how people might view him. He was probably more sensitive to the judgements of others than most. She hadn't taken the time to look deeper when it came to Marjorie, and also when it came to his apparent dismissal of her choir. The fact that Tom had seen this in her didn't feel good.

'I feel a bit like I've been told off.' She laughed weakly in an attempt to make light of the situation but it was an uncomfortable realisation.

He looked troubled by this. 'I wasn't . . . I didn't mean it like that. I wasn't talking about you specifically.'

They were approaching Josie's turn off the main village road. He'd been kind enough to walk her home, and she didn't want him to feel that she was attacking him again but all she wanted was to be inside the cottage now.

'I know you weren't, but you are right. Well, this is my road. Thank you for walking with me. It was decent of you.'

'It was nothing. But once again I feel like something I've said has been taken the wrong way.'

'You just spoke the truth. It's fine, Tom, really. Thank you again.'

Tom didn't look convinced. 'I'll just say goodnight then . . . ?'

Josie couldn't meet his eye. She knew she was acting like he'd upset her, and he had, but not intentionally. Nevertheless she couldn't hide her emotions well enough to convince him all was fine. She felt ashamed that she'd been quick to judge Marjorie, but what she was struggling to admit to herself was that she was even more ashamed that Tom had seen that she'd done this too and had pointed it out to her.

'Yes, goodnight.' She gave him another watery smile before she turned away from him.

As she walked towards Glenys and Harry's cottage she tried to conjure up memories of Matthew to comfort her and soothe the sting she was feeling, but all that did was awaken the guilt that whispered in her ear every day, reminding her that her husband's face was fading from her memory too soon for its liking.

Chapter Fourteen

With the arrival of the post on Monday came confirmation from the Welsh Valleys Choral Competition that the Llandegwen choir would be competing against all the other choirs from the Valleys on Saturday 29 April in Bridgend. Josie felt a shiver of excitement laced with a thread of fear as she read the typewritten letter and glanced over the requirements of their entry. Thankfully things hadn't changed at all from the last time the village competed and they were still required to sing three songs. At least they had already chosen what they would sing and had begun to work on the first of them, she thought. Still, they had just six weeks left to work on the rest and polish them to perfection.

'No problem,' Josie said to herself half sarcastically, half in order to convince herself, as she tucked the letter into her music book. She was keen to get to practice that night, both to see if her work with Mr Evans had paid off and to distract herself from the mortification she felt whenever she thought of her conversation with Tom from Friday night. She also felt a little jittery now that it had been confirmed in black and white that the choir would be competing. She wanted to channel that nervous energy into music as soon as she could.

So it was that Josie was poised at the piano at five minutes to eight that evening to wave everyone into the hall and towards the instrument the moment they arrived. Glenys was already seated, looking red-faced and out of breath as the first of the choristers entered the hall. She hadn't quite recovered from having to more or less run alongside Josie on their way to the hall, such was Josie's haste to get there and to get cracking.

'Practice isn't going to start any sooner with you sprinting there like you're in the Olympics, love,' Glenys had puffed out from two steps behind Josie.

'I just want to get started as soon as everyone gets there. We need to make the most of every minute!' Josie had said as she marched on without breaking her stride, leaving poor Glenys to clutch her side to ease the stitch that was pinching her muscles.

As if the group had sensed Josie's urgency that evening, everyone had arrived fairly punctually and Josie was able to begin the choir practice at just three minutes past the hour.

'Evening, everyone! I hope you are ready for some singing,' she called out in a voice that wouldn't have been out of place at a rally. The final singers to arrive were just hurriedly taking their seats. 'We are officially registered as competitors in the Welsh Valleys Choral Competition in six weeks' time so we haven't a moment to lose. Thanks to those in the know . . .' Josie nodded at Mr Evans and Glenys, 'we have already selected our three songs and the rules haven't changed so we're all set on that front. So now we just need to master them!' She clasped her hands together with a loud clap and beamed at them all.

The group looked a little taken aback. It wasn't that they were surprised at the news of the competition being just weeks away, they had known that from the beginning, after all. They were just used to the more relaxed way the previous rehearsals had begun. Josie was suddenly all business and they were just a beat behind her.

When it looked like no one was going to blink until she took the lead, Josie took her seat at the piano and said, 'Let's warm up with some scales!' Her fingers flew across the keys and the choir scrambled to their feet to be poised to sing before they missed the first note.

As Josie had hoped, Mr Evans had remembered everything they had worked on together at their extra practice and the harmonies that they were working on sounded so much stronger as a result. It really lifted her heart to hear the difference their efforts were making. The rest of the choir could hear it too and as the week passed Josie could see them all growing in confidence, little by little. Shoulders were dropped, chests pushed out and pride and joy filled their voices. They were good and they were starting to feel it in their hearts. Marjorie was doing a sterling job delivering her solos, but Josie worried about how she would stand up against the competition. She had a lovely voice and she could certainly put some power behind it, but did it stand out enough? Marjorie seemed to think so, never one to doubt herself. On Wednesday evening she announced to the group after they had sung the first part of 'Suo Gân' together beautifully, 'It's so much better now that *my* voice can be heard properly. A voice such as mine shouldn't be drowned out, people want to hear it.'

'I worked hard on keeping my voice down so yours could be heard, especially for you, dear Marjorie,' Mr Evans said good-naturedly and kindly, though there was a hint of mischief behind his eyes too. The Thomas men rolled their eyes at one another. They were pretty easy-going men and they seemed to take her comments in good humour most of the time but Marjorie tested their patience somewhat. This was a relief to Josie, as harmony within the choir was essential when they had such a tight timeframe to gel as a group both vocally and as a team. The last thing she needed was anyone dropping out. If that happened there would be no competition for the Llandegwen choir at all. She hated to think of the disappointment that would bring everyone now that all of their hopes were riding high.

Catherine always found Marjorie's outbursts amusing. She exuded calm, Josie had realised after observing her over the past fortnight. She never seemed flustered when a harmony didn't quite work or they had to sing the same bars of music over and over until Josie was satisfied. She calmly carried on, and not only that, she had a knack of rallying those standing next to her too. Everyone had quickly relaxed around Catherine after that first night when no one seemed quite sure of how to take her presence in the group. She had shown them all from day one that she was one of them and wanted to be treated the same as the rest of them. She had no airs or graces, no sense of entitlement, despite the fact that she returned to her grand house each evening, while the rest of them returned to their simple homes and frugal, ration-supplied living. Josie found her fascinating.

Her ponderings over the reasons for why Catherine might have decided to join their choir hadn't yet been satisfied with a concrete answer until that Thursday night's rehearsal when they sang 'Suo Gân' all the way through for the first time at the end of the practice. The choir had sounded wonderful and as Josie turned to praise them all after playing the final notes, she saw Catherine wipe tears from her cheeks. Josie remembered how she had sung this song with such feeling the night they had chosen it to sing at the competition. She had felt then that Catherine was singing it to someone, that the lullaby had some deeper meaning for her. Glenys, who happened to be standing next to Catherine as she tried to recover herself from the emotion that the song had spilled over in her, touched the woman's arm and in a soft voice full of concern said, 'Are you all right, love?'

Catherine laughed a little embarrassedly and fanned her face with her hands. 'Oh, I'm so silly, I'm sorry! I've no idea what's come over me. Ignore me.'

The rest of the group looked at one another uncertainly, not wanting to move on until they were sure everything was OK.

'Really. I'm absolutely fine. I think we sounded so beautiful and that song has such a special memory for me, to hear it sung like that, and to sing it with you all. Well, it was obviously a bit much for my silly heart.' She laughed as she said this and looked at everyone with such reassurance that the room visibly relaxed.

'Wow, were we really that good?' Owen's sarcastic tone broke the tension.

'Well, Josie did say she'd have us breaking hearts. She's a woman of her word,' Michael added, making everyone laugh.

Josie sensed there was more to Catherine's reaction than the explanation she had given them all, and so she wanted to take the spotlight off the woman and wrap up that night's practice. 'Catherine's right, that sounded so beautiful. You are well on your way to melting everyone's hearts. I'm a very happy choirmistress tonight! Keep up the good work and I'll see you all next week.'

The gentle hum of light-hearted chatter filled the room, as everyone prepared to leave but wanted to share their moment of pride at their achievement that night for a few extra minutes. Glenys gave Catherine's arm a supportive squeeze as the two women joined in with the others excitedly but modestly speaking of their great improvement and how they might just be in with a chance of doing quite well at the competition next month.

Catherine broke away from the group so discreetly that no one noticed, and she began to help Josie with putting away the chairs. Josie wasn't quite sure if she should say anything, but Catherine took her dilemma away by speaking of it herself.

'Music is wonderful, isn't it? How it can make a memory feel so real it's as though you are in the moment again.' Her voice held a note of wonder as she spoke.

'Yes, it is. I grew up with music around me, and certain songs take me back to a time or a place as soon as I hear the first notes.'

The two women smiled at one another, knowing they both

understood the sensation Catherine had felt while singing the lullaby.

'I'm really glad to have you in the choir, it makes my job so much more fulfilling to see others share in my love of music,' Josie added.

'I'm glad too. I know it might have seemed a little . . . unusual for me to have come here at first but it was something I really wanted to do.' Catherine paused for a beat and Josie, not being quite sure what to say to this and with part of her curious to know this woman's story, hoped she'd go on. She was relieved when she did. 'It's hard to explain, but I wanted to do something for myself, you know?'

Josie nodded. She had set this choir up partly for that very reason.

Catherine frowned as she searched for the right words. 'Everything I do, I do as the mayor's wife. That's my role. The wife. And don't get me wrong, it's an extraordinary privilege and I know exactly how lucky I am. But sometimes I just want to be Catherine, to be me, doing something I love. Singing makes me so happy and being part of a group as just myself, singing with everyone in the choir, well, it feels good. I'm sure that sounds strange to you.'

'No, it doesn't. In fact it makes a lot of sense. There is something lovely about working together as a group, and you can't be anyone else when you're singing except yourself.' Josie shrugged, she got it. Catherine needed the choir to have something of her own, something she could own without standing to the side or in the background as she had to do as the mayor's wife. Though it was a life Josie couldn't really imagine, so far was it from her own, she could understand the notion of finding yourself living a life where you haven't quite got your own space or purpose. It was how she felt after losing almost everything she held dear and having to move to Wales. Josie knew she was lucky to have someone as welcoming and supportive as Glenys in her life, but she had still felt that she couldn't live in her shadow, that she needed her own thing to focus on. Catherine needed her own thing too.

'You're a great teacher, you know?' Catherine had looked relieved and grateful that Josie had understood her.

'That's nice to hear, thank you. I think I actually get more out of it than anyone though, when I hear you all sounding so wonderful.'

'Well then, we're all helping one another, which is the nicest thing of all, isn't it?'

The two women smiled and a silent and subtle bond formed between them. They were different in so many ways, and their lives were worlds apart, but the choir was something that made them the same, and that was something special, Josie thought.

'It is indeed, Catherine.'

And with that they joined the few stragglers standing by the coat stand that stood at the other end of the hall and who were stretching out the last minutes before they left the warm rays that the evening's choir practice had bathed them in. Within Josie's heart she felt the first fluttering of true happiness, a feeling that had been lost to her for so long that she barely recognised it when it stirred now.

Chapter Fifteen

Had she really been in Llandegwen nearly a month? Josie was stunned that the weeks could have possibly ticked by that fast. The elusive Mrs Moss had posted a note through their cottage door that morning to explain that the monthly village meeting which was due to take place the following week when April took its turn on the calendar had been brought forward by a week due to there being a number of pressing items to be discussed. It meant that Josie would have to move her choir practice to the Tuesday evening, as the village hall would be occupied. Josie just couldn't believe that it had been that long ago since she had stood in that hall, her heart on her sleeve, attempting to convince the committee and the villagers that she was capable of reforming the choir. Her heart swelled with pride when she thought about how far they had come since then.

And it wasn't just the choir that was going well for Josie. Sam had seemed so much happier these past weeks, ever since he started playing football. He no longer grumbled about having to go to school, in fact some mornings he was racing to get there.

They were settling in – something that had seemed so impossible when they first arrived. Josie had been so anxious to make living in Llandegwen work, she had almost not reformed the choir because of it. But everything was going so well she found herself looking over her shoulder less and less. The more time passed in Wales, the more London and her past faded into the background. And though she missed her home and her friends there, she had the memories that she'd always cherish. It was a small price to pay for the clean slate and better life she could give Sam and herself in Llandegwen. And she'd made a wonderful new friend in Peggy. She couldn't believe her luck to have found such a fun and supportive kindred spirit in such a small place.

She and Peggy had taken a walk through the fields and hills outside the village that Sunday and Josie had realised how much she'd missed having a friend her own age to chat about everything and nothing with. Though she often wrote to Rose in London, letters weren't the same as talking easily in each other's company.

'It makes me laugh now to think of myself as a little girl with all those big dreams. You think you can do anything when you're that age, don't you?' Peggy said, a wry smile playing on her lips. Josie had wanted to know what Peggy had hoped for before her life changed so dramatically. It might help her to find a way of helping her friend realise some of her dreams.

'I know. I sort of wish we could keep that belief a little longer though. I'd love Sam to have it for ever.' Josie filled her lungs with the clean air around her and exhaled slowly. 'What were your dreams then? When you were little?'

'Oh, they were big, Josie! I was going to leave little old Llandegwen as soon as I was old enough, and I was going to move to the big city. For me that was Cardiff. I would get a job as a secretary and I would live in lodgings with girls my own age and we would share clothes and help each other get dolled up to go out to dances.' Peggy's eyes were sparkling with pleasure at the telling of her younger self's fantasy. 'And it would be at one of these dances that I would of course meet the man of my dreams.' She nudged Josie playfully as they both laughed.

'Was there never anyone in Llandegwen?'

Peggy laughed. 'I had notions of a much more sophisticated city man than a local Llandegwen boy. But there was one lad, Jack. He was very sweet. We were friends and he wrote to me during the war when he was away. When he came back he said he wanted us to get engaged. But I didn't love him, I would have just been settling and he deserved better than that. I think I broke his heart a little. He lives in Cardiff now.'

They walked in comfortable silence for a moment before Josie asked, 'So what was he like? Your dream man?'

Peggy looked thoughtful. 'I imagined he'd be tall and strong, with a dazzling smile. He'd be chiselled in that film-star way. And he'd be so charming and gentlemanly, I'd be swept off my feet.' Peggy's smile started to fade now. 'But it wasn't to be. No big city, no dances, no dream man.'

Josie put her arm around her friend and gave her a supportive squeeze. 'Life's not very fair sometimes, is it?'

'You know that more than most, Josie. I've a lot less to

complain about. I get to be quite independent, which is a bit of a gift. And thanks to you I might eventually get to that big city finally to compete with the choir!'

'Maybe you'll even meet your dream man there?' Josie turned towards her friend with a look that said you never know. She hadn't told Peggy the full story of why she'd had to leave London. She was still so ashamed of the mess she'd made and she wanted to forget it, bury it. She felt bad for holding back from her friend when she'd been so open with her.

Peggy laughed. 'Maybe. So was Matthew your dream man then?'

Josie smiled sadly as she looked into the distance. 'I suppose he was, though I don't think I had a picture of who he might be before I met Matthew. But I knew as soon as I saw him that he was the man I wanted to marry.'

'Who knew Welsh music had such wooing power in London!' Peggy joked and the two women giggled. 'You must miss him?'

Josie nodded. 'I do. It's been a long time now without him though, and so much has happened. Sometimes I think it was all a dream. If it wasn't for Sam I'm not sure I'd believe he ever existed at all.' She felt sad all of a sudden – she had never voiced the guilty feeling she'd been carrying with her for a while now. Perhaps saying it out loud would help her make sense of what was going on inside her heart. 'This sounds terrible but I find it hard to picture his face these days. I have to look at photos to remind myself of all the little lines I used to know so well.' She looked at Peggy anxiously, hoping that her friend wouldn't judge her for what she was saying.

'It's not terrible. I think it's normal actually. Memories fade with time and perhaps that's for the best. It helps us to move on and not live in the past too much.'

'I've never been able to imagine myself moving on.' Josie was full of doubt.

'Not yet, maybe, but you will. Perhaps sooner than you think.' A gust of wind blew Peggy's wild curls in front of her eyes as Josie took a moment to digest what her friend had said. 'What about Tom Jenkins?'

'What about him?' Josie was confused.

'You said he walked you home the other night and he's been helpful with Sam.'

'And also that he's been rude and told me I'm judgemental!'

'And you think he's handsome.'

'Peggy, no. I'd sooner marry Mr Duffy than Tom Jenkins. He'd say the same of me, I'm sure. Well, maybe not with Mr Duffy in mind, but you know what I mean. And I'm not looking to marry anyone anyway, thank you very much.' Josie had told herself this for so long she hadn't realised that it was perhaps more of a defence mechanism than how she really felt these days.

'I reckon Mrs Duffy would have something to say about that,' Peggy joked.

'Let's focus on you, please. Hopefully there's a tall, film-star good-looking man in one of the Valleys choirs next month,' Josie said, and the mood was light once again.

'Now wouldn't that be nice!' Peggy giggled.

Josie was relieved to see that the message that choir practice had moved to the following night had got through when all ten members arrived that Tuesday evening. Though it transpired that Owen had deliberately kept his father in the dark about the change of arrangements and had found it hilarious that Michael had burst into the hall in the middle of the village meeting.

'You can laugh now, son, but just you wait!' he said good-naturedly after Owen had regaled the group with the story of how Michael had frozen, red-faced in the entrance to the hall, after the loud clatter of the doors opening had caused the entire hall to swivel their heads around to discover the identity of the rude interrupter.

'It did give us all a laugh, Michael. And we were in need of one at that point, the meeting was so dull last night,' said Mr Evans.

'Well, I am glad I entertained you all,' Michael said, giving everyone a little bow.

Josie joined in with the laughter and thought how good it was to see these two men, father and son, so relaxed after initially thinking they'd been forced to join the choir by Mrs Thomas. Everyone was in great form that evening and threw everything they had into working on the next song. Josie had noticed that Marjorie was unusually quiet though. She didn't chastise Owen for playing a trick on his father or for not taking the village meeting seriously, and she didn't even seem to hear Peggy and Michael when they joked about them all wearing funny hats when they competed in the Welsh Valleys Choral Competition. Marjorie's mind seemed to be elsewhere, though she sang with unquestionable effort, and she seemed reluctant to leave the hall at the end of the practice. She even offered to lock up for Josie, which was most unusual. Marjorie said she had wanted to check the kitchen for tea supplies for her meeting with the other women who arranged the church events the following morning. Josie's instincts were telling her something was up with this usually bossy and vibrant woman, but nevertheless she let her take the keys.

'Is everything all right, Marjorie?' Josie asked before she left.

The older woman's eyes flashed with something Josie couldn't put her finger on before she gathered herself and said with a tone that resembled her usual no-nonsense self, 'Of course it is. Why wouldn't it be?' and continued to bustle about the hall, clearly wanting Josie to leave her be.

Josie, never having had a personal conversation with the woman before, decided not to press her further and instead bid her goodnight and thanked her again for doing her job for her. She glanced back into the brightly lit hall from the darkness of the doorway to see Marjorie walk over to the piano stool where she sat and put her head in her hands. Though she couldn't see the tears, Josie could see the postmistress's body trembling in the way that only deep, anguished sobs made it do. Josie hesitated on the threshold, unsure of whether or not she should go back inside and offer her help in some way. But she felt that she'd trespassed on Marjorie's moment of private pain enough as it was. Whatever it was that was causing her this much sorrow, she didn't want anyone to know and Josie would respect that, though she hated to see anyone suffering in silence. She would keep an eye on Marjorie from now on, she decided. Perhaps this tough woman wasn't as steely as she led everyone to believe.

Chapter Sixteen

'Look at love's young dream over there.' Peggy nodded towards Gethin and Bethan, as Bethan let out a sweet giggle at something he'd said. 'That's your handiwork,' she said to Josie, quietly enough so that only she could hear. They were standing by the piano watching everyone gathering their things as they got ready to leave choir practice that Thursday night. Gethin and Bethan seemed to be glued at the hip these days, and the young woman was blossoming as a result. She was so much more confident, joining in with the others when they joked or made suggestions, when she had been too timid to do so before. It was wonderful to see, but Josie had hoped Bethan would sing more confidently too. Though the young woman appeared to enjoy being part of the choir she was still singing with a very soft voice and a little self-consciously. Josie had resigned herself to the fact that Bethan's whispered voice was all she was going to get from her at this stage. None of her tactics to encourage her to sing more confidently had worked thus far.

'I might have given them a little nudge but it's not had the full impact I'd hoped for,' Josie replied, as she put away her songbook and moved to collect the others from where they'd been left on abandoned chairs. Glenys had told Peggy about Josie playing with Cupid's arrow and Peggy had been keeping an eye on the romance developing before their eyes ever since.

'Maybe not, but you've put a twinkle in his eye and colour in her cheeks, and that's impressive work in my book,' Peggy said with a wink.

'Peggy!'

'What? It's a nice thing you've done there.'

They both started giggling until a sharp look from Marjorie made them bite their lips.

Marjorie was back to her usual self by the next time Josie had seen her after witnessing her moment of anguish. Her impression of Marjorie had been altered by what she'd seen, however, and she now felt a little protective of her when the others rolled their eyes at her comments. There was obviously more going on in this woman's life than any of them realised. After Tuesday night Josie had thought about what Tom had told her about Marjorie's husband and his drinking, and she had wondered if that was what was causing this woman pain. She knew instinctively that Marjorie wouldn't want to talk to her about it, if she would talk to anyone. She was such a proud woman and knowing people had been talking about her, even if it was just Tom and Josie, would mortify her, Josie was sure. So instead when Peggy said now, 'You'd think it was a crime to laugh with that woman around,' Josie was quick to defend her.

'Oh, she's not that bad. I think she's just really passionate about the choir.'

Peggy looked at her sharply. 'You're too nice, sometimes, you are, Josie.'

'I just think there's more to some people than meets the eye, that's all. Now let's get these chairs away and we can head off together.' Josie swiftly changed the subject before Peggy could question her on what hidden depths she thought Marjorie might have. She could almost see the words on the tip of her friend's tongue and she didn't want to betray Marjorie in any way. Josie was saved by Glenys who approached them now with her coat on, ready to go.

'Josie love, I'm going to run on ahead if you don't mind. I promised Harry I'd mend his pockets in his trousers for him for tomorrow. Apparently his handkerchiefs keep falling through and dropping out of the legs. He got very embarrassed about it all.'

'Of course, I'll see you at home. Peggy's keeping me company while I lock up tonight.'

'Oh good.' Glenys looked towards the village hall doors and paused, as she saw Gethin and Bethan walking out together. 'Ahh, look at them. I'll give them a little head start.'

She smiled affectionately at the young couple who were oblivious to the three women watching their love story unfold as they walked out into the night.

As a rare treat, that weekend Josie and Sam would have the little cottage to themselves and it was a prospect that Josie was very much looking forward to. Glenys was a wonderfully welcoming hostess but for one night it would feel good to pretend that she and Sam were just a little family of two once again, but this time in a warm and cosy cottage instead of a damp, miserable room. It would also be a relief to spend an evening in the house without the awkwardness that always seemed to be present whenever Harry was around too. Josie had given up trying to win him over. She'd tried so hard over the past month, making jokes, offering him cups of tea, even asking him questions about his time working in the coal mine, a subject she knew almost nothing about and had to really scrape the barrel to come up with a vaguely convincing subject. But it got her nowhere and so now they had fallen into a pattern of pretending the other wasn't there. Sam had a little more luck in drawing conversation from his grandfather. His innocent obliviousness to the situation meant he never hesitated to talk to Harry whenever he was present. But given this wasn't very often, Harry choosing to absent himself whenever possible, even Sam wasn't able to break down the barriers the older man put up. Avoiding one another seemed to suit them all better this way, but still Josie found it hard to completely relax whenever he was in the room. So it was a little bit of a relief to have most of Saturday and Sunday without the heavy cloud that Harry brought with him hanging over her.

He and Glenys were going to visit Glenys's sister Lynn in Aberystwyth, and given the long journey they would stay overnight to make it worthwhile. As they were heading out of the door that morning, Glenys was fussing over Josie and Sam, clearly perplexed at the idea of leaving them to fend for themselves for a couple of days.

'Now, I've made you a pie with a little bit of bacon I had left over as a treat that you can put in the oven for your dinner tonight. And there's coal for the fire in the basket by the fireplace.'

'I know, Glenys, you've told me all of this already. And we're very grateful.'

'I just hate to think of leaving you both alone here . . .'

'We'll be absolutely fine, I promise. Now you both have a lovely time with Lynn and we'll be waiting to hear all about it tomorrow evening when you get back,' Josie said in an effort to reassure Glenys who was wringing her hands and standing with one foot on the doorstep, the other still lingering on the threshold.

'Come on now, love, we don't want to miss the bus,' Harry said gently but firmly to his wife, finally coaxing her to make a move from their cottage towards the path that would take them in the direction of the village. And with that they waved one another goodbye, Sam running out to the rickety gate to watch his grandparents head off down the street.

After depositing Sam at his football club later that morning, Josie decided to pass the time she had on her hands with Peggy, keeping her company while she worked in the shop that day. Their conversation naturally wove its way on to the subject of the choir and specifically how lovely it was to see Fred smiling and seeming lighter in spirit as the weeks had gone on. He had become the focus of their chat after he had dropped into the shop to deliver some eggs for Peggy to sell.

'Are you well, Fred?' Josie had asked, delighted to see him in the village outside choir practice.

'I am. Very well, thank you, Josie.' He clutched his hat in

his hands self-consciously, but he was smiling at being included in the conversation.

'It's nice to see you down in the village,' Peggy said.

'Well, I thought while I was down here I might have a drink in the Plough this lunchtime. Michael and Owen invited me to join them. Might be nice.' Though he shifted awkwardly on his feet he looked happy about his plans for the day. Josie thought how nice it was of the Thomas men to include Fred in their weekend plans and what a big step it was for Fred to join in. She knew his heavy heart had kept him isolated for such a long time and that it was hard for him to feel comfortable around people again when he had first joined the choir. And though he'd never be the most gregarious of men, his natural disposition being that of a quiet soul, Josie had been pleased to see him enjoying the company of others, as well as enjoying the chance to sing that the choir offered.

'That sounds like a fine plan for a Saturday, Fred. Enjoy that. Though I hope you won't be talking about what a tough choirmistress I am when you all get together,' Josie teased.

'We wouldn't dare,' Fred said with a hint of mischief that delighted himself as much as them. And with that, he left.

'Gosh, it's so nice to see him so happy, isn't it?' Josie remarked to Peggy once he'd gone.

'He's like a different man. I only ever used to get a few words out of him when he made his deliveries before. He'd be so keen to get in and out, back off to his farm. I knew his story, of course, but still, I used to feel terribly sorry for him. Now look at him, off drinking in the pub with the others. It's marvellous.'

Their shared moment of delight at Fred's transformation was interrupted by the tinkling of the bell as the shop door opened. They both looked up to see who had entered, and they instinctively straightened up to their full height when they saw that it was Anwen. She was on her own and wearing her pristinely tailored green coat and matching hat, her silky chestnut curls sitting beneath it perfectly. She picked up a bag of flour from one of the shelves and jutted out her chin as she made her way towards the counter where Josie and Peggy waited for her.

'Just this, please,' she said, her haughty tone cutting through the atmosphere like a knife.

Josie had moved to the side while Peggy took Anwen's money and rang the sale up on her till. Anwen was pretending that Josie wasn't there and Josie was silently observing the woman who had made things so difficult for her in her first weeks in Llandegwen, waiting for the barbed comment she was sure would come before she left the shop.

'Here's your change,' Peggy said briskly, placing the coins in Anwen's hands.

'Thank you,' Anwen replied, turning on her heel and strutting out of the store.

Josie was a mixture of baffled, relieved and suspicious. She had never crossed paths with Anwen before without a snide word or dagger look being exchanged. Had she decided to let things be? Peggy thought not.

'What's her game then? Lady Anwen with nothing to say for herself? I don't believe it.'

'Maybe she's realised it's not worth causing fuss any more?'

'I highly doubt that, Josie. She's up to something.'

As Josie stared at the door that Anwen had shut behind her she hoped her friend was wrong.

Chapter Seventeen

As Josie approached the field later that afternoon, Sam was practically flying across the grass, weaving in and out of the other boys with the football between his feet. She was thrilled to see her son bursting with so much energy and loving every minute of what he was doing. He seemed to be quite good at it too.

Just as she got closer to where a few of the other parents were watching their boys play, she watched as Sam booted the ball, sending it speeding past the skinny boy standing in goal to cheers of delight from his teammates. Thoroughly pleased with himself, Sam jumped up in the air in celebration. Josie's heart filled with pride as she saw the other lads gather around Sam and pat him on the back. He looked like he belonged there, in that field in Llandegwen, no longer the outsider, and in that moment one of the knots of worry that had twisted in Josie's stomach since their arrival a month ago released.

They played for a few minutes more before Tom blew his

whistle to bring the practice to an end. He gathered the boys around to offer some final words of encouragement before sending them off home. Josie noticed how they all looked up at their teacher and coach with absolute respect, concentrating on everything he said. Knowing how difficult it had been to get Sam to do anything just before they left London and when they first got to Wales, she was quite impressed with Tom's ability to win the boys over. How was it that he could speak to children as equals but when he spoke to her it felt condescending?

After giving themselves a round of applause Sam ran over to Josie shouting excitedly, 'Did you see my goal, Mummy? I kicked it so hard!'

Josie beamed at her proud little boy. 'I certainly did. Well done, Sammy!' She went to hug him but he squirmed away from her arms in embarrassment before telling her off and returning to his friends to say goodbye.

Josie stood by herself, avoiding eye contact with Tom. The way they'd left things the last time they'd seen one another had been awkward and she didn't know how to smooth it over. He seemed set on ignoring her too, which was a relief in one way but she hated feeling uncomfortable. She hadn't minded the tension when she'd felt secure on her moral high ground, but she'd been knocked off her high horse by the realisation that she wasn't all that perfect either. It wasn't a position she was used to being in.

'Come on, Sam, it's time to go,' she called out impatiently as she moved towards him, ready to take his hand to lead him home.

Before she even knew what was happening, Sam looked

across to his teacher who was tidying the sashes into their box and said, 'Mr Jenkins, do you like bacon and egg pie?'

'Um, yes, I do, as it happens,' Tom replied, a little puzzled.

'That's what we're having for dinner because my grandma and grandpa are away. Do you want to come to our house to have some?' Sam looked at a surprised Tom with a hopeful expression on his little face. His teacher had clearly become a bit of a hero to him.

'Oh, I wouldn't want to intrude on you and your mum tonight, and eat all your dinner.'

'You couldn't eat it all, it's enormous. And it would be more fun if you came too.' Sam was all innocence.

Josie, who had been initially frozen by embarrassment, was now incredibly flustered at her son's brazen invitation. 'I'm sure Mr Jenkins has other things he needs to do this evening, Sam . . .' She really hoped her cheeks weren't flaming. She didn't want him in their home, they couldn't get through one conversation without one of them, usually her, walking off feeling wounded.

'Well? Do you?' Sam asked.

'Actually, no, I don't, but—'

'Brilliant!' Sam beamed. 'Do you know where our house is?'

'Um, yes.' Tom was utterly dumbstruck.

'We have dinner at six o'clock, it's the rules. Be there or be square. Come on, Mummy.' He walked away, satisfied with the arrangements he'd made.

Josie and Tom had been hustled by a six-year-old and neither of them knew what to say.

'Look, I don't know what happened last Friday night. I

know I said something wrong, again, but I don't really know what. My communication skills seem to go out of the window when I'm around you. Anyway, I'm sure I'm the last person you want to have round for dinner, so just tell Sam whatever you want to get out of it. You can even blame me if you like.' Tom finally found his voice and it lacked its usual confidence.

'No, no, I'm sorry Sam has put you in this position. But I understand why you wouldn't want to come. Of course you don't have to if you don't want to.' She thought she might be dying with embarrassment.

'I didn't say I didn't want to come. I presumed you didn't want me to.'

'Do you want to come?' She was asking out of disbelief rather than extending an invitation. She had no idea why he'd want to, given how uncomfortable they were with one another.

'Do *you* want me to come?'

They stood staring at one another, aware that they both sounded ridiculous but both too uncertain to back down.

Tom cracked first. 'Sam was kind enough to invite me so yes, I would. If that's OK?'

Josie wasn't expecting this answer. 'Of course,' she said, flustered. 'See you at six then?'

'Great,' he said, as if trying to convince himself it would be.

They walked away from one another and Josie was pretty sure Tom was just as confused about what had just happened as she was. Josie loved her boy but right now she could throttle him.

* * *

The delicious scent of Glenys's pie wafted through the little cottage that evening, but Josie wasn't a bit hungry. She was too anxious. What would Glenys think about her having a man over for dinner while she was away? Not that her intentions were inappropriate, she reminded herself. She was a widow and Sam would be there, and anyway Tom wasn't even a friend. She cringed every time she thought about Sam dropping them all in it with his completely incongruous invitation. And now he'd be here any moment and she was still all ruffled by the whole situation. Sam, on the other hand, was very excited about their dinner guest. He had even laid the table without Josie having to ask him for his help. She supposed there were some benefits to the situation she found herself in this evening.

The sound of the letter box tapping announced the arrival of Tom and Sam rushed to open the door.

'Evening, Sam. Something smells delicious,' he said easily as he removed his coat and handed it to an eager Sam who had somehow morphed into a little six-year-old butler that evening.

Josie realised she'd only ever seen Tom dressed for work or football club till now, and was therefore a little taken aback to see him looking more relaxed in casual slacks and an open-collared shirt beneath a knitted blue jumper. His sandy brown hair was smoothed to the side. He looked really good and the fact that she noticed unnerved her. His broad frame looked cramped in their tiny doorway so Josie quickly ushered him in to take a seat by the fire.

'Thank you. I brought you some chocolate to say thanks for having me tonight.' He offered Sam the large bar and Sam accepted it with unsurprising keenness, his eyes lighting up at the gift.

'What do you say, Sam?' Josie said stiffly.

'Thank you, Mr Jenkins. Do you want to see a photograph of my dad?'

'Sure,' Tom said kindly. 'I knew your dad, actually. We went to school together when we were around your age.' Sam was wide-eyed at this revelation as he brought over the photograph of Matthew he had taken down from the shelf next to the mantelpiece. 'He was a bit younger than me, but I remember he was pretty good at football too. I'd say that's who you get your football feet from.'

'Really?'

Tom nodded.

'Do you think I'll be as good as him?' Sam asked in earnest.

'I think you already are, lad.'

Josie stood there like a lemon as she observed their exchange. Tom seemed completely at ease and she wasn't remotely comfortable. Maybe people from his background always felt they deserved to be wherever they were.

Seeing how much Sam seemed to idolise Tom and how kind and patient this man was with him, was confusing to digest too. Sam was clearly in need of a strong male role model in his life. His grandfather certainly showed no interest in him, apart from that one night he'd taken the time to talk to Sam when they'd first arrived. But it was strange too to see him bonding with a man who wasn't her husband. Josie felt the familiar twinges of guilt as she tried to picture Matthew here with them now and it was a struggle to summon the image in her mind. She didn't want to think much more about it and so she excused herself in order to return to the kitchen and check on the dinner, where she could busy herself for as long as possible, avoiding awkward thoughts and awkward conversation.

Glenys's pie went down a storm and Josie had been glad to fill her mouth with it as much as possible to excuse herself from talking. Sam had dominated the conversation by asking Tom lots of questions about Matthew, football and the war. Josie had presumed, as was the case with most fit young men, that Tom would've fought in the war and she was right. He obviously kept his stories to those that were funny or exciting – rather than the truth of what he would have seen and experienced on the battlefields – for the sake of the innocent six-year-old in the room. And Josie found that she was listening intently to his stories too. The man sitting at their dinner table talking easily to Sam wasn't aloof or entitled, he was patient and interested. Interesting too. He was different to the Tom Jenkins she'd spoken to on previous occasions. The one who was always so stiff and who struggled to express himself. She had to now admit that she might have got his initial dismissal of the choir a bit wrong. But there was something about him that made her defensive. She didn't want to think too much about why that was, as she suspected it might have something to do with her caring a little more than she should what he thought of her.

After she had put Sam to bed a couple of hours later she had thought he would want to leave as soon as possible. She'd barely said more than a few words all night and he was only really there so as not to disappoint Sam. She could see that now.

'I've realised you've probably heard too much of the sound of my voice this evening and perhaps I didn't let you get a word in.' Tom sounded genuinely apologetic. He was standing by the hearth, hands in his pockets, as Josie came down the stairs and back into the front room.

'It was kind of you to answer all of Sam's hundreds of questions. In any case, I doubt you'd find me all that interesting so it's probably just as well.' She laughed to show him that she was being self-deprecating but it came out as awkward. She smoothed the skirt of her pale grey cotton tea dress to do something with her hands.

'I don't know, I'm quite interested in why you came to Llandegwen, for instance. Life in London must be far more exciting than what you get here. To make that decision is interesting.' To Josie's surprise he sat in Harry's armchair and looked at her expectantly. He wasn't leaving and seemed keen to hear what she had to say.

'Exciting isn't necessarily as fun as it sounds.' Josie was still standing and she was starting to feel foolish. She looked like an intruder in own home.

'How so?' He sat back in the armchair and Josie was forced to sit too, and she did so, on the edge of the sofa like a prim and proper schoolgirl. She couldn't get her body to relax. She'd gone from feeling awkward to nervous. Talking about herself in front of him felt exposing.

'There's a fine line between excitement and danger.'

Tom raised his eyebrows and Josie realised that she was getting herself into risky waters by engaging in this line of conversation so she steered it away from anything that would give away the true danger she had found herself in in her home city. 'I love London, it's where I grew up and it'll always be special to me. But it was a hard place to live, especially after the war. I lived in the East End and so much of it was destroyed, so many lives lost and changed. It was hard. I struggled on my own and Glenys offered to help, and well, here I am.'

'That must have been difficult.'

'It was and I miss it in some ways. But now that we've settled in to Llandegwen life, and I have the choir and Sam's happy, I'm glad to be here. It's better for us both.' Josie smiled, realising she'd meant every word and how good that felt.

Tom was watching her closely and Josie was worried about what he might see in her expression so she directed the spotlight back on to him.

'What made you decide to become a teacher? You could have done anything.'

'Well, not anything, there was really only one approved path laid out for me and that was on the board of the collieries. But it wasn't for me. I'm guessing you've heard some version of my story from someone?'

Josie blushed a little and nodded. She didn't want him to think she'd been involved in gossip about him, but of course she had.

'So I don't need to tell you then that I was left to my own devices after I declined my inheritance. And I had always wanted to do something useful in the community, to prove that not all Jenkins men were all bad. That some of us were prepared to give back. I suppose I had a bit of a chip on my shoulder, to be honest. People around here don't take kindly to the Jenkins name, despite the red carpet they might roll out in our honour. Underneath that is a lot of bad feeling, which I can understand. So I try to do my bit to show I'm prepared to give something back, even if my family isn't. But teaching is more than that to me. I love shaping young minds and seeing them succeed. I get a lot out of it too.'

'Do you see your family much?'

Tom looked pained. 'No, never. I hear from my older brother fairly often. We write. He can't visit and I am not welcome in any of the family homes. But we were always close and he's the only one who understands my position and feels bad about the whole thing. No one else will speak to me, my father has made sure of that.' A flash of resentment lit up his eyes. It was clear that Tom was angry and hurt over his father's actions and Josie found herself feeling his pain. She knew what it was like to have no family, albeit for very different reasons. At least she knew her family had loved her no matter what, even though they were all gone.

'Did you never want to marry? You could have your pick of women. And not just because you're so good-looking but because men are a bit thin on the ground after the war.' Tom looked at her in surprise. 'Sorry, that was really nosy of me. You don't have to answer that. I have a really bad habit of asking personal questions I've no business asking.' Josie cupped her hands to her cheeks to cover her embarrassment.

'I was focusing more on the rather back-handed compliment I think you just gave me. I'm not sure how to take it.'

Josie's light blush turned to flaming heat as she realised what she'd said, but Tom was laughing. He'd clearly not taken it too much to heart, either way.

'In answer to your question, yes, I would like to marry, but again my family name has been a bit of a barrier to that. Women I've known are only interested in being a Jenkins and having the money that comes with that. Only they're very disappointed when they learn I don't have access to that money. They either leave at that point or try to change me so that I give up teaching and go back into the family fold. I haven't met one yet who is prepared to take me as I am.' Tom laughed and shook his head. 'I don't know why I'm telling you all this. I sound terribly pathetic.'

'I think you sound very principled and decent actually.'

He studied her face to see if she were being genuine. 'How is it that I was intending to find out more about you and I've ended up telling you all of my secrets?'

Josie shrugged and smiled. 'It's a knack. I should've been a detective.'

'Ha! Maybe you should've. Anyway, it's getting late, I'd best be off.' He rose from the armchair and moved to take his coat from Josie who had risen too and taken it from the hook behind the front door for him. She held the door open.

'Thanks again for dinner. Next time I'll be more prepared and you'll be answering the questions.'

Josie laughed. 'Goodnight, Tom.'

As she closed the door behind him her shoulders dropped in relief. Somehow Tom had managed to smooth away the strangeness between them this evening and this shift made Josie feel much better about things. Her mind had even jumped further ahead than this and was full of the words 'next time'. Did that mean he wanted to spend time with her again? Or was it just something he'd said flippantly and to be polite?

She was so lost in thought she jumped when she heard

knuckles knocking on the front door. Had he forgotten something? It surprised and unnerved her that she was hoping he might want to talk a little longer. But when she opened the door her heart stopped, paralysed with fear. It wasn't Tom. The smile that had lit up her face seconds before froze, muscles paralysed, and her lungs struggled to breathe. He'd found her.

Chapter Eighteen

'I've been looking all over for you, darlin'.' He was smiling in between drags on his cigarette. He wasn't particularly tall but his stocky frame somehow dwarfed the small cottage doorframe. His slicked-back jet-black hair was as smooth as his manner. 'Aren't you going to invite me in?' He dropped the butt of his cigarette on the doorstep where he put out its light with his boot, Josie following the whole gesture with her eyes while her brain scrabbled to grasp how he was here standing in front of her.

'What are you doing here?' she whispered.

'Like I said, I've been looking for you. You're a tricky girl to find these days, aren't you, Josie? Very tricky.'

Josie's heart was hammering so hard in her chest she thought it might bruise her skin. 'How did you find me, Ronnie?'

He laughed his horrible cold laugh. 'Your lovely friend Rose was very upset to hear that Billy had developed a sudden and mysterious illness and she wanted to help me make sure the news reached you. Terribly concerned, she was. Never was the sharpest bird that Rose, was she?' He smirked and Josie felt sick. Oh, Rose. She'd been trying to do the right thing and wouldn't have known that Ronnie was manipulating her. He was so good at that. That's how Josie had been taken in by him and found herself shaking with fear in front of him now.

'What do you want?' She hated the fact that her voice sounded so meek.

'What do you think I want, girl?' He spat the words at her. 'I want what you owe me. Do you think you can just take my money and disappear? Did you think I'd be mug enough to let that go? No, darlin', that's not how this works. You know that.'

'I don't have your money. I thought it was a loan till I got myself sorted. I can't get you it like that, I told you that.'

Ronnie mimicked her words back at her in a mocking whine. 'Boo hoo. So you thought you'd just do a runner, did you? My heart bleeds. But what about me, Josie? Where does that leave me? Out of pocket and left to deal with a rightly narked load of clients who were all paid up and waiting for Josie Williams to do to them whatever they desired. Didn't think about that, darlin', did you?'

He was leaning his arm across the doorframe, blocking her from shutting the door. He wasn't shouting but Josie had broken out in a cold sweat thinking about whether or not the neighbours could hear. Thank goodness Glenys and Harry were away. But she couldn't let him in, she just couldn't. Not with Sam asleep upstairs. It was too dangerous. She had to get him to go away. No one could find out about him. If they did she'd no longer be welcome in Llandegwen, that's for sure.

'Listen, Ronnie, I'm sorry. You're right, I shouldn't have run off but I couldn't do what you were making me do. I was going to get you your money back, I promise. I will get you it back. Just give me a bit of time. I'll send it to you as soon as I can.' She was trying to appease him but even she could hear how pathetic she sounded.

Ronnie laughed at her. 'Do you think I'm stupid, darlin'? Do you think I've come all this way, to the arse end of nowhere, to get back on the train and wait for you to send me money we both know ain't coming? Do you?' He shouted the last two words right into her face.

Josie winced. 'Please, Ronnie,' she begged him.

'Listen to me, Josie. I want what you owe me, plus interest for the business I lost because you couldn't pay your debts with the only other thing you've got to offer. And I want it soon. If you haven't got the money by the time I'm bored of this place, you're coming back to London with me and you're going to work that delightful figure of yours in one of my fine establishments. I'll drag you back by your hair if I have to, but I won't have to do that, will I, darlin'? Don't think I haven't noticed the nicey-nicey set-up you have here. I've been watching you. Saw your lover boy leaving just now and all. I imagine he'd love to hear about how you have a long waiting list of clients in my brothels back in London and that you're the kind of girl who steals a man's money. And those lovely people you live with, don't reckon they'd be best pleased to learn they've a thief and a tart living under their roof.'

'I'm not a tart, I've never worked in one of your filthy places and I never will.' There were tears of anger behind her eyes.

How could he have done this to her? How had she found herself in this position?

'Best find that money then, sweetheart, and double it to compensate me for my losses. I'll be in the pub when you're ready. But I'll be getting to know your nice new neighbours while I'm here. They all seem very friendly, and keen to know more about you from one of your London friends.' He winked at her and pushed himself away from the doorframe. 'Don't leave it too long. It's good to see you again.'

Josie slammed the door before he could turn his back. She couldn't look at his slimy face for another second. She felt physically sick as her body slid down the door to the floor and the heaving sobs finally broke free from her chest. She'd been so stupid to think she could escape him, that it would be as easy as that. What the hell was she going to do? If she didn't find the money, and find it fast, he would tell everyone that she had run off without paying him back, he'd probably tell them she worked in his brothels too, even though she hadn't, couldn't. It was because he was forcing her to do this that she'd run. He'd told her she'd left him with no other option. Ronnie had made a name for himself in the East End and had several profitable brothels running across the city. He was successful and the amount of money Josie owed him wouldn't have set him back all that much, but he had his name and reputation to uphold. If he let her off paying back her debts he'd be seen as a soft touch and he couldn't have that. Josie had been so naive to think he'd treat her differently because he'd been Billy's friend from when they were kids. And Billy clearly didn't know the kind of man his old friend had become in the years he'd been away. Josie would never have taken a loan from Ronnie if she'd known the price she'd have to pay. He'd told her that if she couldn't pay him back with money she had to pay him back with her body. He told her she had a list of clients waiting for her in one of his brothels the following night and if she didn't show he'd come and get her himself. On the same day, Glenys's letter arrived with the train fare to Llandegwen. She'd hoped he'd never find her here, had even started to believe he wouldn't in the last few days. The thought of everyone finding out about her grubby life in London released a fresh flood of tears down her cheeks. She'd have to leave her friends and the choir – oh, she'd let them all down so badly! It was unbearable.

Maybe there was another way. Maybe she could find the money. She still had her wedding and engagement rings, which she wore around her neck. She pulled the chain out from beneath her dress and looked at the jewellery that was so precious to her. It broke her heart to part with them, but it gave her hope too. If she could pay him off without anyone finding out who he really was, she would be free of him and could carry on living in Llandegwen and she could deliver on her promise to get the choir to the competition.

She wiped away her tears and pulled herself up on to her feet again, though she was still a little shaky from the shock. She wasn't going to give up. But even so, she knew he meant every word of his threats and the thought of him dragging her back to London to that horrible, terrifying, seedy life made her heave with nausea. She was right back in the middle of her worst nightmare and this time the way out wasn't as clear.

Chapter Nineteen

'How shall we be getting to the competition in Bridgend, Josie? Have you given it any thought, because it's quite an important detail,' Marjorie said in her now very familiar officious tone.

The group had just been discussing how much time they had left before the Welsh Valleys Choral Competition at the end of the month and a ripple of excitement mixed with nerves had travelled through the choir at that Tuesday night's rehearsal. Josie was momentarily stumped by Marjorie's question. Her mind had been all over the place since Saturday night. She knew Glenys had been watching her with concern, there was no way she could hide her fear from her, but so far the tiny woman had accepted her lame excuses of tiredness and feeling under the weather. Josie was sure she didn't believe them for a second. Ronnie had been mentally torturing her by showing up all over Llandegwen, mocking her with his smile as he introduced himself as her old family friend from the East End to Glenys and Peggy, and anyone else who happened to be present. He'd been very charming and they'd taken him at his word, pleased for Josie that a friend of hers had come to visit, buying his story that he was passing through Wales on the way back to London from a Dublin business trip. Glenys had even invited him over for dinner, and for one horrifying moment Josie thought he was going to say yes. Thankfully Ronnie had had the sense not to push Josie too far and was content giving the illusion that he was busy with work most of the day and just happy to catch Josie when he could. What was even worse than the constant threat his presence exuded was seeing him manipulate the good people of Llandegwen and her having to indulge his lie to save herself from the worse fate of being found out. She hated it and she hated him. She was still working on how to get her wedding rings valued and sold, but she'd have to go into Castleforth to do that and she hadn't yet come up with an excuse for why she needed to go there.

Marjorie cleared her throat, bringing Josie back into the room and out of her head. The postmistress was still waiting for an answer and Josie hadn't actually given this not insignificant detail any thought. She'd been so wrapped up in getting everyone's voices as strong as they could be and then working out the harmonies for the songs they were to sing that the thought of arranging anything else relating to the practicalities of the competition had completely eluded her.

'Erm . . . actually I hadn't, no, Marjorie . . .'

'Well, it's a good job I mentioned it then. And there's also the matter of what we'll be wearing to be sorted out. I suppose you hadn't thought of that either?' Marjorie was looking at Josie with her eyebrows raised in that disapproving way she had so well mastered, and that made Josie feel five instead of twenty-five years old.

'It's very good of you to mention these things, Marjorie. After all, it's up to us all to think of them, not just Josie. She's got quite enough to do with helping us all better our voices and organising us into a choir good enough to compete. We're a team after all, aren't we?' Catherine said kindly and smoothly, softening Marjorie with her graceful tact that saved Josie's blushes as well as Marjorie's pride. Catherine really was very good at defusing tricky situations, Josie thought, she might have been Britain's strongest negotiator during the war if it weren't impossible for a woman to have had such a role.

Marjorie had been quite prickly that evening thus far and Josie had wondered what might be going on beneath her spiky surface. But now that the question of transportation to the competition had been thrown into the ring her mind had snapped to attention. She had no idea how to arrange such a thing in this small village.

'Marjorie is right, it's a very good question. Does anyone have any ideas?'

'Could we hire a bus?' Gethin suggested.

'That's a good idea.' Bethan beamed at her beau.

'But how would we pay for a bus?' Glenys's brows furrowed in concern at this notion. And she wasn't the only one of them who was concerned about the costs of such a plan. The war had made them all poorer in more ways than one and most of the members of the choir made a modest living, to say the least.

'There must be something we can sort out or think of.' Peggy looked as though her dreams of escaping Llandegwen, even for a day, were being stolen from her once again.

'Perhaps we could raise the money to pay for the bus?' Catherine proposed, making herself one of them even though her situation was very different from the others. Catherine's privilege never seemed to set her apart, she saw everyone as equal and in turn they all saw her the same way.

'That's a good idea, that is,' said Fred.

'It is indeed! And I have just the thing.' Mr Evans's eyes were twinkling with excitement at potentially having found a solution to their problem. He was pacing between his seat and where Josie was sitting at the piano. The rest of the choir had remained on their feet after they'd finished singing 'Calon Lan' and they were now watching the vicar in anticipation. 'Why don't we combine the cake sale we are having this Sunday to raise funds for the new hymn books with a fundraiser for the choir? The cake sale could be for both causes and we could give the village a little song as an incentive for more people to contribute!'

Mr Evans looked at everyone expectantly, grinning from ear to ear at his own brilliance.

'That's a wonderful idea! Thank you, vicar, it's very generous of you to allow the choir to jump on the cake sale bandwagon.' Josie rose from her stool in order to face Mr Evans. His offer was getting her out of a really tricky dilemma. She still couldn't believe she hadn't thought about transportation. What kind of choirmistress was she? Thank goodness for Marjorie, even if she had made Josie feel useless in the process.

'So . . . we're to sing in public? This Sunday . . . ?' Fred's voice trembled a little as he spoke. Josie looked at him in surprise but then she caught the deer-in-the-headlights expression on Bethan's face and saw Michael and Owen looking at one another a little anxiously. Clearly confidence levels weren't as high as she had thought they were, despite how well their choir practices had been going.

'Do you think we're ready to sing to everyone yet?' Catherine ventured on everyone's behalf.

'Oh, but you have all been sounding so marvellous, of course I think you are ready. And it would be good practice for us to perform to an audience . . .' Josie looked hopefully at her doubtful-faced choir. Mr Evans and Marjorie were the only two singers who appeared to be more than completely comfortable with the idea.

'We'll have to sing in front of an audience at some point, so there's no point us being wet about it now.' Marjorie was as intolerant of any kind of weakness as Josie had imagined she'd be.

'We'll just sing them one song, a teaser, if you like. We don't want to reveal our secret star quality too soon, do we? What's it they say in show business, always keep your audience wanting more?' Mr Evans added good-naturedly.

'Just one song . . . how hard can that be?' Peggy said with a watery smile that undermined any attempt she'd made at sounding confident about the whole idea.

'It'll be a walk in the park for you all, trust me,' Josie said, giving them all her most winning smile whilst crossing her fingers behind her back. This would be her first test as the village choirmistress. They had trusted her to form a choir worthy of Llandegwen's history in choral competitions. If she fell flat on her face now she'd be letting so many people down.

The thought of such an outcome caused her chest to tighten and her breathing to become short. She felt the pressure of this responsibility more than ever with Ronnie watching and waiting in the shadows. She couldn't let them down, she just wouldn't let that happen. That's all there was to it.

Josie may have left that night's choir practice determined to help the choir show the village exactly how good they really were, whilst also calming everyone's nerves by playing down the importance of this first performance – 'Think of it as a trial run,' she had said, 'a chance to discover strengths and weaknesses in your performance skills that might give us an edge in the competition,' she had said, 'it's really not a cause for excitement,' she had said – but all of her big talk evaporated when she was approached outside the village hall by a man who introduced himself to her as Peter Philips. She'd been struggling to open the heavy hall doors to enter a little ahead of time for that Thursday evening's rehearsal when she'd heard an unfamiliar voice behind her say, 'You look like you're having a bit of trouble there.'

For a moment her heart had been in her mouth thinking it was Ronnie once again. He'd been waiting for Josie when choir practice had ended the previous evening, only stepping out of the shadows when she was alone and locking up the heavy wooden doors.

'I've been thinking, maybe we can use those musical skills of yours in one of my fine establishments,' he'd said. 'I'm sure the gentlemen of London would enjoy a little extra entertainment.' His voice was lazy, mocking.

Josie was constantly on edge, knowing Ronnie was a time

bomb ticking away and waiting to blow up the nice life she had only just started to make for herself and Sam. His constant presence in the past few days made her feel sick with both fear and shame.

'I told you, I'll get you your money. I will have it for you soon.'

'Yeah, you say that, but I've heard those words before and look what happened then. So forgive me if I don't quite believe you, sweetheart.' He was smiling his nasty smile, locking on to her gaze with a challenge in his eyes. 'I think you'll be a nice little money-maker when I get you back to London.' The way his eyes scanned her body as he said this made Josie feel violated and exposed. She had to get him out of her life. She had no idea if her rings would get her enough money to pay him back completely, but maybe it would be enough to get him to leave till she found the rest. She had to try. There was no way in hell she was going back to London to do . . . that. The thought made her eyes sting with tears, but she couldn't let him see her cry, she had to be strong otherwise he'd know he had won. She summoned some steel from within so her voice would sound strong as she spoke.

'I will get your money and I won't be coming back to London, Ronnie.'

He walked slowly towards her till his face was only a couple of inches away from hers, his toxic breath almost burning her cheeks as he stared down at her with a smirk on his face.

'Let's see, shall we?'

Josie had been trembling so much when she got home that night she'd had to go straight to bed so that Glenys wouldn't notice. And now she was jumping at any voices coming out of the shadows, even ones with Welsh accents that couldn't possibly belong to Ronnie.

'Oh no, I'm fine. They just get a bit stuck sometimes,' Josie replied to Peter Philips after she turned around to see who the voice belonged to. He was about her age, she reckoned, dressed quite smartly in a brown wool suit and matching tie. He was clutching a notebook and pencil in one hand, the other hand buried in his pocket, and he seemed to be constantly moving with overflowing energy. She'd never seen him in the village before and when he introduced himself Josie learnt why. Peter Philips was a reporter at the Castleforth *Gazette* and he was there to write a story about the Llandegwen choir.

'We heard a war widow from London was behind it all and I wanted to come down here and check it out. We're looking for morale-boosting stories and it sounds like your choir might be just the ticket – I presume you are the Londoner in question?' He had an easy charm that Josie thought probably got him quite far in his line of work.

'I suppose my accent gave me away.'

Peter laughed before pushing his agenda once again with ease. 'I believe your choir is giving a performance this Sunday to raise some funds for a bus ride to the competition? I'd love to come down and write about it.'

'Well, I wouldn't say it's a performance exactly . . . I mean, we'll just be singing one song for the villagers. It'll be a small thing. More of a practice run for us really.' Josie was desperately trying to play it down. It was one thing to convince the choir to sing for the village after just four weeks of practice, but it was quite another to put them under the spotlight of the local paper.

'Yes, yes, sounds great,' he said dismissively. 'You're about to rehearse now, aren't you? May I stay and have a listen?' He pulled open the door and entered the hall without waiting for Josie to answer.

He was an arrogant man, that Peter Philips, thought Josie as she watched him scribbling away in his notebook while he swung his legs from the stage where he'd plonked himself for the duration of that night's choir practice. She had worried about how the rest of the group would react to his presence and what it would mean in terms of their singing being written about and printed in black and white for all the surrounding villages and Castleforth to see. Most of them had been nervous enough about Sunday and the idea of singing in front of others for the first time, and so Josie needed to build up their confidence ahead of the cake sale. Any additional stress was not ideal at all. But as annoying as he might be in his presumptions of his presence being welcome, Josie did recognise that he was useful to the choir. If he wrote a nice piece about them that would really help drum up support, which might lead to more help with funding their travels to other competitions, if they did well at the Welsh Valleys Choral Competition. They might even get some new members.

So it was that Josie decided to put a positive spin on his presence when she explained to the choir who he was and why he was there.

'He's going to watch our rehearsal tonight and he'll come along on Sunday too, so that he can tell everyone how brilliant you all are.'

Mr Evans had been predictably thrilled at this turn of

events. 'Well, isn't that something! Our choir is to be in the papers. Welcome, Mr Philips, ask me anything you want. And be sure to write good things!'

'Thank you, vicar. It would be great to speak to some of you about your reasons for joining the choir. But to begin with I'll just be an observer. Just pretend like I'm not even here,' Peter said with that charming smile of his.

Of course no one was able to forget the reporter was in the room, especially as his legs never stopped swinging from the stage. As it happened this turned out to be a good thing as, much to Josie's delight and relief, the presence of an outsider – and a reporter no less – instead of heightening everyone's nerves, seemed to spur the choir on to give the best vocal performances they had given so far.

Josie could barely contain her pride once Peter Philips had bid his farewells just before they wrapped up their practice for the evening.

'Do you think we did all right, Josie love?' Glenys asked nervously once the heavy hall doors had closed behind the reporter.

'You did more than all right, you were brilliant!' Josie gave a little leap as she beamed at them all.

'Do you really think so? Because it would be rather wonderful if he wrote something nice about us, wouldn't it?' Catherine cupped her cheeks with her palms, half smiling and half frowning.

'I really do. And I can't see how he could write anything but nice things about you all.' Especially as he had learnt some of their reasons for joining the choir when he spoke to a few of the members of the group in between songs. Hearing Fred explain how the choir had given him something to look forward to each week, and how it had reconnected him to the village after so many years, made Josie as choked with emotion as she had been the first time Fred had told her this. And knowing competing was giving Peggy the taste of adventure she'd always longed for, and the Thomas men a place to forget the horrors of war that they had both witnessed, made Josie feel validated in her mission to make this choir a success, and she knew too that it would give Peter Philips a good angle for his story.

Only Catherine had held back when asked by Peter about her reasons for joining the choir. She merely stated that she loved to sing and had always wanted to be part of a choir. Josie wondered if she was worried about her husband, the mayor, and what her true reason would mean to him, or perhaps for him publicly. Wanting something of her own was perhaps not an acceptable reason to do anything for a mayor's wife. Not for the first time Josie wondered what Catherine's life was really like. The way this woman sang the lullaby 'Suo Gân' still sparked a curiosity within her. Catherine's heart always looked as though it might break when she sang the lyrics, and therefore Josie couldn't help but wonder who or what memory she was singing to each time. But Catherine's glossy exterior never gave her any more clues.

As she looked at her choristers now she realised that each one of them had their own story to tell when it came to the choir, including herself. And in just a few weeks the choir and their adventure to their first competition would be part of all of their stories. But their first real test would be this Sunday in front of the village and the Castleforth *Gazette*.

'If you all sing on Sunday like you did tonight, you'll be a huge success. I'm sure of it,' Josie told them, and she meant every word.

Chapter Twenty

'OK, spit it out.' Peggy leant her elbows on her shop counter and put her head in her hands as she waited for Josie to answer her. Josie had got into the habit of calling in on Peggy at the shop while Sam was at school. If the shop was quiet they'd get to have a bit of a gossip which was more fun than her getting under Glenys's feet at home in the cottage. However, this conversation had suddenly become not at all fun because her friend had clearly tired of her feeble excuses for her jumpy, anxious behaviour of the past week.

'Seriously, Josie, there's something up with you and it's more than tiredness, and the choir actually seems to bring you back to your usual self after a bit, so it's not stress over that. So, like I say, spit it out.'

Josie made to protest, to come up with even weaker reasons for her odd behaviour, anything to avoid telling her about who Ronnie really was. But Peggy was having none of it.

'Listen, you've been a good friend to me, you've been an ear when I've needed to let off steam about my mam and I can't tell you how great it's been to have someone who winds up Anwen even more than I do,' they both laughed as she said this, 'but friendship works both ways, you know. I'm here to listen to you too and I know something is worrying you. And I think it's something to do with your friend Ronnie, who you don't seem all that keen to have around for someone who's supposed to be your friend.'

Josie's shoulders slumped with defeat. Peggy had seen right through her and there was no way she could hide the truth from her friend any longer. She didn't have the strength to either. Carrying around that burden on her own had been exhausting. Her defences broken, Josie burst into tears.

'Oh God, Josie, what is it?' Peggy rushed out from behind the counter to comfort her friend. 'Is it really that bad?'

Josie nodded. 'It's so bad, Peggy. You'll hate me when I tell you. Everyone will. I've been so stupid.' She choked out the words in amongst sobs.

'I doubt that, but how about you try me, eh?' Peggy said soothingly.

The words tumbled from Josie's mouth, desperate to escape from where they had been kept secret for all this time, never spoken to a soul before now. She left nothing out – what was the point at this stage? None of it was good. She told her about how she had known Ronnie for years, that he'd been Billy's friend, and that her brother had told her to get in touch with him to ask him for help when he was unable to help her himself. Billy had heard that Ronnie had done well for himself, but Ronnie's methods of making money had clearly been lost in the Chinese whispers that had made their way across the Atlantic Ocean and over to Billy in America. Josie was sure that her brother would be horrified to learn of what kind of lion's den he'd led his sister into by putting her in touch with Ronnie. She told Peggy about Ronnie's sudden demands for his money back, and that when she couldn't pay him how he'd told her she'd have to work off her debts as one of his prostitutes instead.

'But I couldn't do that, I would never do that, you have to believe me. And I know I ran away without paying him back his money, and that that technically makes me a thief, but I had no choice. I didn't have the money, I don't have the money and I can't pay it back working as a . . . oh God, I can't even say it, the idea makes me feel so sick!'

'Oh, Josie, I can't believe you've kept this to yourself the whole time.'

'How could I tell anyone here? I'm already an outsider and no one wants this kind of trouble in the village.'

'Look, anyone with a brain here knows you're not a thief and if faced with the same situation they'd probably do the same. I know I would.'

'So you don't think I'm an awful person then?'

'No! Of course I don't.' Peggy smiled sympathetically. 'I think you did the best you could do at the time and that's all any of us can do. This Ronnie is a piece of work, clearly.'

Josie smiled at the feistiness of her friend whose fierce sense of loyalty was kicking in. The relief at having told her secret and been given Peggy's support was overwhelming. But it didn't solve her problem, there was no escaping the mess she was in.

'What are you going to do?' Peggy asked.

'I thought I could sell my rings to raise some money and

hopefully pay him off enough to leave Llandegwen, but I don't know how to get away to Castleforth without Glenys coming with me or wanting to know why I'm going.'

Peggy looked thoughtful for a moment. 'It's tricky, but I'm sure we can think of something. In the meantime, I'm here for you, you know that, don't you?'

Josie hugged her friend. 'I do, and thank you for not hating me.'

'Don't be stupid. Now let's get thinking. We'll get you out of this mess.'

The sun had barely begun to stretch its rays above the horizon and the larks were only starting to stir when Josie and Glenys rose from their beds that Sunday morning. There was so much to do, they needed every minute they could grab. First of all they had to bake their offerings for the afternoon cake sale – every member of the choir had agreed to contribute, given they had to raise enough money for both the hymn books for the church and funding for hiring a bus to take them to Bridgend. Other villagers would be baking their finest cakes and pies too. Nothing said 'community spirit' more than households saving the sugar they'd been rationed to bake cakes to raise money for good causes. Mrs Duffy had told Glenys that she would be making her famous lemon drizzle cake. 'Though why she thinks it's famous I have no idea. The woman has never baked for anything in this village before.' Glenys was incredulous. The cake sale had revealed a competitive streak within her that Josie hadn't seen before and it amused her to see this usually jolly woman getting quite serious over something she clearly felt was her area of expertise.

Mr Driscoll had pledged to donate some of the wares from his bakery to that Sunday's sale, which Josie had thought was very kind of him. And word had spread beyond Llandegwen to Castleforth care of Catherine and her husband.

'We know plenty of people who have money in their pockets and like a drive on a Sunday. I am sure I can get them to come,' Catherine had told Josie and Mr Evans when they had been discussing how to get the message out. And knowing Catherine's powers of persuasion she would be true to her word.

It was the first time Josie had seen for herself how well the community rallied to support the two causes the sale was in aid of. Glenys had told her that the village had always been very good at coming together to support one another, but they hadn't had a chance to do so for many years now. 'It's the choir that's got people wanting to help out, it's something nice for the village to get behind. It reminds me of the old days, before the war. It's lovely, it is.' Glenys had been misty-eyed about it all when Josie had told her about Mr Driscoll and his bakery's donations. Only a month ago Josie had faced the uncertainty from the village around whether or not she was the right person to reform the choir. And now she had and everyone was getting behind them, it should have been the most wonderful feeling but the thought of losing it all and letting everyone down because of Ronnie and because of her stupid mistake was devastating. Llandegwen had been starting to feel like where she was supposed to be, not where she had to be. That was something she could never have imagined thinking at the start of last month after those first few days in Wales. She didn't want to lose her new home. Village life had managed to charm her and she'd abandoned her city-girl ways without even realising it.

Josie smiled to herself as she looked down at her flour-covered apron and then up at the window from which she could see the rolling Welsh hills in the distance beyond the other cottages. She'd well and truly embraced the country life.

'Stop daydreaming, Josie love. We've too much to do!' Glenys commanded. Her competitive streak had turned her into a sergeant major. She was right though. They had to be at the village hall early to have one last practice together as a choir before they were to open the cake sale. Stalls were being set up outside in the April sunshine on Colliers Row and manned by the ladies who volunteered at St Luke's church each week. Josie's tummy filled with the fluttering of nerves at the thought of their imminent performance, and then those flutters turned to pangs of panic as she realised Ronnie was bound to be lurking about the village, watching her and talking to her new friends. In the same moment Glenys, as if she could read her mind, barked, 'Giving that batter in front of you some of your muscle will take your mind off the butterflies, love.' If only she knew the half of it, Josie thought.

Laden down with their offerings, Josie, Glenys and Sam arrived at the tables that had already been set up outside the village hall at midday. The sale was to begin at half past two that afternoon. Harry had decided to go for a walk by himself – he clearly didn't want to get involved in the day's festivities. For the first time Josie thought she saw Glenys look disappointed in her husband's reluctance to join in. She didn't question Harry, but she held his gaze with a look heavy with meaning in the moment of silence that went on a beat too long when he revealed his plans for the afternoon. Glenys quickly brushed him aside with a 'suit yourself', but Josie felt her disappointment all the same. She, however, was relieved not to have his negative presence at what was to be an already quite stressful afternoon.

After they had deposited their baked goods with the ladies in charge, and Josie had left Sam with one of his new friends from the football club and his family, she and Glenys entered the hall. They were soon joined by the rest of the choir, everyone looking a little on edge. Even Mr Evans was a little paler of cheek and poor Michael was green around the gills. Josie crossed her fingers that they'd all be able to master their nerves in a couple of hours.

Just as Josie was about to suggest they get started with some vocal warm-up exercises she realised that they were one singer short, in the shape of Marjorie Davies. Josie looked around the room as if Marjorie might be hiding somewhere quietly, which was of course ridiculous. When was the postmistress ever quiet and ever not in the centre of things? But she was also never late, and it was this fact that troubled Josie the most. So much so that when the church bells chimed the hour at one o'clock Josie was unable to shake the idea that Marjorie might not be coming today at all. The others had also noticed her absence and had started to get worried. She was their soloist and as they were to sing 'Suo Gân', the song they had always felt strongest singing, they needed her there.

'Maybe she's not well?' Owen was the first to address the problem.

'I'm sure she'd have got a message to us if she were. It's very unlike her,' Mr Evans said, perplexed.

'Did she forget?' asked Fred.

'Marjorie never forgets anything.' Bethan knew all too well how organised her boss at the post office was.

'Who's going to sing the solo if she doesn't show up?' Peggy looked cross at the idea of Marjorie ruining their first performance.

'Let's not worry about that yet. How about I pop round to her house now while you all take a little break. I'm sure it's nothing for us to worry about.' But Josie wasn't sure at all. Mr Evans and Bethan were right, this wasn't like Marjorie and Josie couldn't imagine what would keep her from such an important moment for the choir.

Anxiously, Josie grabbed her coat from the stand by the hall doors and made her way outside and down Colliers Row until she got to the Davieses' front door. Marjorie's home occupied the rooms at the back of the post office as well as those on the floor above it. Taking a deep breath first, Josie knocked. There was no answer. She took a step back and looked up at the windows above, wondering more about where Marjorie could possibly be than expecting to see anything. She was just about to walk away, not really sure where to look for her next, when she saw movement behind the lace curtains. Quickly Josie knocked again, harder this time, giving the person who was clearly home the benefit of the doubt that they might not have heard her the first time.

Anxiety twisted in her stomach as, after several seconds ticked by, a panicked-looking Marjorie opened the door slowly and only halfway, revealing just half of her face and body in the process. The half of her face that Josie could see was as white as a sheet. Josie was about to ask her if she was OK, but Marjorie jumped in first. In urgent, almost whispered tones, she told Josie, 'I was about to get a message to you. I'm very sorry but I can't sing today. I'm . . . I'm unwell . . . very sorry to let you all down, but I hope you'll understand.'

Josie's heart sank. What were they going to do without their soloist? Illness couldn't be helped though, and she didn't want to make Marjorie feel any worse than she was sure she already felt.

'Of course we understand and I'm so sorry you're unwell. Is there anything I can do or anything I can get you? Sorry to turn up on your doorstep, we were just worried about you . . .'

Marjorie shook her head to decline Josie's offer of help and in doing so revealed the other side of her face that she had thus far kept hidden. The younger woman wasn't quick enough to hide her shock at seeing a dark purple bruise flowering over Marjorie's right cheekbone. Marjorie instinctively raised her hand to cover her wound. She looked pained and humiliated, and worst of all, anxious.

Josie's heart raced as a terrible picture of what might have been happening behind Marjorie's closed door appeared in vivid colour in her mind.

'What happened to your face, Marjorie?'

'It's nothing. Stupid really. I walked into something. A cupboard door left open.' She was gabbling, clearly desperate to end the discussion. 'I'm fine, really. Just under the weather. I'm sorry. I'll be back to normal soon.' She made to close the door before Josie put an arm out to stop her. Tom's words about Mr Davies's drinking, his aggression that night in the pub, and the image of Marjorie crying when she thought she was alone after choir practice, had all started to fit together like an ugly jigsaw puzzle in Josie's mind. The last pieces being Marjorie's bruised face and the anxious look in her eyes now.

'Marjorie, are you all right? Forgive me, but I can't imagine you getting that bruise from a cupboard. I know we don't know one another very well, but if you ever want to talk—'

'No!' Marjorie almost shouted. She quickly adjusted her voice to one resembling the bossy and in control postmistress that everyone thought she was. 'Everything is fine. Really, Josie. I appreciate you coming round to see me and I apologise for letting you down today, be assured it won't happen again. But I'd be grateful if you'd leave now and if you'd just tell the others that I'm unwell. Thank you and good day.' And with that she shut the door in Josie's face.

Stunned, at least a minute must have passed before Josie was able to move from Marjorie's door. She was torn between wanting to knock until Marjorie answered again and respecting Marjorie's wishes to keep her privacy. She had seemed so on edge and Josie couldn't get the thought of her drunk, aggressive husband out of her head. What if he was hurting her? Shouldn't she do something? But if Marjorie wouldn't talk to her or let her in, what could she do? Maybe she was reading too much into what she saw. Deep in her heart Josie knew that wasn't the case, though. Marjorie wasn't going to speak to her today but Josie would try again. For now she had a choir waiting for her in the village hall, minus their soloist. She had to take care of that. But as she walked away from the post office and back to the choir, she couldn't get the image of Marjorie's bruised face out of her mind.

Chapter Twenty-One

'But . . . what are we going to do without Marjorie?' Peggy was aghast.

The only thing Josie had worked out on her short walk back to the village hall was what not to say. She would keep the details of Marjorie's bruised and troubled face from the rest of the group. Whatever it was that Marjorie was going through, the last thing she'd need was everyone gossiping about her. She was a fiercely proud woman – Josie might not know her well but she knew that for certain. And if Josie had any hope of getting Marjorie to confide in her she would need to respect her wishes and keep what she saw today to herself. So instead she repeated the lie Marjorie had given her.

'She did look awfully pale, and I know she feels really dreadful for missing out on today,' Josie said with sincerity, adding truth to Marjorie's cover-up.

'Oh, the poor dear, I bet she's devastated she's missing out,' Catherine said with genuine concern.

'Yes, poor Marjorie. But seriously, what are we going to

do? We have to sing in an hour and we don't have our soloist!' Peggy looked thoroughly frustrated by how distracted everyone was from the main issue at hand.

'Someone else will have to sing the solo,' Fred said, matter-of-fact.

'But who?' Glenys asked.

'We've worked the harmonies around a soprano solo so it'll have to be one of you ladies. Catherine, would you be prepared to give it a go?' Josie crossed her fingers behind her back.

'Oh! I mean . . . me? Really? I don't think . . . I'm not sure my nerves would serve me well. How about Peggy?'

Everyone turned to face their curly-haired fellow chorister but she quickly begged them to take her hat out of the ring. Peggy had accepted in their first week that her voice wasn't as strong as some of the others and now she was unwilling to leave her comfort zone singing the harmonies.

'I have an idea,' Gethin piped up as everyone looked at one another desperately for the answer that none of them could find.

'No, Gethin, please.' Bethan was pulling on his green jumper to get him to sit down. He looked down at her and muttered something about it being time and that she could do it, but Josie couldn't work out what the pair were quarrelling over.

So it was a huge surprise when Gethin declared, 'Bethan can do it.'

Everyone looked at a scarlet Bethan and then back at Josie. In all of the time they'd been rehearsing they had barely been able to hear Bethan sing. Her quiet voice was sweet but it would be drowned out by the harmonies. No one would hear her. What was Gethin thinking? Perhaps love really was blind.

'Please sit down, Gethin!' Bethan pleaded with him.

Gethin gave her a reassuring look before turning back to the rest of the group. 'She really can do it. I've heard her do it. We thought it would be fun to sing a duet together when we were on one of our walks last week,' Gethin explained as he pushed his dark-rimmed spectacles back up his nose. He was blushing too, which prompted Peggy to roll her eyes. 'Anyway, she sang her bit and she was incredible!'

'Gethin!' Bethan hissed.

'No, Bethan, you have this amazing voice and you should show everyone how brilliant you are.' Gethin turned back to face the others. 'We need a soloist and Bethan is our answer.'

The choir looked unconvinced, but something about the conviction in Gethin's voice and the fact that he rarely pushed for or against anything, generally preferring to go along with the majority, made Josie take him seriously. Bethan had pulled her beau aside and the pair were now frantically whispering to one another. The rest of the group were shrugging their shoulders and looking bemused. Eventually Bethan nodded her head at Gethin and the pair returned to the group. Gethin squeezed her hand in encouragement as Bethan said to Josie, 'If you'd like me to, I'll give the solo a go.'

Josie looked at a mortified Bethan and wondered if her shyness had forced her to hide her true talent. There was only one way to find out.

Smiling encouragingly at her, Josie took her seat at the piano and played the opening bars of 'Suo Gân'. With her eyes closed Bethan's lips parted and the most heavenly sound filled the room. It was a voice none of them had heard before and one none of them expected to come out of the mouth of a timid Bethan. There was a gentle power, and a purity that raised the hairs on the back of Josie's neck. Bethan had the most beautiful soprano and Josie couldn't believe they had had it among them all this time and never heard it before.

Josie couldn't contain her excitement any longer at this revelation from Bethan and so she stopped playing after the second verse. In a moment of stunned silence the room held its breath. They were all entranced by what they'd just heard, and astonished by who they had heard it from.

'Oh, Bethan! That was so beautiful.' Josie clasped her hands together and clutched them to her chest.

'Really?' Bethan asked.

'My dear, that was quite something,' Mr Evans said in awe.

'You're a bit of a dark horse, aren't you, girl?' Michael said, to Bethan's delight.

'I told you she was incredible.' Gethin looked at Bethan with such adoration, Josie felt a twinge of envy. She missed having someone look at her like that.

Shaking herself back into the moment, she focused on the secret weapon the choir had just discovered they had in their arsenal. Josie was already thinking beyond the relief of having a soloist to sing for the village and the newspaper reporter today, and revelling in the knowledge that they had a truly special voice on their hands here, and therefore a real shot at the Welsh Valleys Choral Competition.

'Not only have you blown us all away, Bethan, you have given us our soloist for this afternoon and saved the day!' The room filled with cheers for Bethan and though her cheeks were still flaming red, she looked thoroughly delighted with the praise she was receiving from her fellow singers. 'OK, now Bethan has solved our dilemma, we need to give her a chance to practise before we head out to perform. So let's run through the song all together a few times before we show everyone what we've got!'

When they opened the doors of the hall just before half past two, they saw Colliers Row lined with cake stalls and buzzing with people gathering to hear the choir before preparing to buy the delicious-looking – and -smelling – baked goods.

'There are so many people . . .' Owen gulped.

'Isn't it marvellous?' Mr Evans was rubbing his hands together. Oh, to have the vicar's eternal confidence, Josie thought in that moment, as her own nervous butterflies began fluttering once again.

They made their way towards the stalls where they were greeted by Mr Evans's housekeeper, Miss Smith, who was in charge of the cake sale. She informed them that she would give them a minute or two to arrange themselves and then she would draw the attention of the crowd and introduce them. Everything was set up and ready to go, the stalls were overflowing with mouth-watering cakes and the crowd was in high spirits.

'Right, looks like there's room for no more than five in a row, so gentlemen if you stand in one line, Glenys, Peggy and Catherine, you can stand in front of them. And Bethan, you can stand at the front.' Bethan was wide-eyed with terror at Josie's directions. 'Don't look so worried, it's so that you can see me conducting you as we've just practised, so you're not on your own. Also, you are brilliant and have nothing to fear.

Actually, that goes for you all. You are going to sound wonderful.'

The group exchanged nervous smiles as they organised themselves into the rows Josie had suggested. Josie whispered, 'break a leg' as silence fell over the crowd at the ring of Miss Smith's bell.

'Thank you all for coming this sunny Sunday afternoon. St Luke's church and the Llandegwen choir, who will sing for you in a moment, greatly appreciate your support . . .' Josie tuned out as Miss Smith waffled on about the hymn books and the array of cakes, naming some of the star bakers in the crowd. Josie had spotted Peter Philips, notebook and pencil in hand, and her nerves increased a notch. She scanned the rest of the crowd to distract herself, moving her gaze swiftly past a scowling Anwen, her heart stopping when it fell on Ronnie. She had expected him to be there, knowing he'd hear about it, what with him staying in the pub and his determination to unsettle her by talking to the villagers whenever he could. But he was standing next to Tom and the pair had clearly been chatting before they had been called to silence. Josie felt queasy about what Ronnie might have said to Tom. She found herself caring quite a bit about what he thought of her. She'd seen a different side to him when he had come to the cottage for dinner the previous week and the thought of him knowing anything about her connection to Ronnie made her feel hot with shame. She knew Ronnie had sought him out on purpose and indeed he was taunting her with one of his smirks now, looking her right in the eye as he did so.

Feeling her cheeks burn, Josie tried to block Ronnie from her mind and averted her gaze. She was relieved to be able to turn her back on the crowd as Miss Smith declared, 'I now give you the Llandegwen Village Choir!'

Without the piano to lead them in, it was down to Josie to conduct Bethan, as they had practised just the hour before, straight into her solo before the harmonies came in. As Bethan's pitch-perfect and pure voice filled the air and ears around them, Josie relaxed into the soothing lure of the lullaby. The choir sounded magical and she could see from their faces, even the previously green-gilled Michael's, that they were enjoying their moment. Josie could imagine it felt as good as they sounded. Other than the rustling of a gentle cool spring breeze, there was no other noise, the crowd were silent, in raptures at their very own choir surpassing all of their expectations. The music was working its magic and it felt wonderful.

After the final notes were sung, there was a moment's pause before the crowd burst into applause. Josie even heard an appreciative whistle from behind her. She laughed in delight, applauding her singers as they beamed at one another, thrilled with what they'd just done. And as Miss Smith walked out to officially declare the cake sale open, she turned to face the crowd and take a bow with the rest of her choir.

Josie was enjoying the warm buzz of success as she wandered around the cake sale with Sam and Glenys. The only thing tainting the moment was the pair of eyes watching her from the sidelines, never letting her forget he was there, ready to pull the rug out from under her at any moment he might choose. Josie had decided that she would go into Castleforth next week on the pretext of getting something to wear to the competition. Peggy had agreed to go with her so that Glenys wouldn't insist on accompanying Josie, but finding cover for the shop and someone to be there for her mother was proving to be tricky. Josie had to do it soon though, she couldn't stand the constant threat of Ronnie. He was ruining everything, including moments like this which should be all happiness.

To avoid his glare and with two wedges of Glenys's Victoria sponge in her hands, Josie strolled over to Peter Philips where he was scribbling away in his notebook just beyond the stalls and therefore away from all of the action.

'Did you get everything you need for your piece?' She offered him one of the slices of cake.

Putting his notebook and pencil in his pocket he took it gratefully. 'If this is a bribe, there's no need. You have a fine choir there.'

Josie laughed. 'It's not a bribe, more a gesture of goodwill. And I'm glad you think so. They've worked so hard, they deserve a good write-up.'

'Sounded like you've worked quite hard yourself.'

Josie shrugged. 'Music isn't work for me. It's a passion. It can make even the bleakest of times a little easier to bear. I think it made people happy today.' She took a bite of her cake.

'Inspirational words! Can I quote you?'

Josie nodded. 'When will the paper be out?'

'Next Saturday. I need to get my editor to sign off on it, but I know he's going to be all for it.' He polished off the last of his slice of cake and dusted any lingering crumbs from his hands before offering one in a handshake. 'Anyway, I'd best be off. Thanks for the cake and good luck with the competition and getting your bus ride sorted. Looking at the number of cakes being bought, I'd say you'll have no problems with that last one.'

'Thank you. I was a bit nervous about you coming here today and writing about us, to be honest, but I think we did ourselves proud.' Josie smiled at him.

'No need to be nervous. Us journalists are meant to write the facts, and the fact is your choir is rather marvellous. And on that note, I'll be off to my typewriter to put it all down in black and white.'

'I'll look forward to reading the paper next weekend then,' Josie said confidently before saying goodbye and turning back towards the stalls.

As she scanned the small crowd for her son's and Glenys's heads, she heard a voice behind her say, 'You have become quite the country village sweetheart, haven't you, darlin'? What do you think the good people of Llandegwen would say if they knew their sweetheart was a thief and had debts to pay off in my brothels, eh? You can play the wholesome choir angel all you want, but remember I know the truth and I'm getting bored of not sharing it.'

They were standing in the middle of the crowd and he was speaking quietly into her ear, but that didn't stop Josie from snapping her head around to check that no one had heard what Ronnie had said. Luckily there was so much chatter going on around them no one was paying them any attention.

'Why are you doing this to me? I told you I'd get you your money,' she hissed, desperately trying to keep her voice out of earshot of anyone else.

'And I told you I don't believe you. Plus I'm getting bored and I told you what would happen if I got bored. I've given you a week, which is way more than you deserve. And I only did that because, despite what you might think, I am a decent man. You stole from me so by rights I could've dragged you back the minute I got here. But it's been fun to watch you sweat a little, I'll admit that. But now I'm bored. I want my money or your arse on a train back to London by tomorrow.'

'I need longer than that. Just another day. Please, Ronnie!' She gripped his arm as her desperation began to choke her.

He shook her off. 'Tomorrow, sweetheart, or it's bye-bye, Llandegwen.'

And with that he walked away from her, leaving her alone in a crowd, fighting back the tears as her world was about to end.

Chapter Twenty-Two

'Well, he seems like a charming fellow.'

Josie turned around sharply to find Tom standing behind her with a concerned look on his face. Had he heard her conversation with Ronnie just now?

'What?' she said, for lack of anything else to say, her mind racing.

'I was being sarcastic. Are you OK? I wasn't trying to listen but from what I couldn't help overhear that all sounded a little intense.' He nodded in the direction in which Ronnie had casually walked away.

'Oh, no, that was nothing. Just . . . it was nothing. Really.' She was desperately trying to compose herself.

'It didn't seem like nothing. He seemed pretty aggressive to me. He's quite full of himself too. Or is that just a London thing?'

Josie looked at him, unsure of what to say, wanting to agree with him but knowing it would open Pandora's box if she did.

'That was a joke, before you mistake my meaning again.'

He'd taken her uncertain expression to mean he'd once again caused her offence. 'I know some lovely Londoners. What I'm trying to say, very badly, is that I hope you're OK and that your friend isn't causing you any trouble.'

She didn't want to lie to him, which was strange as she'd been lying about who Ronnie really was the entire time he'd been there. Lying had been her only option and though she'd hated doing it she'd done it without any hesitation. But for some reason she was hesitating now with Tom.

'Thank you, but really, I'm fine. Everything is fine.' She couldn't bring herself to contradict him any more than this. Tom looked unconvinced but he wasn't going to push her.

'I need to find Sam and Glenys,' she said as she backed away from him.

Tom nodded. 'Sure. And by the way, the choir sounded amazing.'

Josie gave him a weak smile before she lost herself in the crowd. She really needed to find Peggy so that she could figure out what on earth she was going to do to be able to solve this mess by tomorrow.

Josie found Glenys and Sam weighing up the pros and cons of having just one more slice of cake before they headed home after all of the excitement of the day. Sam was obviously on the side of the pros and Glenys, unable to resist spoiling her beloved grandson, was struggling with the cons. In the end they had decided to buy a slice each to take home to have after their tea that evening.

'I see you were talking to that nice Tom Jenkins?' Glenys eyed Josie curiously, as they stood by one of the stalls.

Josie busied herself with dusting some rogue crumbs from the front of Sam's jumper. 'Yes, he said he really enjoyed your Victoria sponge,' she lied, not wanting to mention anything about Ronnie.

'Did he now.' Glenys sounded amused.

'Mr Jenkins liked your bacon and egg pie too, Grandma. We let him have some for dinner when you were away. He said he went to school with my daddy.'

Glenys looked from Sam to Josie, a surprised grin on her face.

Josie hadn't meant to keep Tom coming for dinner from her, she just hadn't known how to bring it into their conversations and she didn't want Glenys to think there was anything more to it than there was. She cursed herself; it had been silly of her, now it looked like she'd kept a secret.

'Sam invited him over after football practice. He put us all a bit on the spot, didn't you, Sammy?' She ruffled his hair, a guilty look on her face. 'I'm sorry I didn't mention it before. I hope that was OK?'

'Of course it was OK, love. I'm delighted you felt you could have your friends over, it's your home now too. And I'm pleased you've made such a fine friend.' She did look genuinely delighted, which was both a relief and a little unnerving for Josie. She didn't want Glenys to get the wrong idea. She and Tom were hardly friends and Josie didn't want anything to make Glenys think she was being disloyal to Matthew.

'You know, he's a very nice man, Tom is,' Glenys said cautiously after they had bought their last pieces of cake to take home with them.

'I thought he was a bit pompous at first, I'm not sure he

means to be, but he's been a good teacher for Sam.' Josie wasn't sure where this conversation was going. Sam had run on ahead of them and was playing an imaginary game of hopscotch in the distance.

'You know, it must've been hard for you without Matthew all of these years, doing everything on your own. It must get lonely sometimes.'

Josie looked questioningly at Glenys.

'I want you to know that, when you are ready, there might come a time when you want to open your heart again to someone else. And if that time comes, you should embrace the chance at happiness. If the war taught us anything, it was to grab hold of happiness whenever we get the opportunity. So I want you to know that I want that for you too, and so would Matthew. Do you know what I'm saying, love?'

Josie had no idea where this was coming from or what Glenys was getting at. All she could think about was surviving the next twenty-four hours. The guilt she carried over the fading image of Matthew from her memory had been pushed to the back of her mind but she wanted to reassure Glenys that she had promised to love Matthew for ever and that she wouldn't break that promise, even if he was gone. 'I've never been able to imagine loving someone as much as I loved Matthew, and losing that love again.'

Glenys's expression was pained. 'Maybe not yet, love. But one day you might. And if you do, know that I will be happy for you. And I'll always be here for you and Sam, that goes without saying. You've given me such joy in letting me get to know my grandson.' Glenys squeezed Josie's hand.

Josie was consumed with guilt and sadness. She was going

to let Glenys down so badly if she didn't sort this mess with Ronnie out.

'You've been so kind to us, Glenys. I don't know what I would've done if you hadn't thrown us this lifeline.'

Glenys could hear the emotion in her voice and gave her a supportive squeeze, oblivious of the pain Josie was wrestling with.

'It was just meant to be. It's funny how life works sometimes. Remember that, love.' Glenys gave Josie a meaningful look before she called out to Sam to slow down ahead of them.

Josie's first thought when she woke from a restless sleep on Monday morning was that she needed to speak to Peggy so that she could come up with a plan of action. If she didn't get Ronnie his money today, or find a way to put him off, then she was in no doubt that he would tell everyone she was a thief and that she'd been stupid enough to try to run away from an East End gangster.

She washed with the water she'd filled the small bowl in her room with and dressed. She sighed as she looked at her reflection in the mirror on the bedroom wall above the shelf that held the washbowl. Her blue eyes looked tired and she had to pinch some colour into her cheeks. Yesterday had been a wonderful day in some ways, with the choir wowing the village and those who had come from Castleforth. And Bethan's voice had been such a revelation! Josie should be concentrating on the fact that she had such an exceptional talent on her hands and the dilemma of how she was going to work that talent into the choir at this late stage. Not how on earth she was going to find money from nowhere or convince Ronnie to wait just a few more days.

Her heart sank further still when she thought of Marjorie and what she had seen the previous day. She knew she'd have to find a way to talk to the postmistress about it. Even if Ronnie ruined everything, Josie couldn't just pretend it hadn't happened. But on top of this there was the fact that now the choir had two soloists when they only needed one. Marjorie clearly had enough on her plate without Josie wounding her pride and taking her solos from her. She couldn't do that but she had a duty to the choir to give them the best shot at the competition too, even if it was the last thing she did for them. She felt sick when she thought about the possibility of not taking the choir to the competition and letting them all down. There had to be a way out of this, there just had to be.

Josie carried the weight of the world on her shoulders that morning as she took Sam to school. She was also slightly anxious about seeing Tom at the gates and having him question her again about Ronnie. So the last thing she needed was a dose of spite from the likes of Anwen.

She supposed she'd got off lightly with Anwen lately. Their paths hadn't crossed much and Josie had foolishly thought that Anwen might have become bored with her and moved on to putting her energies into something else. Peggy had warned her not to be so naive but Josie had a tendency to think the best of people, even when they didn't deserve it.

As Josie and Sam approached the school gates that morning, Anwen's haughty tones rang out above the chatter of the children playing in the playground.

'. . . One minute she's batting her eyelashes at that reporter from the *Gazette* in full view of everyone, bringing him cake and the like, and the next she's taking advantage of our poor Mr Jenkins, seconds after flirting with her London friend. And I use the word "friend" lightly. She's probably had a string of men since Matthew. At least now I can see how she bewitched him. She probably tricked him into marrying her. She must have for him to end up with someone like her. It's that East End brass. Men can't stop themselves when it's handed to them on a plate.'

Anwen had her back to Josie and so didn't see her approach. It was only when one of her sidekicks muttered 'Brazen woman', before clocking Josie, her eyes widening in horror at being caught out, that Anwen turned to see what had startled her.

Josie felt sick at the cruel words that had been levelled at her behind her back. She had hoped that Sam had been too distracted by looking for his friends in the playground to hear what Anwen had said, or if he had that he wouldn't have realised the women were talking about her. She knelt down to his level to give him a hug goodbye, plastering a fake smile on her face.

'Off you go, Sammy. Have a good day.'

He beamed at her before hurtling off into the playground, clearly oblivious to the nasty scene they had walked into. Her relief at this was only momentary before feelings of anger and injustice quickly replaced them and she rose to her full height, ready to face the woman who had spoken these spiteful words.

If Anwen had felt sheepish or embarrassed at being caught

talking out of turn, she didn't show it. Her chin jutted out defiantly as Josie's eyes met hers.

'Everything I've said is true, we've all seen you giving Tom those puppy dog eyes, playing the victim after your lovers' tiff with your London friend. Very clever. And you didn't exactly hide away with that reporter. You might get away with that sort of thing in London, but in Wales women have class and standards.' Each cold word slammed into Josie as she faced Anwen.

'How dare you, Anwen,' Josie said through gritted teeth, almost unsettled by the level of her own fury. She saw the group of women standing behind Anwen take a step back. Clearly they weren't as comfortable as their ringleader in telling spiteful lies about a person to their face. 'Nothing you've just said is true. You've twisted it all to fit what you want to think about me, and frankly my life is none of your business.' Anwen scoffed at this, which only riled Josie further. 'Believe what you want, Anwen, but let me tell you this. If you knew Matthew at all you'd know he was too smart to be tricked. His heart told him he wanted to be with me, and mine with him. And you'd know that if he didn't want to be with you it was because that was what his heart was telling him. It was as simple as that. Now that might wound your pride to hear, but honestly I'm beyond caring at this stage.'

Anwen's face had turned white at Josie's cutting words. Perhaps no one had had the courage to tell this woman the truth before, Josie thought. It was one thing for Anwen to play silly games with the choir, but to make out that she was some kind of brassy floozy and doing anything untoward with Tom, Ronnie or anyone else for that matter, and within earshot of her son, that was taking things too far.

'You were right about one thing though, I am an East Ender. And where I come from we don't talk about people behind their backs. You're nothing but a spiteful coward. Stay out of my way, Anwen, I'm warning you.'

Josie caught a flash of fury in Anwen's eyes before she turned on her heel and walked away, only letting the hot tears of frustration escape from her eyes when she was out of sight.

Josie had decided to keep her confrontation with Anwen to herself. Partly because she didn't want to cause a fuss, and Peggy would be livid enough to insist on defending Josie she was sure, but also partly because she couldn't bring herself to say the things Anwen had said about her to anyone else. She knew they weren't true, but it still made her worry that that was how others perceived her too. And if they learnt that she'd got herself tangled up with someone like Ronnie, well, there'd be no defence that would convince anyone she wasn't without morals. In any case, she had to put Anwen to the back of her mind until she had sorted out this mess with Ronnie. And so it was this that she focused on with Peggy.

'Can you put him off? Can you convince him to stay another couple of days?'

'I can try, but he was so definite about it yesterday.'

'I don't think you have much choice, unless you can find a stash of money somewhere.'

Josie put her head in her hands. 'It's hopeless! Why can't life be like fairy tales? Why can't I have a rich benefactor who could save me?'

'Fairy tales have a lot to answer for in giving us false hope.

But how about we believe in the miracle of your powers of persuasion, because, Josie, I think this is your only hope at this stage.'

Josie looked desolate.

'We won't let him take you back to London though. I can put up a good fight.'

Even in her hour of despair Peggy could still make her laugh. She knew her feisty friend would fight for her, but Peggy didn't know who or what she was dealing with. Josie's powers of persuasion were indeed all she had left to buy herself some time. It was no defence at all really, but she'd give it her best shot. She'd just have to brace herself to speak to Ronnie, and sooner rather than later.

Chapter Twenty-Three

As she closed the shop door behind her she walked straight into the man in question – his unexpected presence robbing her of the extra few minutes' walk in which she'd planned to run through everything she was going to say to him.

'There you are, darlin'. Thought you might be tempted to do another runner on me, and I couldn't have that, could I?' He took one last drag on his cigarette and stubbed it out on the ground before linking her arm a little roughly. 'Let's go for a little stroll, shall we?'

As they walked away from the shop and down Colliers Row, Josie tried to relax her body into his grip, thinking that if she seemed calm she could create the illusion that she had everything under control, that he could trust her to get him his money if only he'd give her a few more days.

'Ronnie, I know I broke your trust before, but I won't make that mistake again, I swear. I have your money, but I need to go to the nearest town to get it. I just need a couple more days.

That's all.' She spoke in her softest, most convincing tone but her breath caught in her throat as Ronnie spun round and shook her, his face screwed up and vicious with fury.

'Do you think I'm a mug, Josie? Do you?' he snarled. 'I said today. If you don't have it today it's game over. We'll head over to your nice little cottage now and tell those lovely people what you've done and where you're going. We're getting on a train back to London this afternoon. I'm not mucking around here.'

'No! Please, Ronnie!'

He gripped her arm but Josie managed to shake him off. For a minute they just stood there looking at one another, Josie in shock, Ronnie waiting for her next move. She backed away from him, slowly at first, and then did the only thing she could think of, run in the opposite direction.

'Run all you like, sweetheart, but you won't get far, we both know that. I'm off to have a nice chat with that Glenys,' he shouted after her, laughing.

The tears were streaming down her cheeks and blurring her vision as she ran in the direction of the churchyard. She didn't see Peggy watching her from the shop window, and she didn't see Tom walking down to the post office on his lunch break from school. All she could see was her world crashing down around her.

She didn't know how long she'd been sitting by Matthew's headstone, searching for answers from him and all the other souls whose lives were honoured in that graveyard, when Jerry Collins, the man she'd met all those weeks back when she'd first come to Llandegwen, put a gentle hand on her shoulder.

'You look a little lost, love.'

Josie wiped away the tears she hadn't even noticed were still trickling down her cheeks as she looked up at his kind face.

'I am a bit, Jerry.'

He nodded his head and looked away into the distance. 'No one is ever lost for long. We always find our way back eventually.'

He sounded so sure, he almost gave Josie hope. But then she imagined again Glenys's face as Ronnie told her everything she'd done, taking his stupid loan, running away, and the way he intended her to pay off her debts. She'd have to face Glenys eventually, she couldn't sit in this graveyard for the rest of her life. But what would happen after that, she had no idea. She'd have to get Sam and their things and run again before Ronnie could get his hands on her. The one thing she did know for sure was that she couldn't work for him, she couldn't sell her body, the same body that had loved Matthew and given birth to their son, for money.

'What if we can't? What if we're always running away from something?'

'Then you just have to stop running. Face the thing you're running from and you don't have to run any more.' He made it sound so simple, this kind man who spent his days tending to the resting places of those who had had life taken from them. But she couldn't face the fate waiting for her in Ronnie's hands. She would have to face Glenys though. And the sooner she did that, the sooner she could gather her things, collect Sam from school and leave the village before Ronnie could make her leave with him. She'd just have to be cleverer next time, leave no trace.

'You're a good man, Jerry. Thank you for taking care of Matthew's memory.' She got up and brushed herself down, smoothing her blond hair back into place, while Jerry looked at her a little bemusedly.

'That's kind of you to say, love. Take care of yourself now.'

Josie smiled at him as she prepared herself to face the music waiting for her in the tiny cottage she had come to think of as home.

As Josie approached the kitchen she could see Glenys was bustling about as usual. But despite having her eyes on the task in front of her she had heard the front door clunk shut and was aware that Josie had returned.

'There you are, love. Hand me that saucepan, will you? I got chatting in the bakery to Mrs Duffy and then I went over to see Peggy's mam for a bit and before I knew it the time had flown by and I hadn't even made a start on tea for tonight.'

Josie stood in the kitchen doorway in utter confusion. Glenys was acting as if everything was as normal. She'd expected stony silence, disappointment, and in her more optimistic moments, concern. When Josie didn't move to get the saucepan or say anything at all, Glenys looked up from what she was doing and said, 'Is something the matter, love? Why are you standing in the doorway looking like the world has ended?'

'Sorry, I . . . here.' Josie handed her the saucepan and watched Glenys as she took it and filled it with water. 'Did Ronnie come round earlier?'

'No, love. Were you expecting him?'

He hadn't done what he said he'd do. He hadn't told Glenys anything. Josie would've been relieved if she had understood why. It didn't make any sense.

'No. I just thought he might, that's all.' What was he up to? Had he changed his mind and was he going to give her more time? 'I just wanted to pop back to see if you needed anything from the shop while I'm collecting Sam from school.'

Glenys declined her offer and Josie took the opportunity to leave the house and rush into the village to the Plough to find Ronnie. Maybe she wouldn't have to run after all. She wouldn't rest until she knew where she stood, that was for sure.

As she approached the village pub she saw Ronnie leaving with a bag over his shoulder. Her heart stopped. He was clearly getting on that train back to London, which meant he was still planning to drag her back with him. She'd made a terrible mistake and the reality of this froze her to the spot. He saw her and gave her a nasty laugh as he walked towards her.

'There she is, the woman I could curse ever knowing. Don't look so terrified, sweetheart. It would seem your debt has been paid. I'm not the biggest mug around no more and you must be more charming than I thought. Shame you won't be putting those charms to good use for me, but I reckon you're more trouble than you're worth anyway.'

'I don't understand.' To say she was confused would be an understatement. 'How are my debts paid?'

'Ask no questions, and I'll tell you no lies. I'm sure you'll work it out on your own anyway. But I'm done here.' He shoved past her.

'So you're really leaving? Just like that? Without saying anything to anyone? I don't believe you.' She spoke to his back before he turned around to face her, walking backwards away from her.

'Believe what you like, sweetheart. But don't ever show your face in London again, I don't care what friends you have in high places, I'll pay whatever price I have to to make you pay yours. Mark my words.' He looked her right in the eye as he said this and Josie knew that he meant it. His threat sent a jolt of fear through her body.

She had no idea what had happened or who could have paid him off. Whoever it was must know everything about her though and that thought filled her with shame. But it was a small price to pay for being free. She didn't have to run any more, she wouldn't be letting anyone down, she could still take the choir to the competition, Sam could be happy here. She couldn't believe it. Whoever her saviour was, she owed them her life.

Chapter Twenty-Four

'Is everything all right?' Peggy whispered to Josie on the doorstep of the tiny cottage. She had come to see Josie ahead of choir practice that night, unable to sit still worrying about her friend and what she'd witnessed that day from her shop. 'I knew he hadn't dragged you off to London, Gavin came into the shop just before I closed up saying he'd clipped his ticket himself as he got on the train alone. But I wanted to check on you before choir.'

'I can't say much now but, Peggy, it's the strangest thing. Someone paid Ronnie off. I've no idea who, but he's gone, it's over. And the best bit is he didn't tell Glenys anything, or anyone else as far as I know. I can't believe it!' Josie was beaming as Peggy hugged her.

'Who's that at the door, love?' Glenys called from within the house.

'It's Peggy, she wanted to walk with us to choir practice tonight.'

Glenys appeared behind them both. 'Well, don't just stand

on the doorstep, come in, for heaven's sake, while we get our coats on.'

With her world seeming to end and then miraculously begin again as normal, Josie's heart had barely had a moment to settle. Consequently, the matter of how to delicately handle putting her decision to split the solos between Marjorie and Bethan into action had completely escaped her thoughts. But as it happened Josie found herself with a little more time to mull over her dilemma when Marjorie failed to show up for choir practice that Monday night. The postmistress had, however, sent a message to the choir via Bethan who had held the fort in the post office that day for her employer.

'She was too sick to come down into the post office, she just called to me from the top of the stairs. I've never known her to take a day off work before.'

Josie guessed that Marjorie's bruised face was still too swollen to explain away with the notion of her walking into a cupboard, but she worried too that she might have picked up more bruises in the meantime. Bethan had said that she sounded just like herself, barking her orders for the day from the upstairs landing, which was reassuring. And Bethan suspected nothing more than illness keeping her employer away from her tasks. Still it preyed on Josie's mind as she locked up the village hall that night on her own.

She'd stayed behind to play the piano by herself to clear her thoughts. The music always soothed her. Glenys, thankfully, hadn't asked any questions and had left Josie to her own devices without any fuss. Josie had taken the time to try to lose herself in some of the old songs her pa had taught her as a young girl but her curiosity over who could have paid off Ronnie consumed her thoughts. Her busy mind was clearly making even the simplest of tasks too tricky for her, as she struggled to get the key to slot properly into the lock. She'd even taken it off the loop that held the other keys for the locks on various cupboards in the village hall to see if that would help. She cursed herself as she yanked the key from the lock and then dropped it, watching it bounce off into the grass to the side of the footpath. In the darkness, Josie had to crouch down to brush the grass with her hands, hoping to feel the cold metal.

'Is this some sort of odd choral tradition you do every night, or do you need some help?'

Josie, in the most undignified position of being on her hands and knees, looked over her shoulder to find Tom observing her from the road, hands in his pockets, his face obscured by the darkness. She rose to her feet, hastily tugging down her grey fitted wool pencil skirt that she had hitched up, thinking she was alone, in order to be able to bend her knees into a crouched position. She was flustered and cross that she'd been caught in such a ridiculous situation.

'I can't find the key for the hall door,' she told him pathetically.

'How did you lose it?' He walked towards her, scanning the grass along the path as he did.

Josie smoothed her blond hair with her hands in irritation at her own carelessness. 'I couldn't get it to fit in the lock properly and I might have yanked it out a little too hard.'

Tom looked at her with the same expression he had on his face when he found her crying in the school after Miss Hughes spoke so harshly to her. Sympathetic – he felt sorry for her, Josie thought.

'It can't have gone too far then.' He crouched down next to her and ran his hands over the grass before rising to his feet with a satisfied look on his face and a brass key in his hand. 'I presume this is the key in question?'

Josie rolled her eyes. 'How come it took you all of ten seconds to find it and I was scrabbling around for I don't know how long?'

'A fresh pair of eyes? A fresh mind maybe?'

'A fresh mind?' She looked at him curiously.

'You've had rather a lot to think about with the choir and your . . . friend from London.'

Josie shifted uncomfortably at the mention of Ronnie.

'I hear he's gone. Your friend?'

'Yes, he has.' Josie wanted to forget Ronnie had ever been there, so she changed the subject as they both turned away from the hall and walked along the short footpath on to Colliers Row. She wanted to focus her thoughts on Marjorie and Tom might have more information about the postmistress's husband. 'Were you in the pub just now?' she asked him as a way to open up the subject. She had just posted the keys through Mrs Moss's letter box and they were making their way towards the Williamses' cottage.

'Yes, why do you ask?'

'Was Marjorie's husband in there tonight?'

Tom took a sharp breath. 'No, and I don't reckon he'll show his face in there for a while now after Saturday night.'

'What happened on Saturday?' Josie's heart was beating faster.

'He got himself in an awful state. It's the worst I've seen him. So drunk he could barely stand, throwing his weight around. He'd have fought anybody for any reason, but the landlord threw him out before he could do any serious damage. I don't know what had got him so angry.'

Josie felt sick. If Marjorie's husband had been out of his mind drunk and spoiling for a fight on Saturday night, chances are the bruised and swollen cheek his wife had tried to hide on Sunday had come from his fist. And the poor woman was suffering in silence. Josie might be the only person who could help her. But what could she do?

Tom had stopped walking and was looking at Josie with concern. 'You look upset?'

She hesitated for a moment before deciding that she couldn't keep this to herself any longer. She'd already spoken to Tom about this once before so she wasn't betraying any confidences, and anyway, he didn't seem remotely the gossipy type. If anything he was so aloof he barely spoke to anyone beyond pleasantries. So she filled Tom in on what she had seen on Sunday and Marjorie's unusual absence for the past two days. He was just as concerned as she was and agreed that Josie trying to talk to Marjorie privately was probably the best idea, but he wanted her to be careful.

'She might not want to tell you or do anything about it, if he is hurting her. She's a proud woman and the village is small. Plus, that generation see these things differently. They don't walk away from men like him easily. They can't. Marjorie would have nowhere to go, her life, her home, her family, is here in Llandegwen.'

She was surprised that given Tom's privileged upbringing

he understood Marjorie's situation so well. What he said was hard to accept but she knew he was right. She'd seen more than one woman in Bethnal Green cover their bruised arms with cardigans in the summer heat, never speaking of their pain and defensive with anyone who said a word about their bruises or their husbands. They had nowhere to go, or feared they had nowhere to hide. Her ma had explained that to her once when she asked her why Mrs Dailey didn't leave her husband after the whole street had heard the screaming when he'd dragged her out of their home by her hair once the pubs had closed one night. The neighbours had intervened on that occasion, but it wasn't the first time it had happened and Josie knew, even at thirteen years old, that it wouldn't be the last. It didn't stop her from feeling like she should do something now though.

'I know, it's hard to watch someone suffer. But you can't help someone who doesn't want to be helped. You can only be there to offer them support.'

'But sometimes people need to know they have options, they need others to show them there's a way out even when they can't see it.'

'Not everyone is prepared to listen.'

'Would you really give up that easily?'

'I wouldn't call it giving up. Just respecting someone else's decision.'

'I do respect her decision. But it doesn't stop me from wanting to help her.'

'There's helping and there's meddling where you're not welcome.'

'So I'm meddling now?'

'No. I'm just advising against it. Are you really the best person to judge these situations anyway?' Josie could hear the frustration in his voice but she was unable to let the matter go.

'What do you mean by that?'

'From what I saw of your London friend he was hardly someone anyone would advise getting mixed up with, but you had your reasons and perhaps you wouldn't have listened either had someone told you not to.'

Josie felt as though she'd been winded. Every word he'd uttered wounded her. She knew he didn't know the half of it when it came to Ronnie but the deep shame she felt over the whole sorry situation made her sensitive to the judgements Tom had made from what he'd witnessed. It hurt that he would think her unqualified to help Marjorie, or anyone for that matter, because of any mistakes she'd made. And it hurt even more that he might think badly of her because of Ronnie. Tears stung her eyes as the hurt boiled over into anger.

'How dare you! You know nothing about me, or my life before Llandegwen, or my friends!' She was shouting in the street but she didn't care.

'I know, that's exactly the point I'm making about Marjorie.' His expression was one of exasperation, but Josie didn't notice nor had she listened to what he'd just said, she was too angry.

'You think you are so superior to everyone in this village. You pretend to be the nice Jenkins, giving back to the community, playing the martyr giving up your inheritance, but you still think you're better than everyone else, don't you? You look down your nose at us all and think you know better. Well, you don't. Life isn't as black and white for most people as it seems to be for you. I may make mistakes but I try not to judge others for theirs. You've picked me up for being judgemental, well maybe you should take a look at yourself.'

Tom stood for a moment in stunned silence. Josie had shocked herself with the ferocity of her words, the emotions of the past week releasing in one fierce outburst. But he had crossed a line and judged her for the one thing she judged herself most harshly, and it had burnt.

'I see now that there's no point trying to convince you that I am anything other than what you think I am. I'm sorry I upset you once again, that wasn't my intention. I think it's best if I say goodnight.' He spoke so quietly but his tone had an edge of the wounded to it that didn't escape Josie's notice.

As Tom walked away from her Josie felt a knot of regret tug at her heart but she quickly masked it with the righteous indignation that had fuelled her previous outburst. She had been justified in what she'd said to him. So why did her heart feel a little sick as she turned off Colliers Row on to the street that would take her home?

Chapter Twenty-Five

Glenys was worried about her, Josie could tell. She had been looking at her quizzically since Tuesday morning. The woman was a mind reader, Josie was sure of it. She never failed to notice when something was up, it was unnerving. But none of the troubles on Josie's mind were things she could share with the woman who had taken her into her home. She couldn't share them with anyone, not even Peggy. Marjorie's situation wasn't Josie's to speak of, and the situation with Tom, well, Josie didn't even understand that herself.

Six weeks ago Josie was worried about how well she and Sam would settle into Llandegwen and the impact that uprooting their lives from London would have on them. Now she was so immersed in life in the village, she had made enemies for the first time in her life, other than Ronnie, of course, and she had invested so much of herself in the choir that she felt a sense of responsibility towards them as individuals that was overwhelming – especially in the case of Marjorie. She'd had no idea when she stepped off that train at the end of

February that so much could happen in such a short space of time.

At least she was making an impact, she thought wryly. And the choir was getting so excited about the competition now, it was really satisfying for Josie to see. Singing in front of the village had given them a real confidence boost, they were much less nervous at Monday night's rehearsal. Bethan was truly blossoming, and they were all so relaxed in one another's company, the performance having cemented the bonds that they had made over the past weeks as they'd learnt to sing as a group. And so Josie felt a little for Marjorie when she returned to choir practice that Wednesday night, having missed all of the success of Sunday's performance.

Marjorie's cheek was still bruised, but a much less angry shade of blue and yellow than almost-black purple. A shade easier to convince with the lie that she'd walked into a cupboard door while not paying attention when she was ill. And convince them all she did. No one batted an eye at her story, other than to offer their sympathies. They were genuinely happy to see her returned to the choir and had told her they had missed her on Sunday.

'We were a woman down, so it's good to have you back, Marjorie,' Fred said earnestly. The choir meant so much to him, Josie felt he was genuinely happy to have a full house again.

'Thank you, Fred, that's very kind. I heard you were marvellous though, and that softened the blow of missing out, I don't mind telling you all. I've heard nothing but praise. Especially for you, Bethan.' Marjorie looked at her young assistant affectionately as Bethan's cheeks turned predictably pink.

'She got us out of quite a tight spot,' Michael said, not unkindly and more to cover the awkwardness everyone felt at Bethan not only filling Marjorie's shoes successfully on Sunday, but replacing them with a much bigger and indispensable pair of her own.

'She did indeed and I'm very grateful. I felt terrible letting everyone down. She is too modest to tell you this herself, but I don't mind telling you all, every person who came into the post office today was full of praise for her. It sounds like the solo was made for her.' Marjorie said the last words purposefully to Josie, as though willing her to read her mind. Was she saying it was OK, that Bethan should sing the solo, pre-empting with good grace any attempt Josie might make to suggest it? And as if to confirm that Josie had interpreted her correctly Marjorie continued, 'Might I be able to hear "Suo Gân" with Bethan singing solo? I was so sorry to miss it that it would cheer me up enormously to hear it now.' She looked at her fellow singers hopefully.

Bethan nodded, more than willing to please her employer as Mr Evans boomed, 'Of course we will! As long as you promise to join in with the harmonies, Marjorie? Two days of singing without you is quite enough!'

Marjorie smiled at the vicar, her glassy eyes betraying the emotions swelling within her heart as she tried not to show how touched she was that her absence had genuinely been missed, even if they had discovered a new star among them in the meantime.

Josie was moved by the kindness of the group and the huge gesture Marjorie had just made in stepping aside for Bethan, and putting the success of the choir above her own pride. She knew that that was an enormous thing for Marjorie to do and in the process she had saved Josie and the others from any awkwardness at having to suggest it themselves. Josie marvelled for a moment at this strong woman with a heart of gold as she stood ready to sing with the others in harmony rather than in the spotlight. She might be nosy and critical and bossy at times, but when it counted she put others before herself. No one was as simple as their exterior, there was always more to a person than what they revealed on the surface.

After they had sung 'Suo Gân' all the way through, Marjorie immediately moved to embrace Bethan and congratulate her on her talent.

'They weren't exaggerating, were they, all those people who said you were wonderful. You are, my girl, you are.' Bethan looked so overwhelmed by Marjorie's praise that she couldn't say anything at all, she just beamed at the postmistress. 'Josie, if you don't let this girl sing all of the solos, then you'll have me to contend with. She's too good to keep in the background. We want to win this competition and she's our star singer.'

Josie made to protest, she didn't want Marjorie to feel pushed aside, but the older woman would have nothing of it. She put her hands on her wide hips and puffed her chest out so that the buttons of her blouse strained across her plump frame as she ordered, 'I insist and that's that.'

Josie raised her hands in surrender whilst trying to hide her smile. Marjorie had handled the situation perfectly, and Josie felt foolish for all the hours she'd wasted worrying about how to deal with it all herself. She should have known that no one handled Marjorie. She handled everyone else.

Buoyed by the relief that there was to be no conflict over the solos and comfortable that they could all now celebrate the fact that they had a real chance in the competition, the group swelled with confidence for the rest of that night's choir practice. And for just under an hour, Josie forgot all about the troubles that had been weighing on her mind.

In all of the fuss of Marjorie's return and what that would mean for the solos and Bethan, the choir had become so carried away with their singing that Mr Evans had quite forgotten the news he had for the group.

As everyone began to prepare themselves to leave for the evening he clapped his palm to his forehead and called for their attention.

'I almost forgot! Goodness me, I don't know how I could. I was so excited to tell you all before I got here but then, I suppose I must have got distracted . . .' The group exchanged curious glances as he rambled. 'Anyway, I'm delighted to say that the cake sale was a huge success and Miss Smith and the ladies in charge of it all have informed me that we raised more than enough for the church hymn books and so the choir may have the quite adequate remaining funds for our transportation to the competition!'

It was clear from the looks of happiness on all of their faces that this was most welcome news. Everything was starting to slot into place.

'That's wonderful, vicar,' Glenys said. She'd worked so hard on her cakes, it probably felt more like a personal victory to her.

'It really is,' Catherine added.

'So I suppose now all we need is someone willing to hire us a bus and drive it for us?' Gethin floated the question.

'One of the lads we work with in the coal mine, his brother-in-law drives buses in Castleforth, he can probably help to sort us out. I can ask him at work tomorrow if you like?' Owen offered.

'That would be brilliant, Owen,' Josie said, as everyone agreed that this was a great plan.

'I would like to suggest that we all wear the same colour, as our sort of uniform, when we compete.' Marjorie threw the last detail to be organised out there for discussion.

'How about we all wear something black to show that we're from a coal mining village? You know, black for the coal?' Michael was excited by his idea, despite being one of the most unlikely candidates to chip in on the subject of clothing, being a man who had only ever worn the colour brown as far as Josie could see.

'I think that's a lovely idea, Michael,' Josie said as the rest of the group nodded their heads.

'Black is very slimming on me, I like it.' Peggy sucked in her cheeks and cinched in her already quite narrow waist as she said this, making everyone laugh in the process.

'Well, I think that's every last detail covered. Now all we need to do is practice, practice, practice!' Josie didn't need to do much to rally her choir, she could see quite clearly that they were excited about the competition in just over two weeks' time.

'That we can do, Josie, don't fret about that,' Fred said good-naturedly, as he removed his flat cap from his pocket where it had been rather scrunched up and put it back on his head in preparation for heading home for the night. He tipped it at her as he left the hall, closely followed by the rest of the choir.

Josie was in high sprits as she began to clear away the chairs and songbooks from the hall. Glenys had left, chattering away with Mr Evans. Josie thought that she'd probably sensed that Josie rather enjoyed the quiet time of tidying the hall and locking up by herself or in the company of one of the other choir members, and so she had taken to leaving ahead of her most evenings recently.

However, tonight Marjorie was appearing to linger as Josie stacked up and put away the chairs. The jubilant atmosphere of the night's choir practice had distracted Josie from her intentions to find a way to speak to Marjorie alone to clear the air about what she had seen on Sunday and to let her know that she could come to her if she needed to. Tom's words about her meddling still stung, but she had to admit he had a point in advising her to tread carefully and his words had influenced her approach in a positive way. As annoying as that was to acknowledge. Despite her bruised cheek, Marjorie had been on the best form Josie had ever seen her, which was somewhat of an encouraging factor. But even so, Josie couldn't forget the nervous and vulnerable woman who had tried to hide behind her own front door just days before.

That Marjorie was deliberately delaying her departure now suggested that she too wanted to speak to Josie, which Josie hoped was a good thing. And when the village hall doors clunked shut, leaving just the two of them standing next to the piano in the echoing empty room, Marjorie cleared her throat and revealed that that was indeed her intention.

'I would like to speak to you about our conversation on Sunday and my slightly odd behaviour. I must have looked quite terrible, though I am grateful to you that you've obviously not said anything about it to anyone else. That was kind of you.'

'Oh, Marjorie, I'm not a gossip—'

'I know that and I appreciate it,' Marjorie interrupted her.

'But,' Josie pushed on, 'I am concerned about you.'

Marjorie looked away and smiled sadly. She shook her head and sighed.

'Look, Josie, I'm not going to pretend it was the cupboard door to you, you're too clever for that. But it's not as simple as you might think. My Philip isn't a bad man. Not really. He wasn't always like this.'

Marjorie leant her back against the piano and Josie sat on the stool, not taking her eyes away from the postmistress, fearing she would stop talking if she did. And even though she didn't know what she was going to tell her, Josie felt somehow that it was vitally important she hear it.

'He's always liked a drink, like his father before him. I knew that when I married him. But he was placid mostly, not angry. He got hurt in the war and that changed things. Not physically like others, not in a way you can see, but in his head. He came back a different man.' Marjorie looked at Josie, checking that she was following what she was saying, hoping that she was making herself understood.

'That must have been hard. I heard of that happening to some of the men around where I grew up in London. How did it change Philip?'

Marjorie raised her eyes to the ceiling, perhaps to prevent any tears from falling. 'It made him angry. So angry. He drinks to take away the pain of it all. That's what he tells me after . . . when he . . .' She gestured to her bruised cheek. 'It doesn't happen often, just on bad days, and he doesn't mean to do it, I know he doesn't, and he feels so sad after.' Josie could hear the pain in Marjorie's voice as she paused for breath.

'You shouldn't have to live like that, Marjorie, you could go somewhere—'

'Where?' Marjorie snapped. 'Where could I go, Josie? This is my home. I'm not like you, I can't just uproot myself at my age.'

'But what about your son or your daughter, could you live with them?'

'They can't ever know. I've always protected them from it and I always will. And Lord knows what Philip would do to himself if I left him. No. I couldn't. This is my home, the post office is my life and he is the man I married, for better or worse.'

'But—'

'No, Josie. I appreciate your concern but I don't need it. You're a kind person, but not everyone needs your help. That's what I wanted to say to you tonight. Things are what they are, and you may not understand it, but I need you to respect it and leave things be.'

Josie felt Marjorie's dismissal of her attempts to assist her like a punch in the stomach. Marjorie was so staunch in her determination to draw a line under this discussion and Josie knew she wouldn't get any further. But that only made her feel more helpless. She didn't want to push her away entirely and so she nodded her understanding, making it clear that she was there if ever she needed her.

Marjorie must have seen the anguished look on Josie's face as her tone softened slightly.

'You're a good woman, Josie Williams. But give your attention to those who can be helped. I've accepted my lot in life and that's that. I know it's hard for you to see it that way but that's how it is for me.' She pushed her short plump frame away from the piano and walked to the other end of the hall to put on her coat. But before she opened the hall doors she looked back at Josie who hadn't moved from the piano stool and said in her more familiar bossy tone, 'You get yourself off home now, dear. You're lucky enough to have a good roof over your head, as I'm sure you already know.'

The old Marjorie was back and it was as if the conversation they'd just had had never taken place. Josie knew instinctively that that was how Marjorie had always intended it.

Chapter Twenty-Six

Josie woke suddenly as the sun began peeking its head over the Welsh hills that Saturday morning. The memory that today was the day the article on the choir was to appear in the local paper filtered through her unconsciousness until her body snapped awake. She could hear the faint sounds of movement coming from the kitchen downstairs and she guessed Glenys was already up and preparing to bake her order of cakes. That she had come so close to losing all of this made Josie savour the moment of waking safe and secure in this house.

There was no chance of her falling back to sleep for another hour, so she dressed quickly and quietly so as not to wake a sleeping Sam, before heading downstairs to join Glenys. She might not be a natural baker herself but she could be helpful in cleaning up and assisting with ingredients and suchlike. It was the least Josie could do to pay back the woman who was putting a roof over their heads and on mornings like this one, Josie was glad to have a task to focus her energies on. They wouldn't be able to see a copy of the paper until they made their way into the village later that morning to deliver the cakes to the bakery. There was some time to kill and Josie needed a distraction.

'You're up early, love.' Glenys wiped some flour from her nose as Josie entered the kitchen and pulled on the spare apron that had been hanging on the back of the door.

'The paper is out today.'

'That's right. So it is.'

'I can't seem to think about anything else.'

'Well, beat that butter and sugar together for me there, it'll pass the time quicker. We'll be in the village with that paper in our hands before you know it.'

Glenys had said very little about Ronnie's sudden departure. She'd merely acknowledged it and that was that. If Josie hadn't known how impossible it would have been for her to find anything close to the amount of money she needed to pay back Ronnie, she might have thought Glenys was the one who had saved her. It was a puzzle and one she might never solve.

Later that morning, Josie was a fidgeting mess as Glenys stood discussing business with Mr Driscoll in the bakery. While they had been there delivering their cakes, two villagers had come in and offered their congratulations on the fine article in that week's *Gazette*. But the relief at knowing the piece was a good one wasn't enough to still her anxiousness to read for herself what Peter Philips had written.

'Why don't you run along ahead to the shop, love? Sam can stay with me and we'll follow you over in a moment,' Glenys said with a hint of exasperation. She put her hand over Josie's which had been tapping the counter for who knows how long and clearly irritating everyone in the process. Sam looked relieved to be staying with his grandmother so Josie jumped at the chance to finally get her hands on the paper.

She practically ran across the road to the other side of Colliers Row where Peggy's shop was, and she burst through the door with such force the bell clattered rather than rang to announce her arrival.

Peggy, who had obviously read the article the moment the papers had come in that morning, had already set aside a copy for Josie and had it open on the right page ready for her to read. Peggy was bouncing up and down as Josie made her way to the counter.

'Read it, read it!' Her eyes were bright with excitement.

'I'll read it faster if you stop jumping around in front of me.' Josie laughed as she took the paper from her friend's hands and glanced down at the pages.

'Sorry, I just can't wait to see your face.'

The piece took up half a page, and was longer than any of the other articles that Josie could see. But it was the headline that made Josie's heart almost burst: 'The Songbirds of Colliers Row bring music back to Llandegwen'. The article was full of praise for their performance on Sunday and how hard they were working to get to the competition in Bridgend at the end of the month. Peter Philips had quoted Fred and Peggy on what the choir meant to them, as well as quoting Josie on her motivation for reforming the choir in the first place. The piece finished with the line: 'There is no doubt that their determination and talent will make them hard to beat at the Welsh Valleys Choral Competition at the end of the month, and after their performance on Sunday the village of

Llandegwen will surely be cheering them on all of the way.'

Josie couldn't have hoped for more. The article summed up everything she'd hoped the choir would be when she first set out to reform it, and that a reporter from outside the village had seen everything they had tried to do and praised it publicly gave her the sweet validation she needed to know she had done the right thing.

She was grinning from ear to ear when she looked up at Peggy who gave a little squeal of excitement.

'It's great, isn't it?'

'It really is,' said Josie happily, as the door to the shop opened behind them and Mrs Duffy walked in with Glenys and Sam.

Glenys, seeing the smile on Josie's face, made grabbing gestures with her hands as she rushed to the counter to take the paper from Josie.

'He took my husband's line, did that reporter fellow,' Mrs Duffy said proudly, reading the article over Glenys's shoulder. '"Songbirds of Colliers Row", that's what Mr Duffy called you after he heard you sing that night. I always told him he should've been a writer. He's very poetic sometimes.'

Josie and Peggy had to stifle their giggles. The thought of the very quiet and grumpy Mr Duffy being a secret romantic poet was too ridiculous to contemplate.

'Can I see?' Sam was standing on his tiptoes, straining to see what everyone was making such a fuss about.

'We'll take this copy home with us and we can read it together when you get back from your football practice later,' Glenys promised her grandson. 'I think we should frame it, Josie. Isn't it wonderful? We're famous!'

'I'm not sure Hollywood will be knocking on our doors anytime soon,' Josie said.

'But a bit of local fame feels quite nice. I've never had my name in the paper before. I quite like it,' Peggy said happily.

Glenys had decided to pay Mrs Jones, Peggy's ailing mother, a visit that day while Josie and Sam were up at the field at his football practice. Josie had been dreading seeing Tom but thankfully there were enough parents and children around that they were able to avoid one another easily. Nevertheless, it was a relief for her to return to the shop to collect Glenys on their way back through the village before heading home to the cottage.

The shop was empty as she and Sam entered and Peggy looked relieved to see them.

'It's been so busy in here this morning, I was hoping for a minute to myself but even better to have a chat with you instead,' she said as she tucked one of her wild curls back into place with a clip, not realising that another unruly tendril had escaped from the clip on the other side.

Peggy informed Josie of the morning's gossip that she had picked up from her customers.

'Obviously everyone is talking about the article and the choir, and I'm not going to lie, I have been loving my moment in the spotlight. Lots of people have said they want to hear us sing again before we go to the competition, because they won't get to see us actually compete. So that's something to think about. But the best thing about it all is that apparently Anwen is livid about all of the fuss!' Peggy had that mischievous glint in her eye that Josie had seen before. She was no fan of Anwen's and she didn't even know the latest nastiness she'd dished out to Josie. 'Pamela who is friends with Joan who, as you know is one of Anwen's sheep, told me that Joan told her that Anwen is furious that the paper wrote such a big article on the choir and that the whole village is excited about it. She thought the reporter would write something patronising – apparently she tried to propose that angle to him but he must've ignored her, wise man. Anyway, she told Joan in confidence – I mean Joan couldn't keep a secret if her life depended on it,' Peggy rolled her eyes, 'but probably in a moment of weakness she told Joan who told Pamela that Anwen feels she is "losing her power" in the village.' Peggy's eyes were wide with glee as she quoted Anwen.

'Losing her power? What on earth does that mean?' Josie was baffled by the way that woman's mind worked.

'She means to you.' Josie still looked none the wiser and Peggy sighed in frustration. 'She means people aren't listening to her any more, they're listening to you! Though I never felt she had any such power, to be honest. More like people were scared of her; I don't believe anyone could genuinely like her when she hasn't a good word to say about anyone but herself. She thought of herself as the village sweetheart, but apparently you're all set to take over that role.'

Josie was stunned by this, to the point that laughter began to escape her mouth and before she knew it she was in hysterics. 'But that's so stupid!' she squeaked out in between hoots.

Her laughter was contagious and Peggy had got the giggles too. 'I know! But isn't it brilliant?'

It was hard to take Anwen's nasty words so seriously now that Josie knew she was so concerned about what the village thought of her. She viewed Josie as competition and that meant she'd say anything about Josie to make herself feel better. Therefore, in knowing that, her words lost all their power. And the silliness of it all, of the idea of being the village sweetheart, something Josie had no desire to be, though she was touched by the villagers' support, made her laugh even harder now.

Sam was staring at his hysterical mother and her friend in bemusement as Glenys came out from behind the counter with a panicked expression on her face, clearly believing the shrieks she could hear were those of distress rather than laughter. She began to question the two women on what on earth was so funny when the door to the shop opened with the tinkling of the bell and Tom walked in.

He froze when he came into view of the scene taking place at the counter, not sure what to make of the red-faced doubled-up Josie and Peggy, nor the perplexed-looking Glenys and Sam.

'I don't think we should even bother asking them, Tom. I don't think we'll get any sense out of them,' Glenys said a little huffily, evidently not in the mood for silliness.

Josie wiped the tears of laughter from her cheeks and started to slow her breathing at the sight of Tom. Peggy was still struggling to suppress her giggles. Tom looked like he might want to leave but then realising that would look rude he walked towards the counter.

'I'm sure the joke is none of my business,' he said awkwardly.

Josie's eyes flashed with irritation. 'Yes, well, I know how you feel about getting involved in anyone else's business.' Her tone was haughty and it didn't suit her.

Glenys and Peggy exchanged a look that made the atmosphere in the shop even thicker. Josie wouldn't be able to hide her falling-out with Tom from Glenys any longer now. She should've kept her mouth shut and just left the shop quietly. She moved to take Sam's hand as she told him it was time to go.

'We should be getting back, Glenys. We've distracted Peggy long enough and she has customers.' She gestured lamely at Tom.

'Yes, love. Let's get going. Nice to see you, Tom, bye, Peggy,' Glenys said with an attempt at cheerful that fell a little flat as she walked towards the shop door.

Josie knew that it would only be a matter of seconds before Glenys passed a remark about herself and Tom, she could feel it on the tip of Glenys's tongue as if it were on the tip of her own and she braced herself for it as the shop door snapped shut behind them and Sam ran on ahead.

'He's a nice man,' Glenys said. The moment of silence that followed was heavy with meaning. When Josie said nothing, Glenys continued, 'I've not seen that side of you before, love. What could've made you speak to Tom like that?'

'Glenys . . .' Josie sighed, even though she had known it was coming she really didn't want to have this conversation.

Glenys gave Josie's arm an affectionate squeeze. 'I'm not blind, love. You two have had words. But he's a good man and I just wouldn't want you falling out with him over something you might regret.'

'He doesn't think as highly of me as you do of him, and there has been no falling out. We've never been friends. Nothing has changed.'

Glenys frowned at Josie. 'If you say so, love. But I think his opinion of you is higher than you think.' Josie shot her a look and Glenys raised her hand in defence. 'I'll say no more on the matter.' Josie's shoulders sagged with relief but only for a moment. 'For now anyway,' Glenys said, walking on ahead of her.

Chapter Twenty-Seven

The attention that the newspaper article had shone on the members of the Llandegwen choir over the weekend had quite gone to some of their heads by Monday night's choir practice. Even Fred was puffing his chest out slightly as he spoke of how he'd been congratulated on his mention in the paper by those who had been in the pub on Saturday night. He'd taken to having a pint in there a few nights a week after he'd become better acquainted with some of the other regulars he'd met through Owen and Michael. There was a lightness in his shoulders and a spark of something in his eyes these days. Josie found it hard to imagine the heavy-hearted, detached man she'd first seen that night at the village meeting. The sight of this new, confident Fred made her happy.

Looking at them all that night Josie found it incredible to think of how unsure they all were of singing together just a matter of weeks ago. Bethan, who had been so timid she could barely sing an audible note, was now quietly confident and her voice had become even more powerful in just the last week since she'd revealed her true talent. Josie had watched as Owen, Michael and Catherine had laughed together that evening – two coal miners and the mayor's wife, three people who might never have sat together in any other situation were now firm friends, and seemed to give one another something they had perhaps lacked before they had joined the choir. That seemed to go for everyone. She didn't know all of their stories, but the privileged glimpse she'd been given into some of their lives had shown Josie how what she was doing with the choir was soothing their broken hearts, as much as it was helping mend her own. Even though she'd felt quite helpless with Marjorie's predicament, Josie looked at the smile beaming across her face now, as Marjorie and Bethan told the others about the praise heaped on them in the post office that day. Knowing the darkness that waited for Marjorie above the post office, she was glad that the choir could give Marjorie some light and something to feel proud of.

The newspaper article was really the icing on the cake but they still had a competition to attempt to win.

'Right, everyone, I know we're all very excited about the article and no one is more proud of you all than me, but the competition is in just under two weeks and we still have lots of work to do.' Josie brought them all back down to earth with a bang.

'This journalist fellow said he thinks we're going to win it,' Owen said with mock cockiness.

'That article will have all the other choirs trembling in their boots, don't worry, Josie.' His father backed him up with a smile on his face, making everyone laugh.

'That might be so, lads, but Peter Philips isn't one of the

judges and we'll not be judged on the article but by your fine voices. So let's get to work!' Josie clapped her hands to get them to stand up ready to sing. She received a groan of resistance, she was breaking up their moment in the sunshine and reminding them of their important task ahead, but it was all for show. They were as keen as her to get to work that night. The newspaper article had given them all confidence and now they were determined to do their village proud at that competition. Plus nothing gave them more joy than to sing and nothing gave Josie more joy at the moment than to hear them.

It had been one of the most enjoyable practices Josie had experienced with the choir so far. Their spirits had been high and the choir's added layer of confidence gifted by the praise the newspaper article had bestowed on them had put a sprinkle of something special in all of their voices. They all had an extra bounce in their steps as they prepared to leave the village hall that evening.

Catherine and Fred had offered to help Josie clear away the chairs, enjoying the opportunity to talk more about how much fun they were having singing together. As Catherine lifted one chair in order to stack it on top of the one placed next to it, she did so with such gusto that she caught the golden chain she always wore concealed beneath her blouse on the tip of the chair. The chain snapped with the force of the chair being manoeuvred, freeing the necklace to fly across the room past Josie.

Catherine let out a distressed gasp as she realised what she had done and Josie quickly moved to recover the necklace from the hard wooden floor. When she bent down to retrieve it she found that attached to the chain was a pretty locket that had sprung open when it had hit the floor and now revealed a black and white photograph of a baby wearing a frilly bonnet. The trace of an arm holding the child on a lap could be seen but the person had been cut out of the picture, due to the small size of the locket, presumably. Josie wondered who the child might be, knowing Catherine had no children of her own. But sensing the picture was something personal, she didn't want to linger over studying it too long and therefore look as though she were prying. She quickly rose to her feet with the locket in her hand and walked towards Catherine to return it to her.

Josie caught the look of panic Catherine gave Fred when she could see the locket was open and that therefore Josie had seen its contents. It was a strange look to Josie, as Catherine always appeared so composed. In order to break the sudden tension of the moment Josie said, 'What a beautiful child.'

Catherine was still speechless but Fred jumped in to fill the silence.

'That must be your sister's child, is it, Catherine?'

Catherine looked from Josie to Fred.

'Um . . . yes, it is. Sorry, I'm just so careless . . . I can't believe I broke it.' Catherine took the locket from Josie's hand and quickly snapped it shut. She was flustered. 'Thank you for picking it up, Josie. I need to be more careful.'

She looked so upset that Josie desperately wanted to console her. 'I'm sure the chain can be mended and the locket might need a little polishing but I don't think any serious damage was done.' But even as she said this she felt that Catherine's upset ran deeper than the fact that she'd broken her locket.

'You're quite right. I'm just being silly, I hate breaking things. Ignore me.' She waved away Josie's concerned look as she put the broken locket in her cardigan pocket and smiled her usual winning smile at Josie. 'Now let's put these chairs away,' she added brightly as she marched over to the storeroom next to the kitchen carrying the two chairs she had stacked.

Fred nodded at Josie and shuffled awkwardly before following Catherine with chairs of his own.

It was the strangest thing. Though Josie had been one of the three players on the stage in that moment, the scene she'd just performed felt like a completely different one to the scene Catherine and Fred had been enacting. They were reading from the same script but the meaning was different. And Josie couldn't think for the life of her why.

On Wednesday evening Josie had been lost in thought as she helped Glenys to prepare the tea that they would all eat together before they went to the village hall for choir practice. They had been working together in a comfortable silence as Josie was now more than familiar with what Glenys needed her to do. The distant sounds of clipped voices on the wireless drifted through to the kitchen from the living room where Harry was in his usual spot by the fire, the flames still being lit in the evenings even though they were well into spring now. Sam was working quietly on his handwriting at the kitchen table, preferring the company of his mother and grandmother to his sullen grandfather, even if everyone was silently focusing on their own tasks.

Josie had been thinking again about Catherine and the child in the photograph in her locket. Her nephew or niece,

Fred had said, but he hadn't been close enough to see the picture himself. Maybe he'd seen it before – he and Catherine were friends, she knew Catherine popped to the farm to have a cup of tea with Fred now and then. Perhaps she'd spoken of her family to him before and shown him the photograph. But why would she wear the locket out of sight? This nephew or niece was clearly very dear to her, so upset she'd been at breaking the locket. Why was this child more special than perhaps her other nieces and nephews? Josie thought again about how Catherine always sang the lullaby 'Suo Gân' with such emotion that Josie felt she were singing it to someone in her heart. Was it this child?

'Do you know much about Catherine's family, Glenys?' she asked as she chopped up some carrots.

'Not really, love. She's spoken of an older sister a few times. I think she has a brother too.'

'Does she have many nieces and nephews?'

'I have no idea, she's never spoken of any. But she's quite private, I think. Why do you ask?' Glenys looked up at Josie.

'No reason really. Just curious.'

Glenys accepted this answer easily and Josie returned to the thoughts floating around in her mind. She was very curious, but really it was none of her business. She wouldn't ask any more questions – Josie might have ideas in her head that didn't quite match with the story Catherine, or rather Fred, had told, but there was no need to put them in anyone else's head by asking strange questions. She didn't know where her newfound nosiness had come from. She'd be holding letters up to the light to read their contents like Marjorie in the post office soon if she wasn't careful. And with a laugh to herself Josie put thoughts of lockets and Catherine to the back of her mind.

Peggy was waiting for Josie as she locked up the village hall that night after choir practice. It had been another wonderful rehearsal and Josie had really put them through their paces. Bethan was blossoming in her soloist role and the harmonies were sounding heavenly. There were a couple of wrinkles here and there that needed to be smoothed out, but they still had a few practices left and Josie was confident they'd be ready by Saturday week. Look how far they had come in such a short time already.

'I know it's only been a few weeks but already I can't remember a time without the choir. I don't know what I'd have done if you'd left,' Peggy said as they walked out of the hall doors and out into the night.

'I don't know what I'd have done either.' Josie shuddered.

'You're glad that someone paid Ronnie off then?'

'Of course I am. I just wish I knew who it was. And more importantly, why. I just have no idea who it could've been. Unless Billy somehow got word of things in America, but then I don't know why he wouldn't write to me if he was back in contact again.'

They walked towards Peggy's shop in easy silence, Josie's mind still ticking over the possibility that her brother might have somehow come to her rescue.

'What was all that with Tom the other day in the shop? I know you think he's a bit pompous but what you said to him was pretty harsh.'

'It was much less harsh than what he'd last said to me, believe me.'

'What did he say?' Was it Josie's imagination or did Peggy look a little disbelieving?

'He said I was a meddler and more or less accused me of terrible judgement over my association with Ronnie, even though he knows nothing about it, or about me for that matter. He was judging me based on appearances, which he had no right to do and I told him so. He didn't even defend himself really. I thought for a moment there that he might be a decent man – when he came for dinner that night, he seemed so nice and normal, but it must've been an act.'

Peggy looked pained. 'But what if you've got him wrong? It might just be a misunderstanding? *You* could be judging *him* based on appearances.'

Josie glared at Peggy. 'Why are you defending him? Don't you believe me?'

'No, I do, it's not about believing anyone, it's just sometimes things aren't how we see them . . .' Peggy was wringing her hands and she looked so conflicted that Josie's annoyance with her quickly dissipated.

'Peggy, what are you trying to say? I don't understand why you care what I think of Tom Jenkins. It's not like he's a good friend of yours or anything.'

'He's not, but he's a good friend of yours, if only you knew how good,' Peggy muttered before she glanced at Josie guiltily. Josie stared at her friend, a look of utter confusion on her face as she waited for her to explain herself. 'Oh God, he made me promise not to say anything and before you get furious with me, which I know you will, he'd overheard most of it for himself anyway, I'd never have told him or anyone, I promise.'

They were outside Peggy's shop and Colliers Row was in quiet darkness except for the odd crack of light beaming out of curtain-drawn windows. Josie's heart was pounding in her chest as her friend turned to face her fully when they'd reached the shop door. She had no idea what Peggy was about to say but the anguish on her friend's face was enough to make her nervous.

Peggy took a deep breath. 'It was Tom who paid off Ronnie.' The words tumbled out in the exhale. Josie's mouth dropped open so Peggy rushed on to tell the full story before she might not be able to get a word in. 'He'd overheard what Ronnie said to you at the cake sale and he was really worried about you. He came over to me and asked me if you were OK, told me what he'd heard. I tried to pretend I didn't know what he was talking about, but I'm a rubbish liar and I was worried about you too. He knew there was more to it than I was saying. Anyway, then he saw you argue with Ronnie over there on the street and run off all upset and he marched right over to me in the shop and demanded to know what was going on. I couldn't not say anything, I didn't want Ronnie to hurt you, I was scared for you, so I told him you owed him money. But that's all I said, I promise. I thought with him being so powerful round here, his family owning all those collieries, I thought he might be able to help. And he did.' Peggy had almost trailed off to a whisper. She looked so guilty and Josie knew she hadn't betrayed her. Peggy had had no choice and Josie felt bad for not considering how worried her friend might be in all of this. She'd only thought about it from her perspective.

'Tom paid off Ronnie? But why?' Josie was so confused.

'When I asked him he said it was because no one should be held to ransom just for trying to survive the best they could.'

'He said that?'

Peggy nodded. 'He was really angry. He caught up with Ronnie before he got to Glenys and he told him that he'd get his police chief friend in London who he served with in the war to arrest him and bring down his sordid business empire if he didn't leave immediately and never come back. That's how I really knew that Ronnie was gone, not from Gavin.'

Josie's head was swimming. 'But where did he get the money? He doesn't have his inheritance.'

Peggy shrugged. 'I don't know. I didn't ask him that. I was just so grateful that you were going to be OK and that that creep was gone before he did any damage.'

'I can't believe Tom did that for me. I still don't understand why.'

'That's why I've broken my promise to him not to tell you. I think you've got him wrong. He didn't want you to know he'd paid off Ronnie – even when you thought badly of him, he still didn't want you to know. He told me again not to ever say anything after you left the shop the other day. He didn't want you to feel like you owed him anything. He was very passionate about it. But I couldn't not tell you, I know you'd never speak to him like that if you knew. And he did a good thing, it shouldn't be a secret.'

As Josie remembered what she'd said to him in the shop and, even worse, what she'd said the night he'd helped her find the key to the village hall, the guilt was almost unbearable. He'd saved her from a life of fear and violation without wanting anything in return. He hadn't been judging her for meddling with Marjorie's business or for getting tangled up with someone like Ronnie, he'd been trying to show her that we never really knew why people did what they did, but they must have their reasons. He understood her reasons. That's why he'd said what he'd said, but she had judged herself so harshly for letting someone like Ronnie hold such a position of power over her she had assumed he'd been doing the same.

She'd got him so terribly wrong and the shame burned in her chest. She put her head in her hands.

'Oh Peggy, I've been so stupid.'

Chapter Twenty-Eight

Josie woke with a knot of anxiety in her stomach on Thursday morning, and instead of it unravelling as she distracted herself with her morning tasks of helping Glenys and taking Sam to school, it only pulled tighter. She'd dreamt of Matthew the night before. It had been so long since he'd appeared in her dreams, she couldn't even remember the last time. It had been both a torture and a comfort in the early years to see him when she slept. The nightmares revealing him hurt and suffering on the battlefields were terrifying and Josie would wake gasping for breath in panic. But thankfully these dreams came to her on fewer occasions than the good ones where they were together again as they had been before he'd had to go back to fight in the war. These happy dreams were often worse because Josie felt the loss and heartache of knowing she'd never see him again more acutely after the vivid images of him danced through her mind at night. They made her miss him more.

The dreams had faded over time, as had Matthew's image

in Josie's mind. So it was a surprise to her to find him waiting for her in her unconsciousness that night, having not had one dream about him since living in his childhood home. She dreamt that he'd come to Llandegwen to find her. He was upset with her, he'd been looking for her all over London. He hadn't died in the war after all, he'd just lost his way home. And now he'd returned to Wales to find her living in his family cottage with another man, Tom Jenkins. In the way that dreams play tricks with the mind, Josie couldn't remember what he had said to her when she woke, but she remembered his pained expression, and she remembered the feelings that his words had left her with. She'd felt guilty.

That feeling had twisted within her all morning. That her mind had imagined her living with Tom as husband and wife was unnerving and that she'd felt so guilty about it was even worse. She knew the dream had probably been a consequence of what Peggy had told her but the feelings it had evoked felt too real to brush aside as a silly dream. They were bothering her so Josie took the opportunity to clear her head that afternoon before she had to collect Sam from school. She went for a long walk in the Welsh hills. If the fresh air didn't clear away the tension she was feeling, nothing would.

It was a beautiful spring day, the sky was blue and the sun shone in bursts between white cotton clouds. She still needed her coat, the air still held a chill, but it was comfortable to walk in and the bright sky showed the Welsh countryside at its best. Josie was mentally running through the areas of the three competition songs that she wanted to focus on with the choir later that evening when she saw a figure in the distance walking across the hill towards her. She held her hand to shade her eyes to see if she could work out who it might be before their paths crossed.

Josie could make out the shape of a woman wearing a nicely tailored navy coat and as she got closer she could see it was Catherine Morgan smiling at her warmly as she approached.

'Great minds think alike! It's such a beautiful day for a walk,' Catherine said as their paths finally met.

'It certainly is. I needed to clear my mind and this,' Josie gestured to the wide stretch of green countryside surrounding them for miles, 'is just the ticket.'

'I've been over to see Fred. I often do when I take my walks. He's such a kind man and I like the cosiness of his farm in contrast to my big, cold old house. It's a nice change of scene.'

'It must be nice for him to have the company,' Josie said, thinking of how isolated Fred had been up here on his farm, away from the village.

'It's good for me too. We're both rattling around up here in the hills. I do love the space and the quiet, but we need others around us too.' Catherine sounded a little sad.

'I suppose the mayor is terribly busy with the important job he has to do.' Josie couldn't even imagine what the day-to-day life of a mayor would be like if she were really honest, but it seemed like the right thing to say.

Catherine sighed. 'Yes, it's a very important job.' There was a hint of impatience or dismissal, Josie wasn't quite sure which, in her voice. 'As is the choir. Fred and I were just saying that. It was what we needed, something to work towards, somewhere to be, you know?'

Josie smiled her understanding. 'It was the same for me.

I'm glad my motive didn't end up being an entirely selfish one.'

Catherine laughed. 'Josie, you are the least selfish person. You look out for people, you notice things. I can see that. You've probably kept a few people's secrets too, I'd imagine.' She looked at Josie curiously and Josie felt that she was testing her in some way.

'I don't know about that . . .'

'You saw my biggest secret and you didn't say a thing. Most other people would've asked questions, but you didn't.'

A moment of understanding passed between Josie and Catherine then.

'The child in the photo?'

Catherine nodded. 'No one knows apart from my husband. And Fred of course, but you knew that. Kind Fred, trying to cover it up for me the other night. We've become quite good pals, Fred and I, as unlikely as that might seem. I think we both needed someone to talk to these past couple of years. He talks about his family and I told him about mine. He's kept my secret and allowed me to talk about it.'

Josie just nodded silently. It was the conclusion she'd tried not to jump to, but now here was Catherine confirming it, confiding in her. Josie wasn't sure why, though.

'In a way he wasn't lying, I am her aunt as far as she and everyone else knows. My sister raised her as her own – she was married and I was not, the lie was easy and my family were too proper, too concerned with their standing in society to let their silly daughter ruin things by getting pregnant without a husband.' A hint of bitterness sharpened Catherine's usual calm and soft tone. 'But I was lucky, because I got to know my daughter, even if she thinks of me as her aunt. I've seen her grow into the beautiful young woman she is today. She is in my life and that's so much better than nothing at all. Other than missing out on being with her every day and seeing her grow as a mother should, the hardest thing about it is keeping it a secret. I'm a mother but I can't tell anyone. John and I never managed to have children of our own, and knowing I had before I met him has always been a sore point. The fault can't therefore lie with me. But I have this beautiful child and no one can ever know.' Catherine's voice broke slightly now.

Josie had no idea what to say, there were no words that could change how Catherine was feeling. Instead she asked her about her daughter, giving her the chance to speak as a mother for a moment.

'When you sing "Suo Gân" do you sing it to your daughter?'

Catherine looked at Josie in surprise. 'I was right. You do notice things.'

'You sing it with such emotion that I always felt you were singing it for someone, or to someone in your heart.'

'It's funny, I had no intention of speaking to you about any of this. I knew you'd ask no more about it after you saw my locket. But then seeing you today, walking away your troubles just like me, I don't know, it felt like fate. Like I had to speak about it. Does that sound strange?'

'No.' Josie shook her head but she wasn't really sure it did make much sense to her.

'You'd seen her beautiful picture and I wanted to acknowledge the child I'd had, not lie about her. I wanted, for once, not to be the mayor's wife, proper and perfect, but a woman who has made mistakes but done her best. That probably sounds ridiculous to you, I'm not sure it makes complete sense to me either. But I felt somehow that you already knew the truth.'

The two women smiled at one another.

'Perhaps I did. Mother's intuition, maybe.'

'Thank you for saying that. For saying I'm a mother like you. You have no idea what that means to me.'

'I think I do a little. If you'd ever like to talk about your daughter, I'd love to know more,' Josie said sincerely, knowing if she were to ever be without Sam, a thought she couldn't even bear to consider, she'd want to talk him back into existence.

Catherine gracefully swept away a tear that had escaped from her lashes. 'Thank you, Josie. I'd like that. Maybe next time we find each other on the hill?'

Josie smiled. 'It's a deal.'

Catherine had composed herself again and had regained her natural poise. She gave Josie her charming smile.

'See, keeper of secrets. I told you.' She tapped her index finger against her nose before she bid Josie farewell and walked in the direction Josie had come from.

As Josie watched Catherine's slender figure disappear beyond the slope of the hill, she thought how funny life was. In London she would never have met the wife of the mayor, let alone shared secrets with her. She and Catherine had very little in common, Catherine was only a little younger than her own mother would have been, but Catherine had a privilege and an expectation to live up to that neither Josie's mother nor she herself had ever experienced. Their lives could not have been more different, but yet they had understood one another. Josie had always admired Catherine and envied her effortless charm and ability to fit in with everyone despite being so different from them all. And now that she knew the heavy secret she carried in a locket around her neck, hidden beneath her expensive clothes, she admired her even more. Perhaps she might even consider her a friend. Friends with the mayor's wife – life really was quite funny.

By the time Josie had arrived back at the cottage, she'd forgotten all about her dream of Matthew and Tom, and the confusing feelings it had stirred up. The fresh air, the long walk and the dose of perspective she'd been given by Catherine's secret had not only untangled that sickening knot within her but had blown all traces of it away. Glenys was pleased to see the lightness in Josie's mood on her return. The older woman had been frowning at Josie each time Josie caught her looking at her that morning. Her mind probably rifling through all of the reasons that Josie might be anxious and trying to figure out how to help her, knowing Glenys.

'Walk do you good, did it, love? The hills around here are quite the tonic, I've always thought.'

Josie agreed. All that space, it allowed a person to breathe.

Josie's refreshed outlook carried her through to choir practice that evening where focusing on the task at hand was an even greater tonic.

She wasn't sure if it was nerves as the competition got closer or overexcitement at the attention they'd all been getting due to the article, but Mr Evans's volume levels had gone rogue once again and some of the timing was off when they sang 'Calon Lan'.

'I'm terribly sorry, everyone, I can even hear it now myself.' Mr Evans looked pained about the mistakes he was making.

'It's all right, vicar, we're all a little off tonight, I think,' said Fred sympathetically.

'I don't know what's wrong with me, I keep coming in too soon.' Marjorie, usually so full of praise for herself, was so frustrated she couldn't help but admit her part in the timing faults.

Josie looked around at the troubled faces, staring at her, wide-eyed in panic.

'There's nothing to be sorry for and it's nothing we can't fix,' she said soothingly. 'Just think how brilliant it is that you can hear it yourselves when it's not quite right. You couldn't have done that a few weeks ago. And now that you can hear it, you'll know how to fix it. Let's try it again. I won't play the piano this time, I'll conduct you as I will at the competition when someone else plays. Follow my lead and we'll get it right. OK?'

Ten heads nodded determinedly at her.

'And Mr Evans, just remember to listen to the other voices like we practised before. Use them as your guide.'

'Absolutely, Josie my dear. I remember.'

'OK, Songbirds, breathe, and one, two, three, four . . .'

Josie raised her arm to lead Bethan in first. Her pure solo began the song and she delivered it beautifully. And when Josie turned to the rest of the group to bring them in with the harmony, they followed her perfectly this time, not a voice was early nor late, not a note was out of place. She could see their shoulders visibly relax as they all settled into the rousing hymn. Josie breathed out her own sigh of relief and smiled encouragingly at them all. This was what she was here for, to carry them through the nerves and the hiccups. There was no room for her own butterflies, she was their leader, and she realised in that moment that it made her enormously proud to call herself that. They had just over a week to go but they would be OK. They'd worked so hard to get to this point. There was nothing they couldn't do if they put their minds to it. What she was hearing in the village hall that night was proof of that.

Josie hadn't seen Tom since Peggy revealed that he'd been the one to pay Ronnie off. She wanted to tell him how grateful she was but she hadn't yet worked out exactly what she'd say. The idea that he knew everything, had overheard the truth of the situation first-hand, made her feel queasy with shame. But that he hadn't judged her for it, and more than that, he had felt compelled to help her when she needed it most, despite the fact that she'd mostly been harsh with him, well, she wasn't quite sure how she felt about that. Her opinion of Tom Jenkins was quite changed. He was kind – he'd shown that in the choice he'd made to leave his family's inheritance behind to give something back to the community he thought of as home, and the care and passion he put into his role at the school. The children loved him. But Josie had been too blind to see it. She had chosen only to see the haughtiness, even after he'd opened up to her in the cottage that night. She was so consumed by her own guilt and her own problems that she hadn't seen that Tom had been holding himself back from most people because of his own history with the village and the burden of being a Jenkins in that community.

She would have to find a way to show him that she was truly grateful for what he'd done and that she would pay him back somehow. She was hoping that she might catch him after Sam's football practice that Saturday but there wasn't enough time or enough privacy. Instead, she observed him from the sidelines as he encouraged the children as they played, his athletic frame running the length of the field with them. Why hadn't she looked at him more closely before? He'd been right when he'd said she was quick to judge and now her feelings for him were so confused.

Josie's head was still all tangled up when she saw Peggy in the shop that afternoon.

'I'm still trying to work out what it means, why he would do that for me and not say anything? And not even want me to know?'

'He must care about you.' Peggy shrugged as if this was completely obvious. 'Maybe he's in love with you.'

Josie laughed in an attempt to make Peggy's theory ridiculous but her cheeks had gone pink. 'If that were the case, why wouldn't he want me to know?'

'Because he wants you to love him back for him, not out of some sense of obligation? Because he's a good man? Didn't you tell me he has a weird thing about people only being interested in him because of his money? He gave up his inheritance, so money is clearly something that muddies things for him.'

'That's all true but it doesn't mean he's in love with me. He hardly knows me.'

'If you really believe that then why have your cheeks gone

pink?' Peggy looked at Josie accusingly. 'What would you do if he is?'

'Oh, I don't know! He's not though, so it doesn't matter.'

'If you say so,' Peggy said as she began to busy herself with reorganising the shelf of tea behind her.

Josie stood watching her friend work. The thought that Tom might have saved her because he had feelings for her had her heart hammering in her chest. A ripple of excitement ran through her and she couldn't deny that the idea felt good. But she immediately felt guilty as Matthew's hurt face, the same face that she'd seen so vividly in her dream, popped into her mind. She was living in his home, sleeping in his old room, how could she be thinking of another man in such a way? Even if the man in question was good and kind, and had saved her life.

There was a war of emotions taking place in Josie's heart as she entered the cottage that afternoon. Glenys, as usual, sensed it immediately on seeing her walk into the kitchen.

'Now what's going on in that head of yours, love? Don't tell me it's nothing because it's written all over your face,' she said sympathetically.

Josie was all set to deny everything, but her shoulders slumped in defeat as she lost the will to pretend any longer. 'I don't even know where to begin.'

'Well, let's have a little walk and you can start from the beginning.'

Glenys linked her arm through Josie's as they walked down the garden path and on to the street heading towards the fields where Sam usually played football. The air was clean and fresh; the novelty of no smog had still not worn off on Josie, and neither had her appreciation for the prettiness of the little miners' cottages that lined the village streets. Even the most ramshackle house had its own charm. The lack of tall buildings made the sky seem brighter. Josie hadn't realised how little of the sky she'd seen when she lived in London.

As they strolled Josie gave Glenys the heavily edited version of what had happened with Ronnie and what Tom had done for her. She obviously left out any mention of the hideous brothels and simply explained how she'd had to run when she couldn't pay him back as he had threatened her – with what, Josie had kept as vague as she could. She felt bad withholding the entire truth from Glenys but she just couldn't face revealing the grim underworld of the East End to her and worrying this tiny woman with what could have been. Glenys was horrified enough by the edited version.

'If I'd known I'd have run that rat Ronnie out of Llandegwen myself! I can't believe I'd not seen him for what he really was. I wish you'd told me, love.'

'It was my problem to sort and I hated that I brought it to your doorstep. Anyway, Tom was the one to fix everything and he did it without wanting me to know. I've been so awful to him, Glenys, I don't know how to make that up to him. But I have to tell him how grateful I am.'

'Well, that's a good start,' Glenys said sympathetically.

'And I need to find out why he did it too.' Josie's voice was quiet, as the guilt crept up her spine again at the thought that Tom might have feelings for her and how that thought made her heart flutter in a way it hadn't in a long time.

'Is this what's really bothering you, love?'

Josie nodded as she filled Glenys in on her dream about Matthew and how it had reminded her that she couldn't give her heart away again. Surely Glenys, Matthew's own mother, would understand this.

'But Matthew's gone, love. I wish to God he wasn't, but he is.' Glenys's face showed her sadness at this fact but her simple acceptance of it threw Josie completely.

'But if you saw the way he looked at me in my dream—'

'That's just it though, Josie. It was just a dream. It wasn't real. If anything it was your own fears play-acting in your mind.' Glenys interrupted Josie, her voice that of one determined to make herself understood. 'My Matthew was no saint but he was a good man. I'll always be proud of him for that. But he was also practical and realistic about life. He knew perfectly well what he was getting himself into when he signed up to fight in the war, I remember him telling me when I fussed around him. I was convinced he didn't know what he was doing, but of course he did. I was just being a protective mother. And if he was sure about that, he would've been prepared for the fact that he might not come home to his wife and child too. And my son wouldn't accept that fact and at the same time wish that his wife and son would struggle or be alone for ever just because he never made it home. He'd want you both to be happy. And if that meant you marrying someone else, he'd be fine with that.'

Josie was stunned that her husband's mother could see things this way and yet she had struggled to.

'Trust me, love. I knew my son. He wouldn't torment you like he did in your dream,' Glenys continued. 'And I know you loved him. But I've got to know you, Josie, you have a big enough heart to love another, and just because you might, doesn't mean you never loved my Matthew. If anything, you owe it to him to be happy and live your life to the very best. He fought so that we could do exactly that. Let's not let him down, eh?' She smiled at Josie whose eyes had filled with tears.

'But what if I can't? What if I'm too scared? What if I lose everything again?'

'Oh, Josie, we can't let the bad things life throws at us stop us from enjoying the good. Would you change marrying my Matthew if you'd known he'd be taken from you?'

Josie shook her head fiercely. 'No, I've never regretted marrying him for a second.'

'Well then. No regrets. If you get the chance to open your heart again to love, grab it with both hands.'

Josie wiped away the tears that had managed to escape down her cheeks. And as the older woman hugged her tightly Josie wondered what she'd done to deserve such a person as Glenys in her life. She had saved her in more ways than one.

Chapter Twenty-Nine

'I can't believe the competition is this week! I don't know whether I'm more nervous or excited. Both are making me feel a bit queasy, if I'm honest,' Peggy declared to the group at choir practice that Monday night.

They had been discussing the final arrangements for that Saturday when they would be competing in Bridgend at the Welsh Valleys Choral Competition. The bus and its driver had been arranged through Owen's fellow miner, as he had promised. It would collect them all from outside the village hall on Saturday afternoon in order to get to Bridgend in plenty of time before they were to sing that evening. They had all found something black to wear to represent their village's coal mining history. There was nothing left to do but sing, and the villagers were clamouring to hear them do that once again.

Ever since the article had appeared in the paper after their debut performance at the cake sale, the villagers had been asking them all if the choir would give them a little preview concert before they set off for the competition. Only that morning Mrs Duffy had cornered Josie in Peggy's shop to ask her if she'd arranged anything regarding this yet. The more Josie thought about it, the more she felt quite excited about the idea of giving the village a special performance before they got on the bus to the competition. It could be a sort of dress rehearsal for the choir. They had all been on such a high after the praise they'd got the first time they sang to the village, she was sure that now, with even more practice, they would knock the socks off Llandegwen if they sang to the village on Saturday. The people of Llandegwen would give the choir a real boost that they could take into the competition with them.

Josie was so proud of them all, she also wanted the opportunity to show off all of their hard work to everyone, to prove that they were right to allow the choir to be reformed and to represent them in choral competitions. A little pre-competition concert in the village hall would be perfect.

'Nerves are natural and necessary to give your best performance. I would be worried if any of us wasn't nervous,' Marjorie said without a hint of sympathy for Peggy's queasiness.

'Marjorie is right, nerves are a good thing. And I don't know if this idea will add to those nerves but I was thinking that we should give the village a concert here at the hall before we head off on Saturday. Everyone wants to hear you sing again and I think Llandegwen deserves to have the chance to hear your competition songs before the rest of the Valleys choirs do. What do you think?' Josie looked at them hopefully.

Bethan looked uncertainly at Gethin, and Fred, Catherine and the Thomas men seemed to shrug, but Josie couldn't tell if that was in agreement or indecision. However, Marjorie, Mr Evans, Peggy and Glenys were all for it.

'I think that's a great idea, love,' Glenys said.

'We must give the people what they want. I hear nothing but requests for us to sing when I speak to the congregation after church on Sundays. My sermons are rather less in demand, sadly, but they do seem keen to hear us sing again,' Mr Evans said earnestly.

Marjorie and Peggy had both received similar requests in their roles behind the counters of the post office and village shop and were equally keen to meet those requests.

'Bethan and I shall put up a notice in the post office to let everyone know,' Marjorie decided.

'And I'll do the same in the shop. Word will soon spread if we all mention it when we can.' Peggy was full of energy at the idea of organising an event. Her queasiness at having to actually perform on Saturday seemingly cured for now while the notion of singing in front of a crowd took second place to making sure the crowd was there to hear them in the first instance.

Everyone agreed to spread the word whenever they could and Josie beamed at them as all of the final pieces for Saturday fell into place. There were nerves in the room, there was no denying that, but more than that there was excitement. They were a team, they all belonged to something. And Josie felt her heart swell with the realisation that she'd found somewhere she belonged too.

When Josie had locked up the village hall both Monday and Tuesday nights she had tried to ignore the hope that had flickered within her that she'd bump into Tom on the way home. She wanted to tell him she knew what he'd done and how much it meant to her, but she needed to get him alone somehow.

She was grateful to have the competition to focus on to distract her from the places her mind had a tendency to run away to. Monday and Tuesday's choir practices had been a dream. She couldn't believe that that shambolic first night when they had first all sung together had involved the same voices that sang so beautifully together now. They were more than ready for the competition on Saturday. Josie decided to think only of this fact when she took a walk across the hills that Wednesday afternoon to clear her head. She'd been breathing in the fresh air and staring off into the distance from a high spot on a hill, imagining the choir singing on the stage to rapturous applause, when Catherine Morgan's voice interrupted her thoughts.

'I see we're both fond of this spot. Sorry, I didn't mean to disturb you,' Catherine said apologetically.

'Not at all. I've been on my own up here for a while now, it's nice to see a friendly face.'

'I was just on my way to Fred's for a cup of tea, would you like to come? Maybe we could all do with the company.' There was no pressure in her words but Josie felt unable to decline the invitation, especially as Glenys had offered to collect Sam from school, she was in no rush to get back. And so she found herself not long after this at the kitchen table in Fred's farmhouse with a steaming cup of tea in front of her. As it turned out it was just what she needed.

Catherine had spoken more about her daughter, Violet,

who was now nineteen and working in Cardiff in a secretarial position. Catherine received regular updates in letters from her sister, with whom Catherine was very close. Her sister, it seemed, had always understood the pain Catherine had had to endure in having to keep her daughter secret. Josie could see the light in Catherine's eyes as she got to speak freely about the child she could only love from afar and she felt privileged to hold a space in this small group of three where such a deeply important secret had been shared.

Fred told them stories about his wife and how she would've liked Catherine and Josie, he was sure of it. 'She'd fall off her chair if she were here to see me being so sociable, having guests over for a cup of tea. That was more her thing,' he said smiling.

As Josie listened to Catherine and Fred speaking of the people they loved so dearly but were forcibly parted from, she thought of those she had lost in her life. And then she looked at what Catherine and Fred were doing to live with the absence of those they'd been forced to live without. Catherine had gratefully accepted the chance to be in her daughter's life, even if it was not as her mother. She had taken the opportunity to be something to Violet, rather than letting the pain of giving up her child ruin any joy she could have in seeing the woman Violet would grow in to. And Fred, who had wasted so many years hiding away up here on his farm, nursing his broken heart alone and isolated, was now throwing himself into village life. He'd made the decision to join the choir to enjoy the years he had left.

'I realised that I didn't need to be alone any more. I realised that if Mary were looking down on me she'd be so disappointed to see me wallowing. And David would've got fed up with me by now too. I was letting them down by not living. They weren't given the chance to and here was I wasting mine. That's when Catherine suggested we join the choir. It was my chance to do Mary and David proud, and get my sorry soul living again. I thank you for that too, Josie,' Fred said with such sincerity that Josie had to desperately swallow the lump in her throat that threatened to burst into a sob.

She had thought she'd done everything she could to live fully after losing Matthew and her parents. She'd had to for Sam's sake. But she'd ignored the fact that she'd locked her heart away in the process. The mess she'd made in taking money from someone like Ronnie had made her cautious and too set on survival rather than really living. She would never live life fully if she didn't have an open heart. And she owed it to those she'd lost to live fully. Just as Catherine and Fred had done.

Josie left Fred's farmhouse feeling braver. The first thing she needed to do was to find Tom and tell him she knew what he'd done and what it had meant to her. If he couldn't accept her apology for judging him so harshly, she'd have to live with that, but at least she'd have told him how she really felt. Josie was running through what she might say to him in her head as she made her way over the hill back towards the village, the light in the sky above her fading slightly as dusk began to creep its way in. As she got closer to the road that would take her back into the village she almost believed that she'd been thinking so much about finding Tom, she'd somehow conjured up the vision of him that was now walking towards her. It was as though her imagination was playing tricks on her, but no, the real living and breathing Tom Jenkins was heading her way.

It took him a few moments longer to notice that she was in front of him and she saw him stall slightly as he realised there was no way of avoiding her. That made her heart sink slightly but this was her chance and she had to take it.

As they reached one another, before there could be any awkward hellos or stilted conversation, the mere seconds of tension she'd had to endure already unbearable, Josie blurted out the speech she had been mentally preparing in her head just moments before.

'I know what you did for me. That you paid Ronnie the money I owed him, that you got him to leave quietly. Peggy told me, but don't be angry with her, she told me because I needed to know and I'm glad I do.' She was already out of breath and she'd barely begun. She inhaled and tried to slow her speech so that she wasn't gabbling like a mad woman. Tom's eyebrows were raised, she figured in surprise, but that's as far as she could read his expression. 'I am so unbelievably grateful to you, I can't quite believe you did that for me and I have no idea why you would, I've been awful to you. I thought you were a snob, I thought that you were judging me, but now I see that *I* was judging *you* and I'm so sorry. I really am. And I'm so grateful, did I say that bit already?'

Tom laughed but only nodded his reply.

'Anyway, I will absolutely pay you back. Every penny—'

'That's not what I want. That's not why I did it . . .' Tom was shaking his head.

'Why did you do it?' Josie asked before he could move the conversation on.

Tom sighed. 'Josie, we don't need to do this. I'm glad you no longer think I'm a judgemental snob, particularly when it comes to my opinion of you. I didn't want Peggy to tell you, but if it means I now have your good opinion then I'm glad. But I don't expect you to pay me back nor do I want you to.'

'But where did you get the money from? You don't have your family's money, and teachers' wages are hardly in the same league. Do I have to worry about you with Ronnie?'

'No, no. It was easy for me to do, don't worry.'

'I'm not sure I'll believe you unless you tell me the details.'

Tom ran his hand through his sandy brown hair. He clearly didn't want to tell her but she was leaving him with little choice.

'I sold a pocket watch. It was my twenty-first birthday present and worth a few quid, but it was only gathering dust in a drawer. It really wasn't a big deal, honestly.'

'It's a huge deal to me. That you would sell something precious like that to help me. Please don't act like it was nothing. I know you probably have little in the way of gifts from your family, so to part with that must have meant something. I know you have some idea of what you saved me from so you must know how huge this thing you did for me was. Why did you do it?' Josie searched his face for the answer she was desperate to hear and at the same time terrified of facing.

'Josie . . .'

'Please, Tom, I need to know.' Her blue eyes were wide with expectation and as he looked into them he sighed and shook his head, smiling.

'You are the most infuriating woman, do you know that? You can't leave things be.'

'I'm afraid I can't. I got you very wrong, and I am so sorry for that. But knowing what you've done for me, it's changed everything. I see . . . things, very differently now.'

'The money changed your opinion of me?' His tone was guarded, his defences had gone up at the mention of the one thing that had shaped his life in a way he'd tried to escape the first chance he'd got. He'd told Josie how women had only ever been interested in him for the fortune they thought he would inherit and so she rushed to reassure him.

'No, the fact that you knew what I'd done and what awaited me in London if I didn't get Ronnie his money, that I'd been so stupid and got myself caught up in something so shameful, and the fact that I'd been nothing but rude to you based on silly judgements, and you still wanted to help me, that's what changed my opinion of you. Only the kindest, most decent and open-hearted man would do that.' There was a fervour in her voice that surprised Josie as much as it did Tom.

'You're not stupid nor should you ever be ashamed. You were just trying to survive after life had kicked you in the teeth. Ronnie is a creep and deserved more than the threats I threw at him.' Tom's eyes flashed with a fury and a passion that made Josie's heart flip.

'You don't think I'm a terrible person then?' Josie's stomach was in knots.

'Quite the opposite. You're infuriating, you're stubborn and I don't think I've ever had such a dressing-down as the one you gave me the other night. But I've never met anyone like you. The thought of someone like Ronnie hurting you in any way made me feel sick. And I didn't want you to leave.'

'Even if I was still awful to you?' Josie stepped closer to Tom as she asked her question.

Tom laughed. 'Yes, even if you were still awful to me. You still don't get it, do you?' He was suddenly serious. 'I like you, Josie, a lot, and I hated the thought of you leaving, even if you hated me. I've only ever thought you were incredible, whatever you thought of me.'

'I don't think those stupid things about you any more.'

'You don't?' His eyes were locked on hers and Josie's heart hammered in her chest.

'No,' she whispered, her breath catching in her throat.

'Would I be a fool to hope that you might feel anything remotely like the way I feel about you?'

She stared up at him and shook her head, unable to speak. A soft smile spread across Tom's face as he took her face in his hands gently.

'Well, that's very good news,' he said as she returned his smile. His lips brushed against hers as he lifted her chin to kiss her as dusk fell.

Chapter Thirty

As she walked to the village hall the following evening with Glenys in order to attend their final choir practice before the competition, Josie was glad to have something to steady her mind and maybe settle the butterflies that were fluttering like mad in her stomach. She hadn't been able to take the smile off her face since she had left Tom on the road, his kiss still lingering on her lips. Glenys for once hadn't questioned Josie on her change of mood. It was as if the older woman could sense that Josie needed a little longer to get her own head around the direction her heart had taken her in without the pressure of others giving their two pennies' worth.

With the village hall in sight, Josie couldn't quite believe this would be the last time they would rehearse before they would perform to the village and then at the competition in Bridgend on Saturday. She was so excited to show Llandegwen and everyone at the competition what the choir could do. There was nothing more satisfying than seeing hard work paying off in extraordinary ways. Josie felt a little pressure to offer the choir some rousing final words at that night's practice but she hoped the right words would come to her when the time came.

Josie and Glenys arrived at the village hall ten minutes early as usual, in order to make sure everything was set up for their use. The hall was usually in darkness when they arrived, so it was a surprise to Josie to see a glow of yellow light illuminating the short footpath leading up to the doors, which had been left ajar.

'Someone's here already. We must be later than I thought we were,' Josie said with confusion in her voice, not entirely convinced she'd got her timing so wrong.

'Let's see, shall we,' Glenys said blandly.

As they entered the hall Josie's heart leapt at the sight of the nine other members of the choir gathered by the piano awaiting her arrival. A lovely bunch of spring flowers that had been lying on top of the piano were grabbed now by Fred as Peggy, on seeing Josie and Glenys standing in the doorway, declared, 'She's here!'

'What's all this?' Josie asked, baffled but smiling at the jolly gathering.

Fred walked towards her, offering her the bunch of flowers, which Josie happily took from him.

'These are a small thank you from us lot. We just wanted to thank you for making us sound good and for giving us the choir. I know I'm not the only one who has benefited in more ways than one from it. And, well, it's all down to you. So thank you.' He glanced down at his feet which were shuffling awkwardly as he delivered this heartfelt message on behalf of the choir.

Josie was so touched, she felt a little weepy. She clutched the flowers to her chest as the others all followed Fred in giving her their thanks.

'We only came to keep my mam quiet, but singing all together, I don't know, it's given us something to look forward to when we get out of the mines at the end of the day, so thank you, Josie,' Owen said with a big grin on his face.

'As the lad says, the choir turned out to be just what we needed. Typical of my wife to know that before we did.' Michael rolled his eyes and Josie laughed.

'And I wanted to say thank you for helping me find my voice. I didn't think I was much good till the choir, and Gethin of course.' Bethan flushed as her beau smiled at her. 'Well, until you made me see that I might be.'

'Are you getting a big enough head yet?' Peggy joked as she hugged her friend.

'I don't know what to say! This is the loveliest thing anyone has ever done for me. And I feel quite undeserving because the choir has given me so much too. You've made me feel so welcome here and it's you lot who have made the choir what it is. I couldn't be more proud of you all.' Josie's sight blurred with happy tears and her heart swelled. 'I'm meant to be the one giving you all a rousing speech, not getting all soppy,' she laughed as she wiped away her tears.

'We don't need any galvanising tonight, we're all ready go, aren't we?' Marjorie said bolshily as everyone cheered.

'Let's get singing, shall we?' Mr Evans boomed. They all agreed and made their way to the piano ready for their final practice to begin.

As Josie remained by the hall doors watching them all

taking their places, Marjorie quickly returned to her and gave her a swift but hard hug and whispered, 'You know the choir has been a sanctuary for me. You've done good, girl. And I listened to what you said. Jimmy Griffiths is going to come and live at the post office as our lodger and odd-job man. So Mr Davies and I won't be alone.' Marjorie studied Josie's expression to make sure she'd been understood and when she was satisfied that she had been, she was back with the others by the piano before Josie could blink. Her admiration for the postmistress had just gone up a notch; Marjorie had found a way to be OK, which only made tonight sweeter.

Josie's father's voice drifted into her mind now, reminding her of the magic of music. She smiled to herself at the sight before her, the kind, eager, happy faces of her choir. She inhaled the scent of the pretty flowers that she held in her arms and let out a satisfied breath.

'Right then, let's get to work,' she called out as she hung up her coat and marched over to the piano stool.

'Imagine if we won the competition!' an excited Bethan said breathlessly as they all agreed that they had their best choir practice to date.

'I think we stand a good chance,' said Gethin.

'Let's not get carried away, loves. As long as we do our best, that's all that counts,' Glenys said with the wisdom of someone with more years on this earth under her belt.

'But if we do do well, imagine where we could travel. We might even leave Wales! They have choral competitions everywhere, we could go international!' The travelling possibilities that the choir brought to Peggy's life had always been the biggest appeal of the choir for her. And now that she was finally getting to spread her wings, albeit to a town in the Valleys not all that far away, she was enjoying the thrill of what the adventure might bring. Her wild curls that she always tried and failed to tame with clips and combs bounced as she talked animatedly.

'That would be quite something.' Catherine indulged Peggy.

'We should all get plenty of rest and rest our voices as much as possible,' Marjorie ordered rather than advised.

'I imagine resting your voice will be hard for you, Marjorie,' Owen said cheekily. Luckily Marjorie, now used to Owen's mischievous ways, found this amusing and she simply swatted at him with a reluctant smile on her lips. 'Oh hush, you cheeky devil, you.'

Marjorie had planted a tiny seed of worry in Josie's mind with her words though. It would take just one of the singers getting ill, or losing their voice, and they would be disqualified from entering the competition altogether. They were the absolute minimum number of members required as it was. Looking at all of their healthy beaming faces now, it seemed an unnecessary concern. It was typical of Josie to find something to worry about when everything was going so well. She put the thought to the back of her mind as she tuned back in to the happy chatter of the choir who seemed reluctant to end their last practice. They would perform, all ten of them, on Saturday and they would be marvellous. There was nothing to worry about, Josie thought to herself.

It was almost as if by acknowledging the possibility of something going wrong Josie had not only allowed the seed of worry to be planted, but she had somehow let it grow into a reality. The reality being an anxious-looking Mr Evans wringing his hands on her doorstep that Friday morning. Josie had just returned from taking Sam to school when she'd heard a knock at the door while she was preparing lunch for herself, Glenys and Harry in the kitchen. Glenys was in the village shop visiting Peggy's mother and Josie had decided to make herself useful. Harry was pottering about in the small square of outdoor space they had at the back of the cottage, where he grew some vegetables and a few herbs. Josie was sure he was trying to keep out of her way so that he didn't need to force a conversation with her. He'd been barely visible in the house these past few weeks; it was as if he was trying to pretend that he wasn't there at all so that he didn't have to endure the atmosphere that his silent presence created. And so it was Josie who was left to answer the door.

As soon as she saw Mr Evans's face she knew he had nothing good to tell her.

'Oh, Josie, I have some bad news, I'm afraid to say. I've thought of nothing else but trying to find a way around this, but there's nothing to be done about it. I feel just awful . . .'

'What is it, Mr Evans?' A million possibilities filled her head.

'I can't sing in the competition tomorrow. I have to marry a couple at St David's in Castleforth instead. Their vicar, Mr Price, has been called by the Bishop to Cardiff on urgent church business and as we are the nearest village I have been called to attend to both churches in his absence. It's all been rather sudden and there's nothing to be done. I can't be in two places at once and I am the Lord's servant so I must attend to the Church first and foremost. But I am ever so sorry to let you and the choir down. Heartbroken, in fact.' He looked distraught as he told Josie of his predicament.

It was a disaster, there was no getting away from it. Without Mr Evans they were too few in number to compete tomorrow. They'd all worked so hard to be ready in time for the competition, and they were so excited about it too. It would crush them all to know it wouldn't be happening now. But Mr Evans knew that and was clearly crushed himself, so there was no use in making him feel worse than he already did. There was nothing he could do about it, and so Josie would have to put a brave face on it for all of their sakes.

'Oh, you haven't let anyone down. Please don't think that. These things happen and I'm sure we can work something out. Perhaps we can find another willing singer who is almost as good as you to fill in this time.' But even as she said this she knew the chances of that happening were slim to none. She'd been lucky to get the ten members she'd got to begin with, there was no hope of finding someone who was both willing and, more importantly, able.

Mr Evans leapt on this branch of hope that Josie had offered, and his face visibly brightened.

'Do you think you could? That would be just marvellous, I'd feel so much better about it all. I'll hate to miss out on singing tomorrow, but I'll hate it even more if no one gets to sing. I'll ask the boss up there for a bit of help, shall I?' He glanced up at the heavens, his eyes brighter now that all might not be lost.

'It can't hurt. But whatever happens, promise me you won't worry. There will be other competitions.' She wanted to ease

Mr Evans's concerns but really her heart was sinking. How was she going to tell the others? Was there any way they could fix this?

'Thank you, my dear. You are kind to ease my conscience. I will pray for you all from St David's church tomorrow.'

As he walked off down the path Josie, who didn't believe in things like prayer, thought they needed something more like a miracle. And she wasn't sure she believed in those either.

After sitting at the kitchen table and staring into space for ten minutes unable to form a plan of action, she abruptly pushed back her chair, grabbed her coat and headed out of the door and into the centre of the village to Peggy's shop. She couldn't sit in silence for a moment longer. She needed to speak to her friend, maybe she could help her to come up with a solution.

As soon as she came into Peggy's view on entering the shop, the door had barely shut behind her when Josie said, 'You won't believe what's happened!' at the same time as Peggy declared, 'You'll never guess what I've just heard!'

The two women, wide-eyed with surprise that the other had something bigger to share, stared at each other for a beat.

'You go first,' Josie said, suddenly unsure how to break it to her friend that her dreams of escaping Llandegwen with the choir might have fallen at the first hurdle. In her haste to lean on Peggy for support in this current crisis she'd forgotten the effect that it would have on Peggy herself. She'd be crushed.

'OK, so Joan and Pamela were just in the shop. I'd been out the back when they came in and just as I was heading back to the counter, but was still out of sight, I heard what they were talking about. Josie, you'll never believe what Anwen's tried to do. According to Joan, Anwen called the vicar at St David's in Castleforth and pretended to be the secretary of the Bishop in Cardiff. She told Mr Price that he had to go to Cardiff at once for important church business and that he was to have our Mr Evans cover for him that weekend. Anwen's cousin Pauline is getting married at St David's on Saturday and she knew that if Mr Evans had to marry them instead he'd not be able to sing at the competition. She wanted to stop us from competing, can you believe it!' Peggy was outraged but clearly unaware that Anwen had actually succeeded in her plan. Josie, however, felt sick at the discovery that Anwen was behind poor Mr Evans having to worry about missing out on the competition and letting everyone down, and that Anwen would be the cause of the heartbreak Josie would have to inflict upon the choir if they couldn't find a tenth singer.

'I can believe it, actually. And more than that, her plan worked. Mr Price is on his way to Cardiff and Mr Evans is having to marry the couple at St David's tomorrow.' Josie spoke calmly but anger was boiling within her. Anwen had wanted to sabotage the choir from the moment Josie got involved in reforming it, and now she'd succeeded. Because of her unshakable and unfounded hatred of Josie, Anwen had in one last spiteful move trampled on everything the choir had been working towards and hoping for.

'What?' Peggy gasped.

'Mr Evans told me. I headed here straight after. I've been trying to think of what we can do, but so far I have no ideas.'

'That bloody cow! I could kill her. Do you know what else I heard? It was her who tore down all of your posters when you were trying to get people to join the choir. Pamela told Joan that Anwen had boasted about it to them all at the time. She's a nasty piece of work and what's worse, she's getting away with it all,' Peggy said furiously.

Josie's shoulders sagged under the weight of how one woman's grudge against her could've caused all of this drama. Anwen had fought the choir at every stage and now she'd won. It was devastating and infuriating but Josie couldn't think of a way to fight back.

'This is all my fault. It's me she hates but the choir is suffering for it. I should've let someone else take charge, then you'd all be singing tomorrow.'

'There wasn't anyone else, you were the only person brave enough to reform the choir. We all found our voices because of you. You're the reason we should be singing tomorrow, Anwen's the reason we're not. And don't let me hear you say otherwise.' Peggy spoke these words fiercely but Josie felt so much despair at the situation that they had little effect.

'I just wish I could fix it.'

'I wish I could smack her. She deserves it.'

Josie would've laughed at the idea of her friend raising a hand to Anwen's perfectly made-up face except for the fact that she was trying very hard not to cry. It was hopeless. Anwen had wanted her to fail and now she had.

'I was going to wait for Glenys but I think I'll just head back to the cottage and lick my wounds for a bit till I work out what to do.'

'Wait.' Peggy hurried out from behind the counter and gave Josie a tight hug before she pulled away roughly to look her in the eye as she said, 'Whatever happens, this is all on Anwen. I'll make sure everyone knows it. All right?'

Josie nodded. 'But let me tell the choir. It needs to be me.'

She left the shop with a heavy heart. It wasn't until she found herself sitting in the same spot at the kitchen table in the tiny cottage, this time with her head in her hands, that she let herself cry. If she'd handled Anwen differently maybe this wouldn't have happened. She'd never know now. But what she did know was that she'd let everyone down. And that was the worst feeling of all.

Chapter Thirty-One

She didn't know how long she'd been sitting there like that, sobbing quietly by herself. She didn't hear the kitchen door open and Harry shuffling into the room. She only realised she wasn't alone when his gruff voice said gently, 'Whatever has made you cry, girl, I'm sure it's not as bad as you think.'

She was so startled at him addressing her directly, she just stared at him for a moment. He simply looked back at her patiently.

'I'm sorry, I thought I was alone. I'm sure you don't want to hear my problems.' Her tone was brisk and she made to get up and excuse herself from his company. He had never wanted to engage in conversation with her before now, why would he want to endure her tears?

But to her surprise Harry put out a hand to stop her and sat down at the table with her.

'Stay. Tell me what's happened.'

When Josie looked into his eyes she saw that there was genuine sympathy there. She swallowed the sob that was rising in her throat.

'Go on. I might be able to help.' Harry pushed her lightly.

Josie sighed. 'You won't, no one can, I don't think. I've let everyone down. I promised the choir that I'd get them to the Welsh Valleys competition but now, because of me, we can't compete. They're going to be heartbroken and the village will be so disappointed. They were expecting to send us off to Bridgend tomorrow after the performance we're giving in the village hall. Oh, it's all such a mess!' The tears started to fall in full force again.

'And tell me, why do you believe this is your fault?'

Josie sniffed. 'Because Anwen Lewis hates me for reasons too ridiculous to go into, and to hurt me she's tried to sabotage the choir from day one. Today she's finally succeeded. She's managed to arrange things so that Mr Evans can't sing with us tomorrow, which means we only have nine singers and . . .' A sob forced Josie to trail off.

'You need ten singers to compete.' Harry finished her sentence for her.

'Yes. How did you know?' Josie looked at him curiously.

'Believe it or not, I used to be in the old choir and competed at this very competition back before the war. I remember the rules. We were always a small choir so it was always a worry of ours, if someone got sick or had to drop out at the last minute.' Josie was stunned that someone who lived as much in the shadows as possible, as Harry did, would have ever been part of something like a choir, let alone performed in one. 'But I still don't see how any of this is your fault.'

'If Anwen didn't hate me, we wouldn't have lost a member.' Josie shrugged.

'Exactly. So this is that madam Anwen's fault. Not yours,' Harry said simply.

'But what will I tell the choir? How do I tell them we won't be competing tomorrow after all?'

'Maybe you won't have to. These things often work out in ways you don't expect.' He patted her arm.

These were by a long stretch the most words they'd ever exchanged in one another's company and not only that, Harry was offering to help her. Josie's expression was curious.

'Why are you being so nice to me?'

Harry looked down shamefully.

'I can understand why you might ask that, and I'm ashamed that you've had to. So ashamed. It's no excuse for how I've behaved, how I've treated you and Sam since you came to this house, but you see, when I first saw young Sam he was the picture of my son. And the shock of it, well, it hurt too much to look at the lad. I didn't deal with Matthew's death very well, Glenys has had to put up with a lot, and having you and Sam here when my son was not, well, I didn't handle that well either. And I'm sorry for that. Especially when you've both made Glenys so happy, she loves having you here. And despite appearances, I do too. Sam is a character, just like his father, and you're a bit of a ray of sunshine in this house.' Harry smiled awkwardly.

Josie felt as though she were meeting Harry for the first time. The man sitting next to her, saying these words, was a totally different person to the one she'd shared a house with for the last two months.

'By the time I'd realised all that,' Harry continued, 'I'd been such a miserable sod and you'd both rightly given up on me, and I didn't know how to change things. So I carried on as I was. But then seeing you so upset just now, I thought if I could help you, maybe you'd see I'm not just a grumpy old fool after all.'

He looked at her so hopefully Josie could only feel sympathy for him. All of this time he'd been in pain. She'd seen a glimpse of it back when she'd first arrived but she'd forgotten it with everything else that had been going on and she'd chosen to believe he just wasn't keen on having them there. She'd read him all wrong. It seemed she had a habit of doing that. It must have been so hard for him to deal with their presence while also wanting to find a way to be a part of things. Instead he'd removed himself, choosing coldness over warmth, and he'd suffered as a consequence.

'I haven't quite given up on you,' Josie reassured him.

The relief in his eyes was almost too much for her.

'I'm glad.' He patted her arm again, this gesture from him meaning more than a warm hug from anyone else. 'And remember what I said, these things have a funny way of working out, your choir will compete.'

'I don't see how, Harry. I really don't. But there is something I can do to make myself feel better.'

'What's all this?'

They had been so lost in the moment, neither Josie nor Harry had heard Glenys enter the cottage. She was looking at them, sitting at the kitchen table like old friends, with a bemused grin on her face.

Josie turned to face the tiny woman standing in the kitchen doorway.

'Here, have my seat. I'll let Harry explain. He can tell you about Mr Evans and Anwen Lewis. I need to go out and sort something.'

'All right, love, you do that,' Glenys said, sitting down and looking at her husband in confusion; he could still surprise her after all of these years.

Josie grabbed her coat from the back of the door and pulled it on as she dashed out of the cottage and down the road towards Anwen Lewis's house, two streets away.

It was only when she arrived on Hillside Road that she realised she had no idea which house was Anwen's. She only knew the road because it was the one with the nicest houses in the village, and Glenys had told Josie once that Anwen had done very well for herself and married a man with a good job who was able to provide her with a home on this road. It was a small road on a hill, its relatively steep curve eventually opening out to the rolling green countryside that surrounded Llandegwen, but even so there were ten terraced houses to choose from. Josie's heart was racing as the adrenalin from the morning's events pumped through her veins. She scanned the houses for a clue as to which one might be home to the woman who had tried to ruin everything Josie had worked for. Just then she saw one of the nicely painted front doors open and a teenage girl step out with a basket under her arm, clearly on her way to do some errands. Josie seized her opportunity and politely asked the girl which house belonged to the Lewises. After being pointed to Number 4, Josie stood on the doorstep and smoothed her blond hair, the sides of which she had pinned back in soft rolls to keep out of her face that morning. She waited for the girl to be far enough down the street before she finally knocked.

Anwen was startled to find Josie on her doorstep and Josie used the element of surprise she'd been gifted to her advantage.

'I just wanted to let you know that it didn't work, your nasty plan. We'll have ten members in our choir and we will be singing for the village and at the competition tomorrow, if it's the last thing I do.' Josie was lying through her teeth but she wasn't going to let Anwen win. And maybe Harry was right, maybe it would all be OK somehow.

Anwen looked torn between wanting to know how this could be and protesting her innocence in order to keep up the pretence that she had nothing to do with Mr Evans being called away. In the end she erred on the side of caution.

'I don't know what you're talking about,' she said in her usual haughty manner.

'I know it was you. I know it was you who called the vicar at St David's and had our Mr Evans called away tomorrow. And I know it was you who tore down my posters.'

Josie heard a gasp from behind her and turned to find two women huddled together in the doorway of the house opposite trying to appear as if they weren't listening. Anwen had seen them over Josie's head too, and was determined to save face in front of her neighbours.

'Who do you think you are coming to my door and making ludicrous accusations like this? How dare you!' she said loudly to ensure any nosy ears could hear her.

'You can deny it all you like but sooner or later word will get back that Mr Price was sent on a fool's errand and I'm afraid your friends have loose lips. But anyway your plan will fail and I wanted to be the first to tell you.' Josie was about to turn away but Anwen's pinched face, pink in anger as she visibly struggled with how to respond, made Josie pause. 'Do you know, I actually feel quite sorry for you, Anwen. You have no idea what you've got, have you? You waste all of your time trying to ruin the choir, why? Because Matthew married me and not you? But you have a good husband, he provides for you and your girls, and he's here, he came back from the war when so many didn't. Matthew was killed, Anwen! I lost him. So you could say I've paid a high enough price for whatever crime you seem to think I've committed against you. But you, you still have your husband, and you have lovely daughters and a lovely house, and you're still not happy. There are people in the choir who don't have half of what you have, myself included. But we're all a damn sight happier. Maybe you should think about that.'

Josie saw Anwen's bottom lip wobble ever so slightly and her cheeks were flaming red as her eyes darted between Josie and the neighbours who had overheard every word. She was humiliated, caught out and absolutely furious about it. Even if Josie didn't solve the problem of the missing choir member, the look on Anwen's face had been worth the white lie. Josie turned on her heel and marched away from Anwen's house and back up the street towards her home. She smiled to herself when she heard one of the women who had been earwigging say 'Oh my!' as she walked past.

Chapter Thirty-Two

It was still dark when Josie woke on Saturday morning. How she'd managed to stay in bed until it was a reasonable time to rise she'd never know, she was a bundle of nerves from the second her eyes flew open. She'd made so much noise in the kitchen preparing breakfast, almost dropping cups and saucers and clattering plates and cutlery together, that Glenys thundered down the stairs in her nightgown to prevent her entire kitchen being broken into tiny pieces by Josie's nervous hands.

'Goodness me, love, I had visions of finding my kitchen in ruins, the noise you're making!' Glenys removed the teapot Josie was attempting to fill and led her to the chair she'd just pulled out for her at the table.

'I'm sorry, I'm all butterflies, I don't know what to do with myself.'

Glenys smiled at Josie. 'I can't believe the day is finally here! It's exciting, isn't it?'

It should have been but Josie was dreading having to tell

the choir that they would only be performing for the village and not in the competition that day. She'd not yet told any of them about Mr Evans having to drop out, she was still hoping for some kind of miracle. The choir had arranged to meet at the village hall half an hour before the rest of the village was due to arrive to hear them perform. It would give them time to warm up and have one last practice. She'd have to break the news to them all then.

Harry was a new man when he joined his family at the kitchen table that morning. Josie saw Glenys give her husband an appreciative smile, she had been visibly thrilled with Harry for making such an effort. But Josie also knew that it ran deeper than this for Glenys – she was proud of her husband for opening up to Josie. It meant so much to her that they could all now sit around the kitchen table and talk easily with one another. Josie could tell this from the way she fussed around them all; ever since yesterday afternoon she'd been extra affectionate and cheerful. It made Josie happy too. The cottage felt like a very warm and content place to be that morning. More than ever Josie felt incredibly lucky to have been gifted this family at a time when she thought almost all was lost. Without Glenys she didn't dare to think where she and Sam might have ended up. And Tom too, of course. Josie was still overwhelmed that he had done what he had for her and that he felt the way he did about her after learning her darkest secret. And now they had Harry too, the cottage in Llandegwen really did feel like home. London was their past, Wales was their future. This was where she was supposed to be. If she could just fix the little matter of her number of choristers then everything would be perfect.

* * *

There had been some concern that their choice to wear black to the competition would make the choir look a little sombre. But looking at them all now, standing in front of her on the stage in the village hall – the men in their mixture of black slacks, jumpers and suits, all sported with a crisp white shirt, and the women in a variety of black A-line and pencil skirts teamed with black cardigans and cream or white blouses – they all looked rather smart. Peggy and Bethan had added a dash of colour with bright red lipstick – Peggy's unruly curls were swept up neatly in a twist, while Bethan's silky black locks hung loose with only the sides pinned up in soft rolls. The older women had set their short hair in conservative but well put together waves, while all of the men had got out the Brylcreem, even Fred. They looked very professional, all standing together, and the fact that their choice of colour represented something so vital to the village gave them a sense of unity.

Josie looked at them all with a heavy heart – she was about to crush them with the news she had to share with them. Despite what Harry had said to her, she still felt as though she'd let them all down. As she cleared her throat to speak, the hall doors opened behind her. Harry, dressed smartly in black exactly like the other men in the choir, walked towards the stage and without saying a word stood at the back where Mr Evans should be. For a moment Josie was stunned, unable to say anything at all, but as she made eye contact with him he gave her a small but reassuring smile. The others looked at Harry in surprise, none more so than Glenys.

'Everyone, Harry is to be our newest member and will sing

with us today.' She looked at Harry for reassurance that she hadn't imagined him stepping in silently to save the choir, and he nodded at her to continue. 'Mr Evans has had to drop out unexpectedly and as we need ten members Harry has stepped in to save the day.'

'That's very good of you, fella,' Michael said as he slapped Harry on the back. Glenys was staring at her husband open-mouthed.

'You sang in the old choir, if I remember rightly?' Marjorie asked Harry.

'I did,' was all Harry said in reply.

'That's worked out all right then, hasn't it?' Fred couldn't believe their luck and neither could Josie.

'Shall we do some vocal warm-ups and then give Harry a chance to practise with us while we have the time?' Josie was comforted by Harry's confident exterior but even so she was crossing everything that he would be able to deliver.

And Harry proved himself to be the saviour they so badly needed when the choir began to sing the first of the songs they were to perform at the competition. His voice slotted into the harmony for 'Myfanwy' so easily it was as if he'd always been a part of the choir. Harry had never doubted he could fill Mr Evans's shoes, but the rest of the choir had looked at one another in relief when they heard for themselves that their solution was working. They sounded wonderful and Sam, their one audience member pre-performance, gave them a big clap after they'd sung the final notes. He was sitting in one of the chairs that had been set up in the front row, swinging his legs in glee as he got to watch his grandparents and mother showing off their talents.

'Are we really ready to do this?' Catherine asked before biting her lip after they'd run through all three songs.

'Of course we are. Didn't you just hear us?' Fred said with a smile.

'I think we sounded decent enough,' Owen said as he smoothed his gel-laden hair unnecessarily. There was so much Brylcreem in it, it would take a chisel to dislodge a strand.

'It's all so exciting!' Peggy squealed.

'I feel a bit sick.' It was true, Bethan did look a little green. It was just nerves though – Josie knew that as soon as Bethan started singing her voice would give her confidence.

The villagers would be arriving any minute to bag the best seats in the hall and after the performance the choir would be getting straight on the bus heading to Bridgend. It was Josie's last chance to say something meaningful, to attempt to put into words the mountain they'd climbed together to get to this point. She swallowed the lump that had formed in her throat when she thought of how much these people now meant to her and how they had given her a purpose, somewhere to belong. She stepped away from the piano and took a deep breath as she faced them all. Instinctively they all turned their attention to their choirmistress, eager to hear what she had to say.

'I'm not sure I can quite put into words how proud I am of you all. Harry, you have saved our bacon today, there's no doubt about that, so thank you. And the rest of you, Mr Evans included even though he can't be with us today, you have put everything you have into this choir and these songs. You've shown up every week and given it your all, and you've supported each other and me on this journey to the competition in ways that truly warm my heart. I couldn't have asked for anything more from any of you. I want you to know that no matter what happens at the competition this evening, you are all winners to me and to this village.'

Seeing that everyone was getting a bit emotional at her words was making it hard for Josie to hold herself together. Now was not the time for tears, she had to rally the troops.

'So let's knock Llandegwen's socks off like I know we can and end the day with a bang by blowing away all of the other Valleys choirs in Bridgend!'

'Hear hear!' Michael called out as the rest of the choir cheered.

When the doors to the village hall opened to receive the first members of the audience for their performance, the choir temporarily left the stage and congregated in the kitchen where they could gather themselves and have a moment together to savour what they were about to do that day. The gentle hum of chatter from the hall swelled quickly to a loud buzz as the room filled with eager ears. Village concerts were no longer a thing of the past and the choir had reignited a love of music in Llandegwen. The full house today was a sure sign of this.

When the buzz of chatter reached full volume Josie decided to peek out of the kitchen to assess the crowd. She slipped through the kitchen door discreetly and crashed into a solid chest as she walked down towards the back of the hall, so focused was she on the room full to bursting with Llandegwen locals.

'Oh goodness, I'm sorry!' she said in surprise before she looked up to see whose chest she'd just slammed into. When she found herself staring into Tom's green eyes, she took a step back, trying to ignore the heat warming her cheeks. 'You came,' she said happily.

'I didn't want to be the only person in Llandegwen who missed out on all the excitement. I'd be left out of every conversation for at least the next year if I did.' His tone was sarcastic but he was smiling that lazy smile of his that made Josie's stomach flip. 'But that's not the only reason. I wanted to see you.'

'You did?' Josie laughed.

'Any excuse . . .' He leant in to kiss her but before his lips reached hers Marjorie's bossy voice called out from behind.

'Sorry to interrupt, Josie, but I think we ought to get started if we want to leave on time. The whole village is here and waiting, and the nerves are starting to get to some of the more sensitive members of our choir.' Her clipped officious tone was so familiar now.

Josie looked from Marjorie who stared at her impatiently, hand on generous-sized hip, to Tom who rolled his eyes in mock frustration.

'Yes, of course, Marjorie. I'll be there in a moment.'

Marjorie huffily nodded at this and marched back to the kitchen as Josie turned to Tom.

'The choir, we have to start. I'll speak to you after?'

'Of course. I'll be here. Break a leg, is that what they say?' He kissed her on the forehead and went to take a seat as close to the front as he could get.

Josie couldn't wipe the smile from her face as she moved to introduce the choir and lead them all in their first performance of the day.

As she passed the kitchen she popped her head around the door and when ten heads turned to face her she mouthed, 'Ready?' to which all ten heads nodded half eagerly and half nervously. Josie made her way on to the stage, the butterflies in her tummy in full flight as she cleared her throat.

'Welcome, everyone, and thank you very much for coming to hear the Llandegwen choir perform ahead of competing in the Welsh Valleys Choral Competition later this evening. We will perform for you the three songs we have worked very hard on and will be singing in our attempts to do you all proud at the competition. We hope you'll enjoy what you're about to hear and that you'll give the choir, your songbirds of Colliers Row, a good old Welsh send-off after the performance!'

The hall gave a hearty round of applause as Josie descended and took her seat at the piano, and the choir took to the stage and organised themselves into their positions. Josie gave them a moment to compose themselves before she played the opening notes of 'Myfanwy' and almost physically felt the spirits of those in the hall lift as the voices of the choir filled the room with rousing notes. Josie had her back to the audience but she could feel the emotion of the room in her bones it was so palpable – 'Suo Gân' stirred their hearts, as it had always stirred the hearts of those who were singing, and 'Calon Lan' had everyone on their feet before the closing notes had been sung out into the air around them. Josie had never heard such thunderous applause. She clutched her hands to her chest almost in shock at the reaction of the crowd. It was a glorious sound. She looked up at the choir before she turned around. She wanted to see them enjoying their moment of glory. She wanted them to savour every second of this moment. They had shown everyone what they could do and what they'd worked so hard for. Seeing their beaming faces was the icing on the cake for Josie and she realised she was beaming herself.

Finally, she turned to face the audience as the choir took a bow and left the stage to be greeted by determined villagers eager to be the first to heap praise upon them. Josie laughed to herself as she saw Mrs Duffy wrestle her way to the front of the crowd while shouting 'That was brilliant!' Mr Driscoll approached her to offer her his congratulations, followed by a little old lady who looked as fragile as china but who had such a steely look in her eye Josie knew just by looking at her that she was tougher than her appearance suggested.

'You've done good, girl. Not everyone thought you'd make a decent stab at this but you proved them wrong. Well done. I'll be expecting the keys through my letter box as usual on Monday night,' the old lady said with a wink before she shuffled off.

Josie threw her head back, letting a hearty laugh escape her lungs. The elusive Mrs Moss was a mystery no more. And what's more, she'd given the choir her stamp of approval. Today was just the beginning, whatever happened this evening. The village had shown them that all of Llandegwen expected them to be back at choir practice on Monday evening, win or lose.

As Josie hung back from the crowd, observing from her place at the piano the joy in the room and the confidence almost overflowing from her ten singers as they enjoyed their moment in the spotlight, she caught Tom's eye across the hall. He smiled at her from where he stood raising his hands to clap her. Before she knew it she was working her way through the chairs towards him so fast she caught her cardigan on a splinter of wood sticking out from one of the seats. She yanked it free, not caring about anything else in that moment than feeling Tom's arms around her.

When she reached him she was almost breathless.

'Are you glad you came? I know how you feel about choirs,' she said as he pulled her against his chest.

'I thought we'd cleared all of that up? Anyway, if I get to do this at the end of it, I'll watch a hundred choral performances.'

He leant down and kissed her as she laughed against his lips. Josie didn't want him to ever let her go, and she was so lost in the warmth of his arms that it came as a shock when she heard Owen call out loudly to the rest of the hall, 'The bus is here! Songbirds, off we go!'

'I have a competition I have to get to,' she said as if the idea had just occurred to her.

'Yes, you have. But I'll be waiting for you when you get back,' he said as he tucked a loose strand of her hair behind her ear.

'Promise?'

'I promise.'

She stole one last kiss before she tore herself away from his arms and joined the rest of the choir in the doorway as they made their way to board the bus. All of the villagers had gathered outside to send them off and as the bus's engine ignited with a loud rumble the crowd cheered and clapped.

Josie joined the others at the back of the bus to watch the village of Llandegwen wave them on their way. Everything she wanted was there in that village, she wasn't running from the wreckage of her old life in London any more, she was happy and safe and her heart was full again when for years it had been empty and hollow. Llandegwen had saved her in so many ways and as the village got smaller and smaller as the bus drove away from it she knew that whatever happened that evening, she'd be returning to a place she could now call home.